Tom Holt started his literary career early, publishing a book of poetry at the age of twelve. Since then, he has turned his attention to fiction and has already written one sequel to E. F. Benson's immortal Lucia novels, *Lucia in Wartime* (also available in Black Swan). He is currently a post-graduate student at Oxford University, specialising in Ancient Greek History.

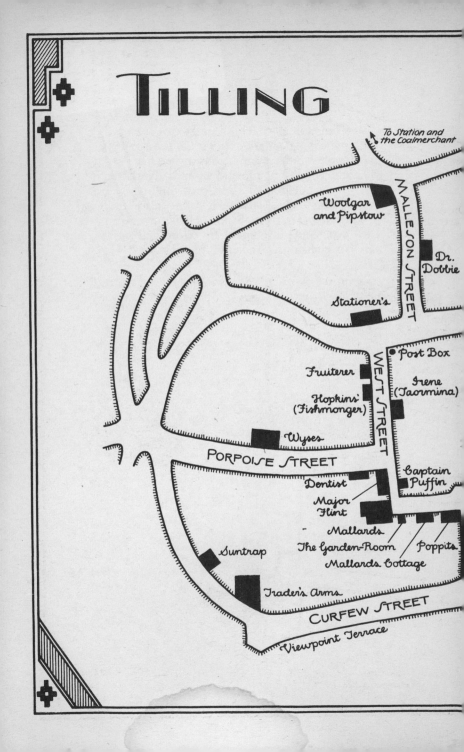

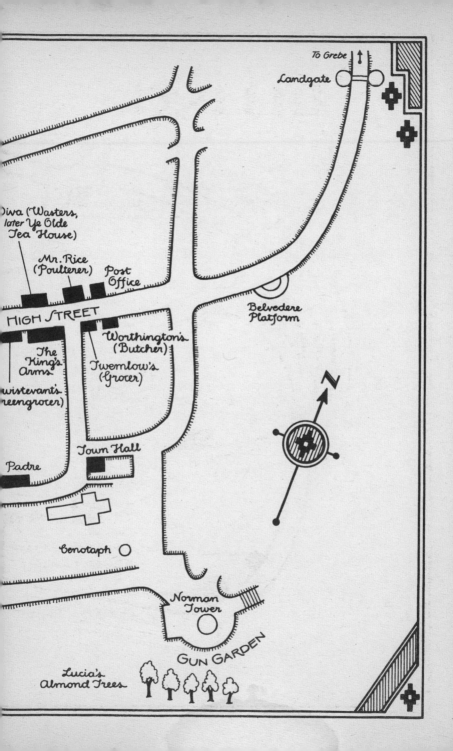

To Grebe

Landgate

Diva (Wasters, later Ye Olde Tea House)

Mr. Rice (Poulterer)

Post Office

HIGH STREET

Belvedere Platform

Worthington's (Butcher)

The King's Arms

Twemlow's (Grocer)

wistevant's reengrocer)

Town Hall

Padre

Cenotaph

Norman Tower

GUN GARDEN

Lucia's Almond Trees

Also by Tom Holt
LUCIA IN WARTIME
and published by Black Swan

LUCIA TRIUMPHANT

Tom Holt

Based on the characters created by E. F. Benson

BLACK SWAN

To My Father

LUCIA TRIUMPHANT
A BLACK SWAN BOOK 0 552 99281 X

Originally published in Great Britain by
Macmillan London Limited

PRINTING HISTORY
Macmillan London edition published 1986
Black Swan edition published 1987

The author acknowledges with gratitude the permission kindly
granted by the Estate of K. S. P. McDowell to base this novel on
the characters created by E. F. Benson.

The map of Tilling shown on pages ii and iii is adapted from
E. F. Benson: Mr Benson Remembered in Rye, and the World of Tilling,
by Cynthia and Tony Reavell (published by Martello Bookshop,
Rye), and is reproduced by kind permission of the authors.

This book is set in 11/12pt

Black Swan Books are published by Transworld Publishers Ltd.,
61-63 Uxbridge Road, Ealing, London W5 5SA, in Australia by
Transworld Publishers (Australia) Pty. Ltd., 15-23 Helles
Avenue, Moorebank, NSW 2170, and in New Zealand by
Transworld Publishers (N.Z.) Ltd., Cnr. Moselle and Waipareira
Avenues, Henderson, Auckland.

Made and printed in Great Britain by
The Guernsey Press Co. Ltd., Guernsey,
Channel Islands.

LUCIA TRIUMPHANT

1

Mrs. Emmeline Pillson, 'Lucia' to friends — and all the inhabitants of Tilling were her dear and devoted friends — sat in the window of the picturesque garden-room that was such an outstanding feature of Mallards, her elegant Queen Anne house. From this vantage point she had a unique view over her little Protectorate (for Lucia was in every respect the Lady Protector of Tilling, being Queen of its social life and Mayor, for the second year in succession, of the town itself). At her feet, so to speak, was West Street, cascading down to join the High Street along which passed all the traffic of the town, while to her right she guarded the way to the Church Square and the church itself. Thus her high seat kept watch over Tilling temporal and spiritual, and very little evaded her sharp eye.

It was not so many years since another watcher had held this place; a less benign guardian, Elizabeth Mapp-Flint, had long been the owner of Mallards. She too had delighted to sit on the conveniently situated hot-water pipes in the garden-room window, taking full advantage of the fact that nearly all her subjects (for before Lucia's arrival in Tilling several years ago, she herself had been the Queen of Tilling Society) were under her eye: Diva Plaistow in the High Street, quaint Irene Coles in West Street, Mr. and Mrs. Wyse just round the corner in Porpoise Street, and the Vicar and his wife in Church Square. Like the Lord our God (whom she did not in the least claim to resemble in other respects) she observed their going out and their coming in, and used to the full her exceptional analytical powers to work out exactly what they had been doing and why.

Lucia was not nearly so intrusive. If she happened to observe the comings and goings of her friends out of the corner of her eye (which she could hardly fail to do, given the nature of her favourite sitting-place) and chanced to be able to remember when she had seen them and where they had been going, it was simply a tribute to her keen powers of observation and recall. Conscious spying was beneath her altogether.

It was to this eyrie that she generally repaired when black melancholy assailed her, as it occasionally assails even the most vital and dynamic of men and women. The wide views and the realization that she was the first citizen of this almost unbearably beautiful and historic town very seldom failed to raise her spirits. But on this cold, bright January morning the prospect had itself caused her sadness, for it was not the deteriorating international situation, nor yet the depressed national economy that occupied her thoughts; a purely local stagnation oppressed her like the heaviness of an approaching thunderstorm.

To be precise, now that she had secured a second term of office, what was she to do with it? All her considerable ingenuity had gone into providing herself with innocent employment during her first year of civic supremacy. Everything that a mayor could reasonably do, she had done. No proposal for the betterment of her fellow-citizens, however imaginative, had been lightly dismissed. No worthy cause had been allowed to evade her benign persecution. Nor had she been content to sit and wait for opportunities to present themselves; rather she had exhausted her own creativity in the search for something to do. Yet the year had slipped by and the council elections had come round again, and before she had been able to substitute achievement for activity, she had been compelled to fight off a very real threat to the well-being of Tilling. Elizabeth Mapp-Flint, whom she had appointed her Mayoress in an access of generosity (and to keep her from making mischief) had, like the Emperor Tiberius, reverted to her own essential character, and had gone about to subvert the loyalties of the other Councillors with the aim of becoming Mayor herself. Since the other Councillors were leading tradesmen, she had sought to buy their adherence with lavish orders for coal and chickens and preserved ginger. But they were made of truer stuff, and Lucia did far more entertaining and was thus a far more valuable account than Elizabeth, so the plot had foundered. Indeed, Elizabeth had lost her place on the Council; worse yet, she had lost it to quaint Irene, her sworn enemy.

Miss Coles had been, ever since Lucia's arrival in Tilling, her most fervent admirer — quite embarrassingly fervent at times — and had resolved to remove this threat to her idol once and for all. Being a fine *extempore* orator and young and attractive (despite the extraordinary garb she felt it necessary to wear as a daringly *avant-garde* painter), she had successfully espoused the Socialist cause and beaten Elizabeth by a full five votes. Nevertheless, Lucia had reappointed Elizabeth as her Mayoress, to the latter's indescribable fury.

Apart from that, however, what had she achieved? As Lucia listlessly turned the pages of her Shakespeare (her resort in times of tribulation) her eye caught the second scene of the third act of *Macbeth*. 'Nought's had,' she read, 'all's spent, Where our desire is got without content.' She could hardly have encapsulated her feelings better herself.

'Here I am,' she mused, 'Mayor of the most charming town on earth, and apparently baffled for want of any worthy thing to do. There must be something. . . . My immortal predecessors in this high office would be ashamed of me. Why, they dealt with floods and fires and plagues of rats, fought with the smugglers and were smugglers themselves. Yet they had such thrilling things to deal with, and I have no such excitements to bring out the best in me. Why can't the man produce the hour, rather than the hour producing the man? History is like all the other traditional products of our nation; it is no longer made in small cottages but in the great factories of the cities, and all that is left to us here, like so many abandoned mines or disused mills, is the tradition and ceremonial of which unhappily I am the unworthy guardian. Yet I do my best. There was the Tilling Festival that I planned. Fancy Mr. Bernard Shaw not wanting to *première* his new play here! And Mr. William Walton did not even reply to my letter. How little interest my fellow-citizens took in the project! How complacent, how self-satisfied, how truly provincial they are at times!'

Her husband, Georgie Pillson, intruded upon this meditation. He was feeling rather bright this morning, for he had just renewed the brilliant auburn of his apparently abundant hair, and was feeling young again. As Tilling's *jeune premier*, he had a duty to 'keep young and beautiful', as Mr. Eddie Cantor puts it in his song, and there was no more zealous slave of duty than Georgie, in this respect at least. It galled him slightly that his brilliant artifice must be kept secret, but here was surely a supreme example of the art that conceals art. He was therefore at peace with the world, for it is not in the praise of others that the true artist revels, but in the knowledge that he has satisfied himself.

'Have you seen my embroidery needles?' he asked cheerfully. 'I believe I left them lying about here somewhere. They're in their red felt case with my initials on. I had them yesterday evening and now I can't find them anywhere.'

He's dyed his hair again, thought Lucia. If only there was a kind way of telling him not to. It does so strain one's credibility.

'Alas, *caro*, I have not seen them. Have you looked in your pockets?'

'That was the first place I looked and they weren't there. It's too tar'some, because I wanted to get on with those hassock-covers I'm presenting to the Church to celebrate your second term. And I'd thought of a brilliant idea. Instead of just doing flowers and things, I thought of showing a view of the town from the Harbour, with the Landgate and the Norman Tower and all the red roofs.' He put his hand in his pockets and felt something suspiciously familiar. It was the needle-case, but he could not bring himself to declare it, having just vowed that he had looked there already.

Lucia was silent for a moment, resting her chin on the tips of her long, beautiful fingers. It was one of her more exquisite poses and denoted Thought. Generally it was reserved for civic matters (it was very hard to keep up for a prolonged period) and Georgie was surprised that she should assume it over so apparently trivial a suggestion. Then he recalled that Elizabeth had vowed a hetacomb of hassocks to the Church during her election campaign, which vow, despite her defeat, she presumably meant to make good.

'I believe you may have something there, *Georgino mio*, the kernel of an idea, perhaps the idea itself. Yes, yes, I can see it in my mind's eye. I seem to see something on the lines of the Bayeux Tapestry — but it was not a tapestry but an embroidery, as I recall — stylised and quaint yet immensely vivid and immediate. Realism without naturalism, Georgie, is a leading *motif* in Modern Art. There is a move away from the struggle to perfect the reflection of Nature in Art's mirror, which I attribute to the all-pervading effects of photography. But I digress. It's quite an inspiration, Georgie. I insist that you make a few preliminary sketches, based on Norman and Carolingian originals, but incorporating you own unique talent, for you must serve the tradition without being its slave. Remember you are an artist, not a draughtsman. *Kinde, schaf' neues*, as Wagner is reputed to have said.'

'Well, I won't be able to *schaf* anything unless I find my needles,' declared Georgie, who had patiently borne this stream of twaddle. 'Perhaps they're in the drawer of your desk.' And he slipped the case into the palm of his hand like a conjuror.

'I don't think they are, dear,' she said absently, but

9

Georgie, opening the drawer and slipping the case into it, contradicted her with a cry of triumph. 'How strange!' she said. 'I was looking in that drawer only a quarter of an hour since. How careless of me!' By which she meant that she had deduced that he had found the needles in his pocket and pitied him for needing to be forever in the right.

'Well, now that I've found them, I can start right away,' said Georgie, unabashed. 'So glad that you approve.'

'There is a book of illustrations in the bookshelf on your right,' she said, and returned to her musing, for Georgie's idea had spawned another in her mind. It, too, was only the kernel of an idea, but should the seed germinate, who knew what it might grow into?

At her house called Grebe, a quarter of a mile outside the town, Elizabeth Mapp-Flint sat and imposed tea upon her long-suffering husband, Major Benjamin Mapp-Flint, whose disdain for such weak liquor was universally known. At present, however, he thought it politic to acquiesce in his own slow-poisoning in the interests of diplomacy. His was a happy marriage, a lesson to those who would declare that a middle-aged bachelor and a spinster past her first youth are too set in their ways contentedly to pull the yoke of matrimony. Yet he could not help feeling that it would be happier still if his wife were not such a paragon of frugality. For his eye had chanced upon a smart little three-wheeled motor, displayed for sale outside the garage at the foot of the hill below Porpoise Street. He had been sheltering from the rain under the garage's copious awning at the time and therefore had been some minutes in the machine's company. The more he had looked at it, the more it found favour in his eyes; it was gracefully built and rather dashing (for it was open-topped), and motor-racing had of late been featured prominently in the newspapers. Like the Cyclops in Theocritus' poem, the more he looked the more he loved, the more his heart was touched within him, so that by the time the rain had passed away to soak some neighbouring town, notions of owning it, which in his brain were yet fantastical, had assailed him.

For surely he could not persuade his wife to make such a purchase. Besides her economical instincts (an excellent thing in a woman, but not always), there was the fact that they had owned a motor before, which they had been forced to dispose of (as scrap) after an unfortunate collision with the corner of Malleson Street. Although neither of them had been injured, he felt that the incident might prejudice his wife against another venture into the exciting world of motorism. And yet it was a most attractive vehicle in every respect. He had noticed that it was made by the Birmingham Small Arms Company, and although he knew nothing of their motor-vehicles, he had heard during his military service that their staple products, according to those who had business with such things, were most serviceable. Secondly, the dealer had assured him, on his subsequent visit, that both the previous owners of the vehicle, two spinster ladies of a neighbouring town, had spoken warmly of it, selecting for especial praise its accurate steering and awesome powers of acceleration.

In his mind he rehearsed various arguments in favour of the purchase. There was, for a start, the long walk into town every day. Although he had never managed to ascertain exactly how old his wife was, he felt sure that the daily exertion must be as tiresome to her as it undoubtedly was to him. The tram-fare to the golf-links, which he loved to frequent, had recently increased by a whole penny. He was no mathematician, but surely the savings on tickets and shoe-leather would rapidly offset the eighty pounds demanded for the motor. And time was of the essence. He did not know whether fishmongers were wealthy men, but he had seen Mr. Hopkins eyeing the vehicle. In fact, Mr. Hopkins passed by it every morning on the way to the Harbour to buy fish; how long could he resist so desirable an object? In addition, Mr. Hopkins had the misfortune to be a bachelor, and so could spend his money on whatever he chose.

11

Therefore it was necessary that Major Benjy should drink humble tea and speak comfortably to his wife, at least until the motor was in his possession. But the problem of how best to broach the subject remained, and the more compliant he was, the more his wife would suspect him of an ulterior motive and harden her heart against any proposal he might make. He therefore resolved to speak at once, boldly, as befitted a military man, putting his fortune to the test to win or hazard all.

'Been to town today, Liz?' he enquired.

'Yes, dear.'

'Shopping, I'll be bound.'

'Yes.'

'You know, girlie, I'm worried about your carrying heavy groceries all the way out here every day. Not right that you should be put to the trouble.'

'But I'm not put to the trouble, dear. All the tradesmen deliver, albeit erratically, as you would know if you were in more often during the afternoon. But I do not begrudge you your little games of golf. Exercise is so important, after all, and golf is a manly game. There is no need for you to give it up just to carry my shopping basket for me. But sweet of you to offer.'

He didn't remember offering, but that was not unusual. He often could not recall making the promises on which his wife was wont to take him up.

'Still, it's a deuced long way in and out of town — one and a half miles if it's a step, the way the road curves round and about. And there's the danger of twisting an ankle on the cobbles. Very irregular in places.'

'I know, dear. I have complained personally to our beloved Mayor on more than one occasion, but when it comes to something that would be of real service to the community, she seems to be rather lackadaisical in her attitude. Perhaps she would listen to you.'

'I must mention it when next I see her. But it's such a nuisance having to walk into town on these dark nights, now that winter's here again. It takes all the pleasure out of seeing our friends, especially when it's wet. On the other hand, we're admirably settled here at Grebe. Nice spot, quiet, peaceful. So what are we to do?'

Elizabeth studied him carefully over the rim of her tea-cup. She had missed the little ritual of teatime which they invariably performed: Major Benjy would say that he quite fancied a spot of whisky and she would persuade him that he did not. Yet today he had accepted tea without a murmur. Now this unwonted concern about her well-being prompted her to wonder whether he had some foolish plan in mind for which he was anxious to secure her approval. If he had, she would, of course, dismiss it at once.

'There's something else, too,' he ground on, unaware that his guile was in vain. 'Now that you've been appointed Mayoress a second time — the least she could do after getting Miss Coles to stand against you, and who voted for her I can't imagine — you'll be wanting to keep up with civic affairs just as much as ever before, if not more so. Next year to think of, after all. I tell you what, though. I think I know why you didn't get elected this time.'

'Oh, do tell me,' said Elizabeth acidly.

'Well, it's obvious really. There's Miss Coles parading up and down all day, while you're stuck out here where nobody can see you. No wonder they voted for her and not for you. Out of sight, out of mind, don't you know.'

'On the contrary, Benjy. I would have thought that the more the voters saw of Miss Coles, the less they would have liked her, given the tasteless eccentricity of her costume.'

Even as she spoke, it occurred to her that her husband might for once be right. In politics visibility was all, as Lloyd George would undoubtedly have confirmed. At the same time, an explanation for his concern for her political career began to suggest itself. She could read him like a book, although what sort of book he most closely resembled she did not like to imagine.

'It is possible,' she conceded, after a sip of tea, 'but there we are. We cannot carry our dear little house on our backs like snails, to be busy in town during the day and cosy in the country in the evenings. So we must make the best of things.'

'But we could make up for that, you know,' he replied. 'I've often thought it a crying shame that we — I mean you — don't get an official car as Mayoress.'

Elizabeth smiled. So he was thinking those foolish thoughts of which she had not deigned to suspect him.

'What sweet nonsense you do talk at times, dear,' she purred. 'Now you wouldn't want us to be like those dreadful Wyses with their Royce when they drive the fifty yards to Mallards instead of walking. And Lucia herself, with that enormous chariot that she never uses. Too ostentatious for words. Besides it would strike at the very heart of my economic strategy for Tilling, which is, as you should know by now, the ruthless elimination of unnecessary expenditure. It would be a fine thing for me to preach frugality from the back seat of an official Daimler.' Fine indeed; she could just picture it.

'Oh, I don't mean that we should get a Rolls or a Daimler like the others,' he said. 'Something much smaller. More economical. More dignified. Less ostentatious. Why have four wheels when three will do just as well?'

Elizabeth broadened her smile and her perfect teeth (no random work of nature but the product of human craftsmanship) shone like the desert sun on a man dying of thirst.

'Alas, I doubt whether we could persuade Lucia and her Council — as she will insist on calling it, and I'm glad I'm no longer a member of it — to buy us even the most modest of cars, one with no wheels at all, let alone three. And since we obviously cannot afford to buy one ourselves, there the matter must rest. Now if Lucia were still living here at Grebe, I expect she would have a private railway built at the rate-payers' expense, and have her own liveried coaches, all in the interest of creating employment, you understand. What a sweet hypocrite our dear friend is. So amusing!'

14

Benjy snorted, no doubt at the thought of Lucia's hypocrisy, and turn to contemplation of his tea, which was cold. But Elizabeth, instead of persecuting him further as she would normally have done, sat awhile in silence. Why shouldn't they afford a motor, so long as it was small and not liable to involve them in ruinous maintenance? Of course, she, not her husband, would drive it, thus eliminating the risk of further collisions. Driving was easily learnt, so she understood, and she was a quick learner. As for the expense — well, Benjy must never know, but she had recently sold some unprofitable shares and reinvested the money wisely. Eighty pounds might be raised without undue strain, and that would surely be enough to secure a nice little car.

She consulted her watch; it was nearly time to dress for dinner at Mallards, to celebrate Lucia's second term of office. Lucia had, as usual, offered to send the motor over to collect them; as usual she had declined the kind but unnecessary offer. As she rose from the table, rain began to rattle against the window-panes.

Irene Coles, artist, Fabian, free-thinker and Town Councillor (an impressive *curriculum vitae* for one who had not yet reached her thirtieth year) sat in her oilskins in the shadow of the Landgate and surveyed the dark clouds over the estuary. The driving rain had extinguished her short clay pipe, so that only a little black silt remained in the bowl, but she was unconscious of that as of all else but the grandeur of the scene that Nature had laid on for her benefit. Shortly she would have to abandon the spot, for she was bidden to attend Lucia's dinner party and Lucia's wish was her command. But she hoped to absorb a little more of the atmosphere if she could (she had absorbed a great deal already, and it was starting to trickle down the back of her neck) for her next work. This was to continue her series of masterly allegorical sketches, in all of which Lucia had appeared as the representative of freedom and civilisation. This latest was to be a version of the Second Coming (Lucia's Second

Coming into the Mayoralty), with her darling riding into town on the wings of the storm while the voters of Tilling pulled down and smashed to pieces an enormous statue of Elizabeth Mapp-Flint. Her work on this masterpiece had been frustrated by a period of relatively clement weather, so that she had not been sure where, so to speak, her next thunderstorm was coming from. So she was determined to make the most of this one.

The Mapp-Flints, wet and bedraggled as two animals entering Noah's Ark, scuttled wearily under the ancient arch and shook the water from the small, crooked umbrella which alone stood between the elements and their evening clothes. Had they been less wet and weary, they might have noticed Irene just outside the arch, and so been more reserved in their speech. As it was, they shouted to make themselves audible over the pelting of the storm and so were overheard by an audience they would not themselves have chosen.

'See what I mean, Liz old girl?' roared the Major through his chattering teeth, and Irene's acute ears recognised his voice at once. 'Now, if we'd had a little car, with a nice waterproof hood —'

'Oh Benjy, how frail you old soldiers are!' cried Elizabeth, loud and shrill above the fury of Nature. It took more than a thunderstorm to silence her.

'What was that?'

'I said how frail you old soldiers are!' shrieked Elizabeth playfully. 'A little spot of rain terrifies you so much and yet you faced all those ferocious Pathans and tigers in your Army days. I wonder that the enemy did not attack during the monsoons, for you would never have come out to fight and risk getting wet.'

Had Elizabeth known that she was saying all this before one who would take it all down, albeit not in writing, and use it in evidence against her, she would have silenced the batteries of her brilliant wit. Instead, she fulminated on.

'Why, anybody would think that you were made of sugar and liable to dissolve in water. Sugar and spice and all things nice, Benjy, that's what you are made of.'

'You're as wet as I am,' replied he, 'so I don't know why you're being so deuced funny about it.'

'Don't be a cry-baby, nuisance, we'll soon dry out in front of Lucia's nice warm fire, always supposing that Her Worship allows us near it, of course.'

Benjy muttered something about a sure path to pneumonia and they were silent for a while before a dainty little Morgan three-wheeler sped through the arch, spraying them both with water as its tyres cleaved the deep puddles. Elizabeth was briefly vituperative about motorists in general, but from her tone of voice, Benjy (and the fascinated Irene) were able to deduce that her hatred was not untainted with envy.

'Now be fair, Liz,' said Major Benjy. 'Wouldn't it be pleasant, and sensible too, to have a trim little craft like that for getting about in when it's wet? And there's our health to think about too. I hope I won't sound selfish when I remind you that my constitution was broken on the wheel of the Indian climate.'

Did climates have wheels and, if so, how many? But Elizabeth's resolve that her finances should not be broken on the wheel of the Birmingham Small Arms Company was waning fast. The rain showed no sign of letting up. . . .

'Be that as it may,' she said with an effort, 'finding the money would be a problem. You know that those wretched mining shares have gone down yet again.' So they had; how lucky she no longer had any. 'Faced with that sort of risk to our capital it would be sheer reck-lessness. . . .'

Irene, hidden from their sight by darkness and foul weather, grinned broadly. As Tilling's foremost mimic, she would rarely get such an opportunity for gathering the sinews of satire. Unfortunately, she grinned too broadly and sneezed, thereby betraying her position. Elizabeth at once realised that her words had been over-heard and offered up a short prayer that it should not prove to have been Irene who had overheard them.

17

'Hello, Mapp. *Qui-hi*, Benjy. When shall we three meet again, I wonder? What a lot of weather we're having, except that you seem to have taken most of it and secreted it about your person. Mind you give it back later; that's public weather, and I'm a Government official now.'

Elizabeth snarled, but could think of nothing to say. Irene often had that effect on her, like a fly that buzzes and buzzes and cannot be caught.

'The owl and the pussy cat will need a beautiful pea-green boat if they're to get back to Grebe this evening. Or a beautiful pea-green motor-car might do at a pinch, I suppose. What a shame you're too poor to buy one after your speculations on the Stock Market. When we socialists are in power, of course. . . .'

Elizabeth suddenly seemed to recover her powers of speech, and she drove the fly from her presence with a radiant smile.

'So you overheard our little plot, did you, dear one — I shall never get used to calling my little friend "Councillor Coles". Well, you shall be the first to know, in that case. Benjy-boy and I are to have a dear little motor-car to drive about in. . . .'

'But I thought you said. . . .' interrupted her husband. She ignored him.

'. . . and there'll always be the dickey-seat for you to ride in if you wish. My dear Benjy has seen such a dear little car, and since I cannot refuse him anything —'

'Except whisky, or so he says,' snapped Irene. 'Well, that will be a sight to see, unless you get rammed by Malleson Street again. So careless, those street-corners, always bumping into people and flattening their motor-cars. Well, good luck to you both. I'll tell you what, though. I could be your chauffeur and drive Major Benjy round the public-houses while you're out of the way. That would be fun.'

'Oh look,' said Elizabeth brightly, gazing fixedly at the howling storm. 'It seems to be clearing up. Come along, Benjy, we're late enough as it is. See you at Lucia's.'

18

'Save me a place by the fire,' Irene called after them as they splashed their way through the puddles. 'Rain suits you, Mapp. Makes you look like a Rhinemaiden.'

Lucia's party proved to be a great success, but not for Lucia. Instead, Elizabeth held the stage, while Benjy, revived by warmth and sherry after his shock under the Landgate, prompted her with technical details concerning her forthcoming purchase.

Elizabeth had, in her characteristic fashion, become a whole-hearted motorist now, and her only fear seemed to be that someone else might buy the motor-car before she managed to get to the garage first thing next morning. She was not deterred by the fact that she was getting one less wheel for her money than she would have liked, while Benjy's enthusiasm was not entirely destroyed when he learnt that Elizabeth meant to be the driver, for he was sure that she would soon despair of it and leave him in charge of the driving. To be sure, eighty pounds was a small price to pay for the glances of envious admiration in whose radiance they bathed that evening.

The Wyses, Tilling's foremost motorists, had been made to feel that their enormous Rolls-Royce was both antiquated and grotesquely over-sized, whereas Lucia, whose motor rarely left the garage and was retained only to provide employment for Cadman, her chauffeur and husband to Georgie's irreplaceable parlourmaid Foljambe, was made to look more foolish still. Of the pedestrians, Evie Bartlett, wife of the Vicar (or Padre, as Tilling was pleased to call him), had wasted no time in reminding her husband of the many occasions on which he had declared how useful a small, unostentatious car would be for getting around the parish. He had replied in the curious composite-Scottish dialect that he spoke in preference to the language of his native Birmingham, that it was sair muckle work to get about a district so full of hills on a bicycle.

Diva Plaistow, whose late husband had once briefly owned a second-hand Darracq, and who therefore felt a great nostalgia for the lost joys of motoring, said that it sounded lovely, and spent much of the evening trying to work out how she might raise eighty pounds to buy a car. But she was no business-woman, and, although she had the idea of making pin-cushions and selling them on a commission basis in the draper's shop, she feared that it would take her some time to raise such a sum in that fashion.

Lucia was thus on the horns of a dilemma, for the gage had been clearly thrown at her feet and the challenge fairly issued. Elizabeth meant to become great in the land by her motoring, and although Lucia could have no possible objection to poor Elizabeth's making herself conspicuous if she felt it necessary to do so, she did not wish to see Tilling swept by some foolish craze when she might soon have need of their energies for some worthy project of her own. Yet she could not simply pour scorn on motorism in general, for she did not wish to offend the Wyses, nor indeed to dispose of her own motor. For if Cadman left, Foljambe would leave too, and Georgie had declared, over and over again, that life without Foljambe would be intolerable; no one else would ever be able to run his bath to the temperature he liked, or care for his things as they should be cared for — it was impossible. So Foljambe and Cadman, and the car, must stay. She was therefore faced with a choice between pouring scorn on Elizabeth's car and that alone (which would be highly invidious and might provoke unwelcome and distracting reprisals) or else substituting some craze of her own, cheaper and more attractive to the temperament of her fellow-citizens, and also in some way related to that lofty project which she had yet to decide upon. . . .

It was a thorny problem, and yet there was something that Georgie had said that might resolve all. Therefore, once her guests had departed into the night (Elizabeth and Benjy as prospective motorists being driven home by the Wyses in the Royce), she set to thinking, with the aid of strong coffee and a bag of peppermints.

Whether it was the coffee or the peppermints or a night's rest that provided the inspiration, she awoke the next morning with the whole idea, like Coleridge's 'Kubla Khan', fully fledged in her mind. Fortunately no intrusive visitor from Porlock interrupted her (since Porlock was over two hundred miles away, the danger was slight in any case) and she was able to write out the bare skeleton of her plan before any of it could evaporate.

Tilling, its history and heritage, was to be her January stunt, and the instrument of her destiny would be a Tilling Tapestry (or rather embroidery) depicting the whole history of the town from mythological times down to the present day. It would be a work to rival the handicraft of the good wives of Bayeux — greater, indeed, than theirs by as much as the scope of her subject, which was broader and more comprehensive. Roman Tilling, Saxon Tilling, Norman Tilling (that sounded like somebody's name, but never mind), the French incursion in the Middle Ages and the prosperity of the Wool Trade, Elizabethan enterprise and Hanoverian elegance, culminating in modern science and achievement. As a counterpoint to this lofty abstract she would interpose the human specific, uniting this mighty tale with some great continuum; and for that purpose, what could be better than the great tradition of the Mayors of Tilling, their portraits running like a commentary below and above the main action?

In this noble project she could profitably find employment for her husband. She was far too perceptive not to have noticed that at times her civic role had tended to overawe him somewhat, to make him feel excluded and unimportant. She had felt uneasy about this before now, but had steeled her heart (for duty must come first, and there is a dignity hedges round a mayor that a mayor's husband must learn to live with). Now she would have an opportunity to involve him closely in her official work, almost (but not quite) let him be her partner in it. For Georgie was a very fine embroiderer, proficient at both

gros and *petit point*, and successful products of his pro-
lific needle decorated many of the chairs and cushions
of the house. Other, less successful efforts decorated
the interior of a large chest of drawers in the box-room.
Georgie, then, would be her chief assistant and master
craftsman, while the rest of their circle would act as his
apprentices, filling in, doing backgrounds. The finished
embroidery would, of course, hang in the Town Hall,
unless it became necessary to build special premises to
house it. As it so happened, she had made a couple of
rough sketches for a Tilling *Festspielhaus* to accommo-
date the ill-fated Tilling Festival. With a few alterations,
the same concept could be used for the tapestry, and the
Town Hall would thus be spared the disruptions to its
activities that must of necessity be caused by the enormous crowds which would regularly flock to see so great
a work of folk-art.

'And all that,' she mused as she rang for breakfast,
'came from Georgie's hassocks and Elizabeth's motor-
tricycle. Fancy!'

Georgie had, unusually for him, come down to breakfast as well. Generally he preferred to breakfast in his
dressing-room, being aware of the damage that sleep
and the early morning were capable of doing to his
youthful appearance. But Lucia had been pensive last
evening, and so he had decided that it would be advisable to be up and about early to take whatever steps
might be necessary in the event of Lucia having one of
her ideas. Should she decide to trump Elizabeth's
planned motor-car by taking up aviation, for example,
he wanted to be in time to dissuade her from ordering an
aeroplane.

'*Georgino caro*,' exclaimed she, 'what an early riser!
Not a particularly fine day to wake up early for, I'm
afraid. More rain, perhaps even snow, for it is distinctly
chilly, and I fear a cold front closing in from Iceland.'
(She's read that in the paper, thought Georgie, but he said
nothing.) 'And now I suppose you would like some breakfast. I will get Grosvenor to bring us some fresh tea.'

'Most thoughtful,' said Georgie politely.

This cheerfulness was ambiguous. Had she determined to ignore Elizabeth's *coup* entirely — an established tactic, most irritating to the innovator, but hard to sustain over long periods of time — or had she already evolved her counter-strategy?

'Is there anything in the papers this morning?'

There had been nothing except the weather report, so she replied, 'Nothing of any great importance, *Georgino*. How little seems to happen nowadays! We must all lead very uninteresting lives if the announcement that poor dear Elizabeth is going to buy a motor-bicycle and ride it up and down the Military Road all day sends us all into fits of excitement. Yet that is the spice of life, it appears, and boring old civic affairs interest us not at all.'

'It wasn't a motor-bicycle,' said Georgie firmly, 'it was a three-wheeler. And there aren't any civic affairs to bore or interest us. I thought that was the whole problem.'

'I dare say you are right about Elizabeth's motor-vehicle. I can't say I paid much attention to what she was saying. I feel we all lack employment in Tilling these days. Idle hands, Georgie, make for idle minds.'

'I should hate to be employed and have no time for my needlework and my painting and playing the piano and seeing people. I find I have little enough spare time as it is.'

'Rubbish, *caro*, one can find time for important things if one makes an effort. And I've just had a tremendous idea.'

'Shall I like it?' asked Georgie gloomily, for it was as he had feared. 'Or will it be just another festival? That fell awfully flat when all those tar'some people said they couldn't come. And I'd bought a new dress-suit to wear, but I hadn't the heart when it was just us.'

'No!' exclaimed Lucia, her lofty plans temporarily driven from her mind by this exciting news. 'Why didn't you say! And why haven't I seen it?'

'It was to be a surprise. Mohair with silk facings. And

23

now I shall have to wait until it's summer again before I can try it out, because the cloth's too thin to wear in the winter. It's most frustrating, for it was quite expensive. But you were telling me about this scheme of yours. And I was saying —'

'That you hoped it wouldn't be just another festival. Well it isn't. It's even so much better than that, you'll see. There's lots for us both to do. In fact, there's more for you than for me. You'll be terribly important. Can you guess what it is?'

'No,' said Georgie without trying. 'You'd better tell me.'

So she did. The more Georgie heard, the more excited he became, so that as soon as Lucia had finished her most eloquent presentation, which she made with hardly any reference to her notes, he hurried away to the garden-room to start on his preliminary sketches. So involved did he become in this engrossing and gratifying work that Grosvenor had announced lunch before he remembered that he hadn't had any breakfast.

2

Elizabeth's new car, with Elizabeth proudly at the wheel, made its maiden trip into Tilling just three days later. Triumphant was Elizabeth's progress up the hill and under the Landgate; indeed, she had all the air of a successful Roman general, with fascinated crowds to stare at her and Major Benjy to play the *rôle* of the slave who rides beside the conqueror in his chariot and whispers in his ear 'Remember that thou art mortal.' In fact, Benjy was more concerned with his own mortality than his wife's, for her driving, although not at all bad for a beginner, nonetheless made him feel somewhat nervous.

Only one of the Tillingites who observed that spectacle failed to evince the awe and wonder that is associated with Esquimaux who see their first steam-locomotive. Quaint Irene had been sketching at the Belvedere Platform and saw the motor-car coming. Without stopping to fold up her camp-stool or dismantle her easel, she abandoned her sketch to the risk of theft (although, given the nature of her work, that risk was slight) and sprinted up the High Street to her house. Just inside the front-door, laid ready for just this very emergency, was a peaked cap and a small purpose-made red flag. She lay in wait at the corner of West Street until the motor approached, darted out in front of it and proceeded to walk at a slow march all the way down to the Porpoise Street turning where Elizabeth was finally able to overtake her and leave behind the throng of small children who had gathered in her wake.

Rather than attempt to turn the vehicle round in the

road, she made a complete circuit of the town before turning up into Church Square on her way to Mallards (for she particularly wanted to drive past the garden-room and, taking one hand daringly from the wheel, wave gaily to her dear friends within). Unfortunately a baker's van with a brewer's dray behind it was coming in the opposite direction, with the result that three-wheeler and van were soon bumper to bumper in the attitude of two rutting stags locking horns to decide supremacy. The van-driver refused to back, pointing out that he had a team of horses behind him, while she was but six yards from the turning-place. Elizabeth, for her part, instructed Major Benjy to get out and order the man to go back. The Major complied with the first of these instructions only too eagerly but disregarded the second part; in his opinion she really should go back and he would give her directions. So clear were his directions and so skilled was Elizabeth in the manipulation of her vehicle that it took but a quarter of an hour to accomplish the manoeuvre, and the van-driver was then free to travel on his way, which he did. He also gave both Benjy and Elizabeth a good deal of useful advice as he passed, not all of it to do with motoring. When this distasteful incident was over, the Major did not resume his place in the passenger-seat: it was his opinion that his extra weight was making the machine difficult to handle at times, which would no doubt account for occasional spells of erratic steering. He would walk, or if necessary trot alongside as she drove, but get back in he would do under no circumstances.

As the Athenians to the Pnyx, the antique Romans to the Campus Martius, or our Nordic ancestors to the All-Thing, so the folk of Tilling flocked to the High Street for *extempore* parliament. Diva, taking the chair in the doorway of Twistevant's, was of the opinion that Elizabeth was to be admired for her daring and locomotive skill; the name of Miss Amy Johnson was cited as a parallel. Quaint Irene (leader of the opposition) snorted daintily and expressed grave concern for the public safety should the menace of powerful motor-vehicles in the hands of untrained drivers remain unchecked. A similar opinion was expressed by the Lords Spiritual (the Padre), who had watched the scene in Church Square with fascinated horror from his study window; he had recently had his garden planted out in crocus bulbs at some considerable expense. The motion was then thrown open to the Floor (consisting of Evie Bartlett), who had not yet formed an opinion and could only squeak excitedly.

'' 'Tes a diabolic contraption to be exercising within sight o'God's ane house and my wee bittie o' garden so recently planted out wi' bulbs,' exclaimed the Padre. 'And do ye no mind the interference wi' the rightful users o' the King's Highway?'

'You don't object when the Wyses or Lucia drive their motors in Church Square,' objected his wife, who had wanted the front garden planted out with roses. 'I think it's terribly brave of Elizabeth and she's only just bought the vehicle.'

'Then she should learn somewhere else,' retorted Irene. 'It's all rank imitation of Lucia anyway, and very appropriate. Mapp's just a potty little three-wheeler chugging along behind a Mayoral Rolls-Royce.'

Diva generally opposed Irene in debates of this nature, for Irene had once whitewashed her Irish setter, Paddy, for a joke. 'That's nonsense,' she said. 'Just because Lucia does something, it doesn't follow that everyone else who does it is copying her. I had a kipper for breakfast this morning but it doesn't mean that I invented the idea.'

To complete the parliament came Mr. and Mrs. Wyse, representatives, surely, of the Lords Temporal — for were they not related to the Wyses of Whitchurch and, by marriage, to the Italian aristocracy? They were on foot, for the Royce had developed some curious wasting disease and was even now under the spanner. They had thought of hiring a motor for the day, but since no suitable machine could be procured and the furthest they

27

might go from their front door would be a hundred yards, they had opted for a little exercise. As a result, they had witnessed Elizabeth's *début* as pedestrians, susceptible to the glamour that all can vouch for who have trudged along on foot as others purr by on four (or even three) wheels.

As was usual in Tilling, the presence of the Wyses curbed the tongues and improved the manners of those around them. Even Irene was quiet for a moment, but the excitement of combat was upon her like the berserk fury and she now sought to enlist the support of these most distinguished allies.

'Hello, Mr. Wyse, Mrs. Wyse. No motor today?' she enquired sweetly.

'Alas, no,' replied Mr. Wyse after his customary round of chivalrous greetings. 'The Royce has unfortunately developed some slight mechanical disorder and so we must perforce do our little round of shopping on foot. No doubt we shall benefit greatly from a little pedestrian exercise. I have become too, too indolent of late — my bicycle hangs neglected from the rafters of the garage, so my worthy chauffeur tells me.'

A silence generally fell on the company after Mr. Wyse had finished speaking; his language was so fine, so Augustan that it seemed a pity to defile its memory with effusions in the vulgar tongue.

'What rotten luck!' said the quaint one, with an effort. 'If Mapp had bought a proper car she could have given you both a lift. Then you could have worn your sables, Mrs. Wyse.' This was a good point to make if she wished to win round these new allies. Susan Wyse was the proud owner of a magnificent fur-coat which she wore even in the height of summer. Such was its weight, however, that motorised transport was needed to move it about and, now that she was confined to walking for a day, she had reluctantly been compelled to leave it at home.

'But that's typical of Mapp,' continued Irene, 'going and buying a two-seater. You're always offering people lifts in your car. Why should a dog, a horse, a Mapp have transport and thou no car at all?'

'You couldn't expect Elizabeth to drive a great big thing,' objected Diva.

'Why not?' chirruped the quaint one. 'She drives Major Benjy — to the point of distraction, or so he says — and he's a great big thing if ever I saw one.'

This was a tactical error on Irene's part, for Mr. Wyse gave her such a refined look than even her self-esteem was sorely tried. 'I quite agree with you, Mrs. Plaistow,' he said. 'The gentle sex cannot be expected to cope with the physical effort of controlling full-sized machines. Yet they should not be denied the use of motor-vehicles. I believe that young ladies of the most exalted families nowadays drive themselves about in small motor-cars. They are to be seen in Hyde Park and in Norfolk.'

This was weighty evidence indeed and again the gathering was silent as they digested its full implications. But the Padre was a man of conscience to whom principle was more important than expediency. Besides, his crocuses had not been planted in Hyde Park nor yet in Norfolk, but in Tilling.

'I ken that a' ye say is sooth,' he said, choosing his words carefully, 'but yon exalted folk of whom ye spake are responsible, God-fearing men and women, mindful o' the public weal. But 'tes a sinful thing to venture forth in charge o' a hazardous engine an ye no have the complete control on't. There is risk to life and property.'

So well chosen were his words that a pause was required for mental translation and while this process was being carried out, Lucia, basket on arm, and Georgie joined the little throng.

'Risk to life and property!' she exclaimed, after greeting her friends in a cheerful tone. 'What can this be? Padre, I trust you speak but in jest. As Mayor of Tilling, I am in duty bound to protect both life and property.'

'Then get Mapp off the roads,' exclaimed Irene. 'She's worse than a Zeppelin raid in that motor-car of hers.'

Lucia laughed her silvery laugh as expectation hung heavy in the air. For Lucia represented Government and actual power; could she not pass an ordinance sweeping her turbulent Mayoress from the streets?

'My dear, is that all ?' warbled Lucia. 'I was afraid that you were serious. I have every confidence in dear Elizabeth's abilities as a motorist, for has not Major Benjy taught her the craft? And we all know how proficient he is.'

Irene begged her to consult the corner of Malleson Street on that point but Lucia seemed not to have heard. Although her hearing was excellent, she had that gift to temporary deafness that is granted to so few.

'I am sure that Elizabeth will soon be driving exquisitely; she will do this as well as everything she turns her versatile hand to. Now let us consider the benefit to us all that her new departure will bring. We shall see so much more of our dear friend now that she has transport of her own. I own that when I lived at Grebe I was content to walk in and out of town but I had only myself to please. Elizabeth has public duties to perform. In fact, I must ask my Council whether some small allowance — a mere token, you understand, so as not to appear offensive — cannot be found to contribute towards the upkeep of the vehicle, since it was doubtless the thought of her public duties that prompted her to purchase the machine. There was an ordinance in the fourteenth century providing the sum of five shillings a year to buy an ass to transport the Mayor into town if he lived outside the boundaries; if that ordinance has not since been repealed, we might revive it for dear Elizabeth's sake, suitably modernised of course.' And so saying, she passed on into the shop where Mr. Twistevant had been eyeing with growing frustration the knot of customers that had been standing outside for a full quarter of an hour. The Parliament was left with very mixed emotions. Did they really want to see so much more of their dear friend? And what was Lucia up to?

The same question vexed Georgie as they walked back

to Mallards, their marketing over for the day.

'I can't understand it,' said he. 'You were practically venomous about Elizabeth's motor this morning and you said you couldn't wait for her to apply for a maintenance allowance so that you could throw it out.'

Lucia laughed, so that the street seemed full of little silver bells. 'Georgino, how literally you take everything. What possible exception could I take to poor Elizabeth wanting a car? She is getting on, you know.' In fact, she was younger than Lucia but that did not mean that Lucia's statement was incorrect. 'And I suppose that hill up from Grebe is in places a little steep. And since Elizabeth is clearly anxious to make some small sensation, to bathe herself in the public attention which you know I so heartily abhor, why should I deny her the pleasure?'

'I don't know,' confessed Georgie, 'but somehow that's the way it always seems to happen. Whenever you start a particularly good thing, Elizabeth always tries to put you down — I don't think she's ever forgiven you for coming to Tilling in the first place. And then you always do the same to her, because you say it's good for her not to be allowed to get away with making herself conspicuous. And you're right, I suppose. She can be an awful nuisance when she thinks you've put her down, so you have to put her down to stop her doing it again.'

'Quite so, Georgie,' said Lucia, who had not understood a word. 'In this instance, however, my only fear — on her behalf — is that she might continue to make herself appear as ludicrous as she did this morning in Church Square. That van-driver, caro, such power of expression! If his views were less intemperate, we could use him on the Council. But she will soon become aware of the risk to her dignity — she is not totally insensitive to the opinions of others — and will quietly abandon her stunt. You will object that I, as her friend, ought to warn her of the danger she is in of becoming a laughing-stock and perhaps advise her — tactfully, of course — to dispose of her motor in the interests of her own physical safety, at the very least. But I have greater responsibilities than to my friends, I regret to say. Suppose I did act to suppress Elizabeth's motor, privately or even publicly.' (So she had thought of passing an ordinance!) 'Imagine her wrath, Georgie, her bad humour! She would be sure to seek reprisals, perhaps even attempt to undermine the success of the Tapestry. And that I could not allow.'

'You mean it's to be peace between you and Elizabeth until after the Tapestry?' cried Georgie, horrified. The prospect of a cessation of hostilities was appalling, for this warfare provided him with the excitement that no other occupation could hope to offer. 'Isn't that a bit drastic?'

'As far as I am concerned, there has always been peace between me and dear Elizabeth,' said his wife as she swept into Mallards. Georgie paused on the threshold for a moment as if hesitant to enter the habitation of such a perjurer lest it should be struck by lightning. Then a thought occurred to him and he hurried after her.

'But Lucia,' he said, 'what if she tries to disrupt it anyway? If she thinks you've become weak and are letting her get away with the car, she might attack the Tapestry in any case, just to show that she's on top.'

'Just let her try,' said the pacifist grimly.

Lucia's remarkable speech (no one doubted for a moment that it was a speech — and they were quite correct) had caused a stir the like of which Tilling, that place of excitements, had not seen for many a year. Someone even suggested ringing the church bells to celebrate the armistice, but that was considered inadvisable since they had not heard Elizabeth's views on the matter.

It was coming on to rain and since Diva had closed down her tea-rooms until the summer season, there was no public place that was sheltered from the rain where prolonged discussion could take place. Yet public discussion there must be; so everyone went back to Diva's

32

house and she was told off to telephone Mr. Georgie.

'Is Lucia listening?' she said.

'No,' said he, 'she's in the garden-room working on — something or other.' He did not know if he was meant to tell everyone about the Tapestry yet.

'Then make some excuse and come round to Wasters at once. We're all dying to know what Lucia is up to.'

Georgie rang off and went to find Lucia. As it happened, she had come back into the house to pick up a book and had heard the telephone ring. Therefore when Georgie said that he had forgotten something and was just popping out for a moment, she deduced at once what the telephone call had been about and decided to tease him before letting him go. Besides, she thought, they can wait for a minute or so. It will increase the suspense.

'What have you forgotten?' she enquired sweetly.

'Sealing-wax,' he said quickly.

'But I have some in my desk, *caro*. No need to go out in the rain.'

'But it's not the right sort,' he said, desperately. 'It's red and I wanted green.'

'Green sealing-wax! Fancy! Off you go then. And should you happen to bump into any of our friends, you might just drop the tiniest of hints that we have a treat in store for them worth twenty motor-cars. And do buy me some green sealing-wax. It does sound rather delightful.'

It was therefore as a holder of the Mayoral warrant that Georgie went forth to Wasters, hatless and running despite the risk to his *toupée* in the high wind. 'Now, shall I tell them all about it, or shall I tease them too? And where on earth am I going to find green sealing-wax? Infuriating woman!'

There could be only one word to express Tilling's reaction to Georgie's narrative. It fell to Evie Bartlett to say it.

'No!' she said. 'How exciting! But why? It's most unlike Lucia.'

Georgie felt he ought to rebuff what was, on balance, a slur on Lucia's name. But he could not in all honesty do

so; and besides, the remark could just as well be inter-
preted as a tribute to her vitality and indomitable spirit,
so he let it pass.

'She breaketh the bow,' said the Padre, who was a
man of peace, 'and knappeth the spear in sunder, and
burneth the chariots in the fire.'

Talk of chariots returned the conversation to the subject of the motor-car.

'So she'll let Elizabeth keep her motor?' demanded
Evie. 'My goodness, how disappointing! I was looking
forward to there being all sorts of excitements.'

'So was I,' admitted Georgie, 'but there will be plenty
of excitement to look forward to soon, and all in a good
cause, too. Is that the time? I must be going.'

This clumsy attempt at suspense-brewing deceived no
one, for he made no effort to move. He had expected a
barrage of breathless enquiries, but none came. Finally,
Mr. Wyse, whose acute social sense detected some
embarrassment in the silence, took it upon himself to
speak.

'May one enquire as to the nature of this excitement?'
he asked. 'I trust I am not proving ill-mannered in asking
you this in so blunt a fashion, but I believe that you did
mention that this undisclosed event would serve the
common good and I am sure that we are all anxious to
assist the Mayor in any of that most excellent lady's
worthy projects.'

'It's probably just the old scheme to put up those
dratted plaques everywhere,' said Diva, 'saying where
the fire started in fifteen-whatever-it-was and this was
the site of the Anglo-Saxon fish market. And since we've
all agreed that we don't want the wretched things on our
houses —'

'No, it's not that,' said Georgie hurriedly, 'although it
is something to do with local history in a way. Shall I give
you a clue? No, I'd better not, for it is a sort of Government secret and I wouldn't want to end up in prison.'

'Why not?' demanded Irene coldly, for she was most
upset to hear that Mallards was to be at peace with

34

Grebe. 'You'd have no end of fun embroidering the mailbags.'

'Oot wi'it, mon,' boomed the Padre. 'Ye can trust our discretion.'

'Very well, then,' said Georgie, rather nettled, 'but only a little clue, and you must work it out for yourselves. Just two words to help you — "the Normans". And now I really must be going, for I have to buy some sealing-wax for Lucia. Goodbye.'

By some remarkable chance, there was green sealing-wax to be had and he bought three sticks, one for himself and two for Lucia — 'Not that she deserves it, persecuting me like that. She can use it for official letters and make them look important. Oh dear, it wasn't a terribly good clue. I hope they won't be misled.'

For a while then, motorism was unchecked in Tilling. Yet the knowledge that conflict was not likely to result from it between the two great powers tended to diminish interest, and whatever interest there was likely to be seemed destined to be in such disasters as might befall Elizabeth as she pursued the science of motor-driving. Further admiration seemed unlikely. Some saw in this (or thought they saw) Lucia's foresightedness and strategic cunning. She had, they argued, foreseen that Elizabeth could only harm her *kudos* by continuing her stunt, and so permitted her to continue — in fact encouraged her. One of the chief proponents of this argument was Elizabeth herself and although she said as much only to Major Benjy, the view somehow reached a wider audience. On one thing all were agreed, however: Lucia had scored a notable victory but life was far less interesting as a result. On the fundamental question of motorism itself, only the Padre and Irene continued to discuss the matter, and, since they were agreed, there was little scope for further expansion of the theme. The Padre did make one last effort; he preached a fiery sermon in fluent Scotch on the text 'On thy belly shalt thou crawl', developing the theme that God had provided us with feet to walk upon and that any form of locomotion in which the feet did not touch earth (or move pedals, for the Padre rode a bicycle) was in effect a contempt for the Creator and an attempt to improve on His work. In order not to offend both Lucia and the Wyses, however, he was compelled to dilute his finest passages with gentle speech, with the result that most of his parishioners took the sermon to be about a proposed road-widening scheme down by the Harbour.

Elizabeth, meanwhile, was not finding the skill of motorism as easy to master as she had at first expected. What she needed, she decided, was practice and this must be obtained as far from home as possible. With this in mind, she raised the subject with her husband as they drove back from town one day.

'I think we might manage a holiday this year,' she shrieked over the shrill whine of the engine.

'For God's sake, engage third gear!' replied Major Benjy, helpfully.

'I am in third gear,' said Elizabeth and by the time she had finished making it the statement was true enough. 'I thought we might motor down along the coast to Devonshire. Dawlish is recommended at this time of —'

Benjy had seized the wheel briefly and a dog had thereby been spared destruction. 'I don't think you're quite ready for a long journey yet, old girl,' he said, returning the wheel to her hands. 'A bit more practice might be in order before you get too ambitious.'

'Nonsense, Benjy, I've quite got the hang of the thing. But a nice long drive in the country wouldn't hurt, I grant you, where the roads are empty and we're away from the prying eyes and mocking tongues of our so-called friends.'

'You didn't object to eyes and tongues when you started,' said her husband. 'Quite the reverse.'

'How hurtful you are sometimes, Benjy. You make it sound as if I welcomed their interest. You know very well that I hate to be the centre of attention — unlike some I could mention.'

They had returned to Grebe, and the motor, with an

unbattered edge, was parked up for the day. Major Benjy jumped down, rather unsteadily, and handed his wife down from the vehicle.

'Besides,' she went on, 'I feel like a change of surroundings. It will be pleasant to leave Tilling for a week or so and let our friends miss us. They'll soon tire of Lucia ordering them about.'

Major Benjy racked his brains for some reason to stay put. It was a long drive to Dawlish and it would seem longer still with his wife at the wheel.

'But your official work as Mayoress,' he insisted. 'Can't just abandon your post like that. Most unsoldierly. Court-martial offence.'

'I am the public's servant, not their slave, and the humblest parlourmaid is allowed a little holiday. I'm sure Lucia can manage without me for a while and if she can't it might teach her not to take me quite so much for granted in future. Withers, tea and a small whisky-and-soda. A treat, Benjy-boy, to warm you up after the cold air.'

Benjy regarded her warily, for he feared wives bearing gifts. Clearly there was something else behind this project of a Devonshire holiday besides motoring-practice. He counter manded the whisky-and-soda.

'I still say it's too much. Too exacting, too tiring. I'll tell you what, though. We might share the driving, if you like, fifty-fifty or sixty-forty. Then you can get your practice without wearing yourself out.'

Elizabeth's countenance showed no emotion behind the fixed smile that was her defensive visor. 'How thoughtful! Yet I shall never learn unless I do it myself. It's very sweet of you to offer, but I'm sure I can manage.'

'I insist!' cried the Major, thumping the table with his clenched fist. 'No wife of mine will ever exhaust herself with hard physical labour. No, by God, not while there's breath in my body. Either I shall do my share of motoring or we will not stir from the house.'

Elizabeth leaned across the table and put her hand on his. 'Very well then,' she said, 'we shall see. But you must let me have some practice. Else how shall I be able to drive all the time when we get back?'

Major Benjy relaxed. The threat to his life had partly abated and he began to wonder what had so worried Elizabeth about staying in Tilling that she could allow herself to be overruled in this fashion. He wondered also whether it might not be possible, after all, to get that whisky-and-soda.

'So that's agreed,' continued Elizabeth gaily. 'Now let's have our tea and discuss where we are to go. So glad you decided against having a glass of whisky, Benjy. Tea is so much better for you than spirits.'

Withers, the Mapp-Flints' long-suffering parlour-maid, brought in the tray and informed her mistress that Mrs. Pillson had telephoned while they had been out and would she call back as soon as she returned?

'*Elizabetha mia!*' warbled the Mayor's voice, and even electrically transmitted it seemed to fill the room like a miasma. '*Molto grazie* for returning my call *prestissimo*. Just a quick word to inform you that we've just had a Council meeting — how we miss your good judgement and common sense, dear! — and the Town Clerk thinks that the old ordinance can be brought up to date and that you are to receive an allowance of five pounds per annum towards the cost of petroleum and vehicle maintenance.'

Hairs began to rise on the back of Elizabeth's neck. Lucia was definitely up to something or other and she thanked her guardian angel for putting it into her mind to leave Tilling for a while.

'So thoughtful of you, dear. So typical of your sweet, generous nature, but I cannot in all honesty accept. It would be too wrong of me to take the rate-payers' money. Why, when I had the privilege to serve on Your Worship's Council, my policy was always economy, frugality and the ruthless control of waste. And besides, you over-praise me if you think that I intend to use my motor for civic business alone. Why, Benjy-boy and I have just now resolved on a motor-tour of Devonshire —'
There was a loud bump at the other end of the wire and

Elizabeth correctly deduced that Lucia had dropped the receiver.

'No!' Lucia exclaimed when she had recovered the instrument from the waste-paper basket, into which it had fallen. 'How splendid! And you are entitled to a holiday if anyone is after your tireless efforts for the community and the strain of the recent elections. But not too long, mind. You know how much we rely on you even now, both in public and in private life.'

Lucia hung up the receiver, leaving Elizabeth at her end of the wire as stunned as she was herself. For if actual coals of fire had been heaped on Elizabeth's head rather than merely scriptural ones, she could not have been more astonished. As for Lucia, this unexpected stroke of luck made a rosy prospect almost blood-red.

'Better and better, Georgie,' she cried. 'She's going away for a holiday.'

'No!' said he, echoing her reaction. 'That's most unusual. What can she be up to now?'

'Let me think,' said Lucia, in mock contemplation. 'Ah, I have it. She's going away to practise her driving where no one can see her and where she can bump into as many trees as she likes. Then she'll come sweeping back and impress us all with her virtuosity.'

'Why, of course!' cried Georgie. 'That's the reason. How tar'some she'll be. Can't you dissuade her? Think of something for her to do as Mayoress?'

'That would be rather small-minded, don't you think? Let her go to Devonshire. It is a sparsely-populated district where there will be far less risk of her killing, or injuring anyone in the course of her studies. Meanwhile, we can proceed with the Tapestry without any fear of her malice. By the time she gets back, everyone will be so deeply involved in the project that even if she wished to disrupt it — and I think we sometimes overestimate her malice — she would not be able to. But I hope that she will be swept up in the general enthusiasm on her return — yes, and Benjy too. I am convinced that deep down they would be only too delighted to be part of a project that can only bring glory on the town we all love.'

Georgie remembered something about someone who addressed people as if they were public meetings. It would apply very well to his wife, he thought sadly. Nevertheless, from what he could gather, it seemed as if the Tapestry would soon be under way and he was glad of that.

'So we can start as soon as she goes?' he asked. 'How thrilling!'

'I think so, dear. I have already got the shape of it in my mind, the outline, the narrative thrust — and I have been reading my source material very closely. Now, tell me what people think of the idea.'

Georgie saw that the pretence of green sealing-wax had been cast aside. 'Oh, I didn't tell them about the Tapestry in case they told Elizabeth. I just hinted. I mentioned "the Normans" to them and told them to work it out for themselves. I don't think it was a terribly good clue.'

'Never mind, it will stimulate their minds and create a sense of expectation. What is that word the cinema people use? Subliminal. They will be thinking about history, Georgie, our mediaeval past, our heritage.'

'I've been thinking about that too. There's the riots and the plague and the infestation of rats in the reign of Queen Matilda. Apparently, they came ashore from some ships and ate all the corn in the granary.'

'Admirable,' said Lucia, with distaste. 'But I think we might include some of the more cheerful episodes as well.'

She rose and went out to the garden-room, where her notes and sketches, and Georgie's own preliminary work, formed a thick pile of papers on her desk. It was a reassuring sight that seemed to promise her a world of future achievement. She ought to get down to the work of ordering and consolidating her material but she could not resist the temptation to fit in some additional episodes of an exceptionally charming nature that she had come across in an old guidebook. Certainly the project would not be lacking in scope. There were, at the last count, ninety-seven completed scenes and only a little exertion would be needed to fill up the round hundred. At the rate of one scene per worker per day, the project would soon be completed and ready to display. The only drawback, as far as she could see, was that this invigorating and enjoyable exercise would so soon be finished.

She looked out of the window at the darkened streets and considered how much the effect of that view upon her had changed in the last few days. To think that such an inspiring scene could have seemed to taunt her with lack of achievement! Now it was almost as if West Street were a triumphal route waiting for her conquering foot to take the first step towards that contentment which only comes with fulfilment of noble designs. She felt like some Classical heroine — but which one? There was sad Procne, who wove into a tapestry the history of Tereus' abominable crimes — that did not seem to strike the right note. Then she remembered patient Penelope, whose everlasting needlework had safeguarded her honour and found immortality in Homer's transcendent verse. That, she felt, was rather more like it.

Had she paused to consider the implications of that all too appropriate authority. . . .

3

The Mapp-Flints departed with great grinding of gears, waving of handkerchiefs and promises of postcards, and Lucia at last felt herself free to launch the great project. Norman fever had settled on Tilling and only the Mapp-Flints, with other things on their minds, had remained unaffected by it all. Everything connected with the Conqueror had been investigated to see if they could cast any light on Georgie's mystic utterances.

'I think it's something to do with the Norman Tower,' said Diva, as she took tea at the Vicarage. 'It's the most Norman thing I can think of. Perhaps she's going to have it restored.'

'But it is in excellent repair as it is,' said Susan Wyse. 'I am sure that our dear Lucia means something far more important, and besides, I do not see how we could participate in any programme of renovation of the Tower. On the whole, I think Mr. Georgie's clue had some subtler meaning. There is, after all, a direct line of descent from William the Conqueror to our present monarch. A Royal Visit, perhaps?'

'Then why did he say "the Normans"?' Diva persisted. 'Why not the Tudors or the Stuarts?'

'I believe my dear Susan is on the right track,' said Mr. Wyse, 'although I do not believe that she has arrived at the actual truth. Our English aristocracy, you must remember, is of Norman stock. The expression "the Normans" may therefore be a cunning periphrasis for "the nobility", such is the subtlety of Mr. Pillson. Some connection with an exalted person or persons. . . .'

"Tes my opinion that our bonny Mayor has some historical project in her mind,' intoned the Padre. In truth, he had no notion what Mr. Georgie's remark could mean, but the linguistic possibilities of mediaeval vocabulary had excited him greatly. A copy of *The Canterbury Tales* was open on his desk and beside it a small exercise-book in which he was noting down the most quaint and archaic of Chaucer's usages for possible inclusion in his own everyday speech.

'Well, we'll know soon enough,' said Evie. 'I've invited Lucia and Georgie to tea and they've accepted. But how thrilling! I can't wait to find out what's going on — Norman Tower or Royal Visit or aristocratic whatever.' She did not include her husband's pet theory for it was by definition too ludicrous to be taken seriously.

The door-bell rang and soon the Pillsons had joined the company. Georgie was wearing a new pair of trousers made of linen and the colour of terra-cotta. When he had tried them on in his dressing-room they had seemed to be the very essence of the Riviera; walking round Church Square, however, he had suffered a sudden loss of confidence in them and had wanted to go home and change but Lucia had been impatient to make her revelation and had assured him that they were perfect. But since nobody now seemed to have noticed them, the whole thing seemed a trifle academic. . . .

'Padre! Evie dear! How kind of you. And so many dear friends all together in one place. No Elizabeth? But of course, they are on holiday. Such a curious time for a holiday, don't you think — the end of January — and especially for a motor-tour, with snow forecast. What it is to be young and carefree! So sorry to keep you all waiting for your tea but *mio caro sposo* and I were held up — official business — too tedious for words.' (Lucia had been at the Town Hall, but there had been nothing for her to do, as usual.)

'Now then, Your Worship,' demanded the Padre, 'yon folk and I have a' been on tenterhooks tae learn just what it was your mon meant by "the Normans". Ye'll pardon my bluntness but will ye no tell us the truth on't?'

Lucia laughed a silvery laugh and lightly slapped Georgie across the back of his hand. Georgie blushed until his face matched the colour of his trousers.

'Oo vewwy naughty *Georgino* to tell. Me never trust you with important secrets again. Fancy you tell on poor Lucia.'

'Me so sorry,' said Georgie, dutifully.

'Well, since you all seem to know about it already, I suppose I had better confirm your suspicions, for you have doubtless all worked it out for yourselves. Georgie, such an obvious hint! No challenge at all! It is but a wild hypothesis — a mere suggestion — and I do hope you will not be too harsh on me as you point out the flaws in it.'

Then, using gestures with which her looking-glass was now all too familiar, she outlined her plans for the Tapestry. Tea grew cold in the cup and melted butter congealed on the tops of patient muffins for no one remembered them; before the eyes and ears of the assembly, a Great Thing was unfolding, a *Kunstwerk*, a wonder, if not of the world, then at the very least of the south-east coast. And how nobly, how excitingly, how brilliantly did Lucia present her project! At times her voice was low and deep, grave and statesmanlike; then she would reach up a whole octave, her clear, bright voice conveying a message of hope and enthusiasm that seemed to come from a younger, less cynical world where all things were possible. To accompany her eloquence, she emphasised each finely made point with movements of her long, delicate fingers and never once did Evie Bartlett have occasion to fear for her porcelain cake-stand. All the while, she fixed her listeners with her piercing eyes, so that each in turn felt himself to be caught in the spotlight of Destiny. When she was done, and the great peroration had at last reached its inevitable conclusion, there was not one of the company assembled in the cosy room who would not have followed her to the ends of the earth.

As suddenly as it had come, the enchantment faded and their own, sensible, down-to-earth Lucia was before them again. 'Only an idea, the fruit of a few moments' musing which I offer to you to see if you can make something of it. Evie, dear, might I possibly have some fresh tea? I have foolishly let mine go cold. How I do chatter on sometimes and how polite you are to bear with me!'

Evie, deeply moved, rang the bell and conversation gradually resumed, as in the interval of some mighty concert. A rubber of Bridge followed but it was unusually subdued for no one could muster the necessary acrimony and bad-feeling required for the game as it was generally played in Tilling. Although Lucia revoked quite palpably, Susan Wyse could not bring herself to chide her partner with any of her usual vigour, for it would have been most disrespectful. Diva had no appetite for nougat chocolates and pushed away the second plate untasted. Even Irene behaved in a reasonably civilised manner for she had been loftily silent during the preliminary speculation before Lucia's arrival, adoringly silent during the speech and thoughtfully silent after it, and went home without having been rude to anybody. It was all most unusual.

It was a propitious start to an extraordinary spell of activity. The next day, work began in earnest. Lucia started by ordering from the library a complete set of Geoffrey of Monmouth, Holinshed and various other ancient sources and a number of authoritative works on mediaeval textiles and the techniques of needlecraft. As she perused this mountain of literature, she would make vague but useful notes in a large ledger or pursue cross-references, her pencil behind her ear like a clerk. While she was thus engaged in creative study and design (for she realised that her earlier work had all been far too unambitious), her agents moved through the town whipping up a near-hysterical fervour for the town's past. Tilling had long been due for a new craze, for there had been nothing of any real substance since last year's epidemic of cycling. Therefore the enthusiasm of its busy folk had been stifled and frustrated, as Lucia had devoted herself to public work (or such public work as she managed to make for herself) and Elizabeth had concentrated all her formidable powers on preventing her from doing so. Leaderless, Tilling had not been able to concentrate its attention on any one hobby; the Padre had tried to introduce sword-dancing but Evie had championed the cause of barbola work, while Diva had ploughed a lonely furrow as a proponent of butterfly-collecting.

Georgie, as principal artistic director, organised a sort of examination. Everyone who wished to wield a needle had to produce a piece of their own unaided work, illustrating a set theme. The subject was an ambitious one — a Mayoral procession passing through the Landgate. Diva's effort resembled the Ashford Express passing under a tunnel. Susan Wyse, having expressly forbidden interruptions by the distractions of the world and having sent out for mellow-gold silk, produced a most lifelike rendition of a large, black whale gobbling down a tiny goldfish. Quaint Irene's interpretation fully justified her reputation as a leading spirit of the *avant-garde*, while Evie's approach was so traditional as to be virtually unrecognisable.

Nevertheless, the great project gathered momentum and Georgie gave a brief series of classes in remedial embroidery which enabled all to satisfy his exacting requirements. Hessian was procured (at a discount for taking in quantity) from the draper, who began to speak freely of affording a week in Frinton when the rush had died down, while needles and coloured wools of every conceivable hue poured into Mallards by the hour. Lucia prepared yet another set of designs which the Padre and Mr. Wyse converted into finished sketches, and their efforts were hung in a continuous line which extended from Lucia's front-door all round the hall and half-way up the stairs. Indeed, had creativity been allowed to continue unchecked, the line might well have extended right up the stairs and out on to the roof. But even the history of Tilling could not be made to extend that far.

At last the day dawned when the first stitch was to be made on the cloth itself. Brutus, legendary founder of the British race, was to be represented setting sail up the sinuous curves of the Rother. Beside him in his ship was an anonymous hero, the first chieftain of Tilling, who bore in his hands a pennant emblazoned with the borough arms, ready to leap ashore and plant it on the future site of the Town Hall. This historic moment, the first stitch, was to be Georgie's. All Tilling Society and various local worthies were gathered in the garden-room, craning their necks to see the needle's point sink into the hessian. Georgie, as crimson as the wool he was to wield, threaded the needle, pricked his finger, said 'Oh, how tar'some!', and drove the hard steel home. There was a popping of flashbulbs, like a brief electric storm, for Lucia had hired a photographer, and some applause; then tea was served.

'*Finalmente*,' sighed Lucia, when the last guest had departed, 'the work is in progress. Nothing can stop us now.'

Georgie was looking at the first stitch. In his excitement he had put it in the wrong place and it would have to be unpicked. Nevertheless, he felt proud and happy, for this was to be his project too.

'I think Brutus should have black hair,' he said. 'He was Greek, after all.'

'Trojan, *caro*, or Troyan, as our ancestors would have said. He fled from Priam's city as it burned and set sail for the Tin Islands — that's Britain. I wonder if there can be any truth in that old tale?'

'Well, Trojan then. But I want his robe to be golden, so his hair will have to be dark or no one will know where his head ends and his collar begins. Oh look, someone's dropped cigarette-ash all over the cloth.'

Lucia was not listening.

'It is my aim,' she said, her eyes uplifted, 'to use this Tapestry to weave together the disparate strands of our community. There! What a clever epigram! I must remember that for the *Hastings Chronicle*. Achievement,

Georgie, our name written in a strong clear hand across the Vistor's Book of Time. How wonderful it is to be busy again.'

While Lucia gabbled away in this vein, Georgie was busy with Brutus and his ship. As he drew the thread through the close weave of the cloth a slight feeling of unease manifested itself in the very back of his mind. He could not, however, identify it and so let it pass. He contented himself with the outline of the sail; his School (as even now he termed it) could see to the rest.

The first stitch had been thrilling, the second, third and fourth invigorating. The hundredth and even the thousandth were resolutely, if not enthusiastically, made by the needle-women of Tilling. As the work progressed, conversation came less easily to the creators of the Tapestry, for there was no longer anything to talk about. Elizabeth and her car had, so to speak, floated Brutus down the Rother, but by the time the ensign was planted there was little more to say on the matter, for the good folk of Tilling spent all their time in the garden-room, laboriously filling in Georgie's outlines, and could not manufacture the news that Tilling Society consumed at such a rate. There was nothing to tell and hear and be the first with, for nothing except the Tapestry was happening. Still, the first episode had been completed within a week of the start, leaving but ninety-nine more to be done. At such a rate of progress, working from ten to six with all hands to the needle and strictly limited intervals for lunch and tea, they could hope to have the thing finished within two years.

The ten-o'clock train drew out of Tilling's picturesque station, leaving behind it two passengers and a small heap of luggage. Elizabeth Mapp-Flint (for it was she) sent her husband in search of a porter and a taxi and, sitting on an upturned trunk, reviewed the situation.

Certainly it had been unfortunate that the engine of her — their — new motor had fallen clean off between Poole and Southampton and most embarrassing to be told by the mechanic who arrived to repair it that they had been fortunate to escape so lightly, considering the appalling state of the machine. Anyone with any sense, he told them, would never have bought such a pile of old junk; what had held it together for so long defied logical explanation. On the other hand, it was better that this disaster had taken place in a foreign land, so to speak, where no one of any consequence could observe it, rather than under the eyes of Lucia and quaint Irene Coles. Yet she must somehow account for her pedestrian status and her return by rail. The car could not be returned from Southampton for at least a week so great was the amount of work which would have to be done to render it innocuous, and the appalling cost of these repairs would be crippling, were it not that she would certainly recover them from the villain who had sold her the machine. Until she had been fully reimbursed, there was no question of being able to use the thing for anything but decoration. Then again, she had, by dint of furious practice, at last managed to learn the rudiments of vehicle control, and as long as her speed did not exceed fifteen miles an hour (which was quite fast enough) she could drive without risk of injury to herself or others. It would be tragic if she had no machine to drive after all her effort. More tragic still to have to sell it and be laughed to scorn.

She furrowed her brow and thought hard. Someone returning to Grebe from the direction of Hastings need not drive through the centre of town, and so it would have been perfectly possible for her to have returned from holiday without being seen, even if she were still at the wheel. If she could only get home unobserved, therefore, she could claim to have completed her holiday and sent the car to be serviced straight away, and her temporary reduction to the status of pedestrian need have no other significance. Her only problem, then, would be to get back to Grebe without being seen by the keen eyes of her fellow citizens and this might be accomplished by crouching down in the back of the taxi.

All went splendidly, for the High Street was unaccountably deserted as the Mapp-Flints, rather uncomfortable but undoubtedly invisible, were conveyed along it. Their luggage was swiftly unloaded, the taxi paid and dismissed, and Elizabeth and Major Benjy, having resolved unanimously to ameliorate the slight coolness that had existed between them over the past few days in the cause of presenting a united front to the world, set off to walk into town.

As they passed under the Landgate they became aware of a strange feeling of emptiness in the town, reinforced as they continued on their way by the fact that none of their friends was to be seen. This was most unusual for it was the height of the marketing hour, when shopping-baskets should be colliding outside Twemlow's and the traffic backing up behind Susan's Royce as it made its way from shop to shop. The upper window of Wasters, at which Diva always sat and watched the street, was closed and shuttered. In Church Square there proceeded from the Vicarage no hesitant piano-playing or tuneless singing of Highland ballads. In West Street no sweet mockery assailed them from Taormina, where quaint Irene was wont to lay in wait. If they were neither out nor in, where were they? All was still and silent, and only tradesmen and other persons of no consequence jostled each other in the empty streets.

'Can't understand it,' muttered Major Benjy darkly. He had anticipated being, if not the centre, then at least near the centre of that knot of eager enquirers who always assembled round a returning traveller.

'They'll all be at Mallards, you mark my words,' snarled his wife. 'I knew Lucia was up to something, and the moment my back was turned. . . .'

As they rounded the corner by the crooked chimney from Church Square, they saw through the window of the garden-room a sight so pitiful that it would have touched the heart of Lord Shaftesbury had he been alive. Seated in a semi-circle, with the despondent air of Nibelungs forging gold for their tyrannical master, sat Evie and Diva and Susan Wyse, while Georgie, spectacles on nose, directed their labour with, if anything, a greater air of misery. Their faces were unusually pale, like those of coal-miners who see little of the sun, and no word seemed to pass between them. Only Irene seemed to be enjoying herself, and since it was generally accepted that Irene rejoiced when others would grieve and grieved when others would be inclined to rejoice, her mirth was not inconsistent. At the back of the room, Elizabeth could faintly discern Lucia, directing the Padre and Mr. Wyse in their attention to an enormous length of cloth.

Within, the air of gloom was real enough. The second panel of the Tapestry was a battle-scene of great complexity, illustrating a rather obscure tale from the pages of Geoffrey of Monmouth. It had gone wrong at the first attempt, although not before several days had been expended upon it, days of forced, grudging toil under the relentless glare of the electric light. The unacceptable version had been unpicked and a second version begun, with various alterations and additions inserted by the Mayor. Had the author of the 'Song of the Shirt' sought an illustration for that graphic work, there could have been no better than this vignette of misery and despair.

Lucia, who had felt a trifle uneasy for the last two days, suspended her work on the design for the fifty-third panel (she could not be bothered to wait for the others) and came over to inspect the progress.

'Charming!' she cooed. 'Exquisite! Such neatness, Susan dear, although you might place the stitches even closer together. Look, teeny little cracks of cloth are showing between them. Could I be terribly cruel and get you to do that bit again?'

'But it's taken me all day to do that much!' groaned the wretched woman.

'A stitch in time saves nine, dear,' countered Lucia,

and passed on. 'Excellent, Diva, but perhaps you might consider adhering a little more closely to Mr. Georgie's outline. Bravo, Evie! Slow but sure!'

In desperation she turned to Georgie, who had stopped working altogether. He was massaging his wrist and would say nothing but 'I've pricked my finger and it hurts!' and 'Won't somebody open a window — it's so terribly stuffy in here.' So Lucia left him in peace and came thankfully to Irene, whose needle rose and fell with pleasing regularity.

'What ho, Lucia!' exclaimed the quaint one. 'Isn't this grand? It's so wonderfully like Russia, isn't it, in one of the People's factories. Everyone working together for the Cause. This is Socialism in action. I've a good mind to write to the Webbs about it!'

Evie said something which Lucia did not quite catch.

'Dear Irene, what an example to us all!' She caught sight of the figure that the Example was working on and uttered a strangled cry.

'What's up?' asked the quaint one in surprise.

'Why isn't King Tyl wearing any clothes?' demanded Lucia. 'He should have a purple robe.'

Irene guffawed. 'But, Lucia, he was the Defender of the People, or so you said. Obviously a Socialist, an Ur-Trotsky. So I've stripped him of his badges of rank and made him as other men are, pre-eminent in his qualities alone. That's why he is a bit taller than the others.'

'But Trotsky wears clothes, surely?'

'Not all the time,' replied Irene merrily, and returned to her task with renewed effort.

Georgie demanded of his wrist why he bothered if people were going to change things without asking him first, but Lucia ignored him and retreated to the back of the room. The Padre was consulting his watch.

'Alas, Worshipful Leddy,' he said, 'I mun perform a sairvice o'baptism at noon, so I mun be awa' to ma hoose.'

'But it's only quarter to eleven.'

'Ah weel, there's the holy water to prepare and my

vestments to see to, and a' the bonny green chalk to lave fra my hands.'

It was true that the chalk with which he had been marking out the cloth had considerably marked him. But an hour and a quarter seemed a long time for a wash.

'Of course,' she sighed, 'but please be quick.'

'The Lord's work canna be hurried, Mistress Pillson,' said the Padre emphatically. 'I dinna think you would see a newborn babe's soul put in jeopardy for want of a few minutes.'

'Yes, yes, but we must get on. We won't be stopping for lunch until half-past one, and we'll have to resume at quarter to two. I have instructed cook to prepare chicken broth and sandwiches.'

The Padre fled with a groan and was intercepted by Elizabeth as he turned the corner. She had sent Major Benjy home, but could not bear to return herself until some explanation had been elicited. Therefore she had spent ten minutes on an obdurate shoelace in the hope that someone might come out. It was some time before the Padre was sufficiently coherent to be understood, and when his powers of speech were returned to him he spoke pure Birmingham; the Highland dialect did not contain words capable of expressing the emotions he felt. At first his narrative was all of chicken broth and only fifteen minutes for lunch, but a sharp word from Elizabeth brought him back to the point, and he unfolded the whole history of the Tapestry.

'Poor, dear Padre,' she cooed, and her heart sang in her bosom like a nightingale. 'After you have concluded your christening, you must come over to Grebe and have a proper lunch with us. You can tell Lucia that the god-parents were late! I can't wait to hear the full story.'

And so she did. After a long and leisurely lunch had been eaten and properly digested, and coffee lingered over to an extent unusual even in Tilling, the Padre went sorrowing away for what he termed the afternoon shift, while Elizabeth sat and devised in her mind the over-throw of the Tapestry.

She could declare a war of mockery and derision on the project and be sure that the oppressed workers would rise up and defect at her call. Yet to do so would be an overt act of hostility, and Lucia (so vindictive!) would blame her for the collapse of her precious hobby. A harder but better course of action would be to subvert it from within, smiling and smiling and being a villain, so to speak. And it so happened that she had within her luggage a secret weapon of unbounded potential, brought back from Southampton for just such a purpose. But now this mine could be exploded within the enemy's citadel, rather than simply laid under her walls.

She rose and went to the telephone. A number was demanded; she was put through. Foljambe's voice answered at the other end.

'Mrs. Mapp-Flint wishes to speak to Mrs. Pillson,' she said, and soon Lucia's voice, shrill and sharp as ever, came through the receiver.

'Lucia, darling, it's your Elizabeth here. Yes, dear, a simply lovely time, I must tell you all about it when we meet. But, first, I have just heard from the Padre about your marvellous Tapestry; such vision, dear Worship, so full of praise for your clever idea. Lucia, you naughty one, how could you bring yourself to be so unkind to your old friend as to let her go away on holiday and start work without her? Hello?' She's dropped the receiver again, thought Elizabeth. 'Do be sweet and reassure me that there's still something left for me to do — that's if you think that I'll be up to it, of course!'

Lucia reassured her that there was plenty for her to do; only too delighted.

'Splendid! Shall I bring my own needles? No? How thoughtful. And thread? That too! Such organisation. But, of course, I forgot, I am speaking to the Mayor of Tilling, after all. Very well, then, I shall run all the way to Mallards.'

Curiously enough, Lucia entirely failed to catch the significance of Elizabeth's promise to run all the way (surely unnecessary for a motorist), for her mind, like

Macbeth's was full of scorpions. She knew only too well that her own declaration of peace had been Machiavellian policy. What else could Elizabeth's gratuitous and unprovoked gesture of friendship be but another such? And, if so, what diabolical scheme had that dark intellect devised?

4

Lucia sat alone in the darkness and gazed at the tangle of wool and needles that represented the shipwreck of her project. Four days had elapsed since that woman had come Assyrian-like out of the West, bearing in her hand that terrible, ruinous cardboard box.

At this time the room should be full of industry and effort, the electric light gleaming on the points of a hedge of needles. Instead she sat alone like desolate Sappho and could not bring herself to touch the fallen temple, her Tapestry. Even Georgie — perfidious, heartless Georgie — had deserted her for the seductive gaiety of Grebe, the meretricious glamour of the brightly coloured board, the tantalising fall of the dice. *Et tu, Georgino?* Then fall Lucia.

Elizabeth had not made good her promise to run all the way to Mallards but she must have walked ever so swiftly, for she had arrived shortly before the company was due to break off for tea. Under her arm had been a brown-paper parcel, long and flat and rectangular like a painting. She had left it on the hall-table — 'Just a little *memento* of our holiday' — and had been shown the work in progress, Brutus and the battle of the cannibals against King Tyl, which she had seemed to admire greatly. There had not been time to start her at her work before tea, so the trays had been brought in and the table cleared. Elizabeth had spoken briefly, modestly of her holiday, and the subject had almost been successfully closed. Then Elizabeth had, as an apparent afterthought, remembered her parcel — 'Just let me show you the silly little toy we brought back with us from Southampton.' The parcel had been opened and a red and white cardboard box, with the incongruous word 'Monopoly' written on the lid, had been revealed. It was a game, Elizabeth said, with dice and counters, rather childish as all such things were but strangely gripping once you got into it. Should she just open the box? Would it be a terrible bore to everyone if she just briefly explained the rules? Well then, just a quick demonstration, a few throws of the dice, but they must be sure to start work again at five or she would feel terribly guilty. She had come to work, not to play.

Not a stitch more had been added that day, and Lucia had been hard put to it to evict the eager players by half-past seven. The game, it seemed, could go on for an awfully long time, and the longer it went on the more exciting it became. They could not bear to leave it half-finished with Fenchurch Street Station as yet unclaimed and the Padre still languishing in jail. Just a few throws more, and the game must resolve itself. Elizabeth did appear to be in a commanding position, but things could change so quickly. . . .

Work on the Tapestry had resumed the next morning, but at such a pitifully slow rate that hardly anything worthwhile had been done, and there had been no end of careless and botched stitches to be unpicked and done again. The only pleasure seemed to be in discussing Monopoly, with the result that Lucia, who had not participated in the game, was left alone and unregarded. Even Irene had dawdled over her needle, and her usual creative drive had deserted her for she did exactly what she was told. Only Elizabeth had displayed any enthusiasm for the Tapestry. She had laboured tirelessly, drawing the wool through with neat, careful fingers, never looking up and appearing wholly reluctant to discuss the wonder she had brought to Tilling. Indeed it was Elizabeth almost unaided who finished off the second scene, so that for a moment Lucia believed that the Mayoress had come to help, not to destroy. But this illusion was swiftly shattered.

'There now,' she had cried, 'that's that finished. I do think we might stop for a moment, Lucia, and have a little rest. We shall work all the better for it afterwards.'

The break had lasted until lunch-time, and the soup and sandwiches were quickly eaten. But before Lucia could order resumption of the task Elizabeth had produced apparently from thin air (Lucia could have sworn she did not have it with her when she arrived) the accursed Monopoly set, and play had begun at once. The rattle of the dice and the excited cries of the players had driven her from the room; when she returned she found Georgie sitting at Elizabeth's side, watching with rapt attention and expressing heartfelt admiration for her tactical skill and foresight. That he should have succumbed to temptation surprised her not at all, for she knew her Georgie. But the speed of his capitulation disappointed and wounded her.

The game had continued all afternoon and almost until evening, when finally Elizabeth, with pretty words of commiseration to her victims, rose the winner and swept the pieces back into the box. But there was no sulking or bad feeling, such as might follow a game of Bridge, only a general feeling of catharsis; the battle had been hard but fair, and the best player had won. As if to compensate her opponents for their defeat, Elizabeth broadcast invitations to dinner at Grebe. It was only with difficulty that Lucia herself avoided accepting, for Georgie was most keen to go. There would be Monopoly before and after the meal and tactical talk during it, for Elizabeth had declared that she would open the treasury of her experience of the game to all the novices, and Georgie was convinced that he would be at a great disadvantage were he not to be present. As a result he had been sullen and uncommunicative at dinner and had not seemed to hear any word she spoke about the Tapestry, even though she was careful to praise his quite shoddy work during the day. No one had turned up next morning to resume the project, and at half-past ten she heard Georgie gabbling away in a loud whisper on the telephone. Shortly afterwards he muttered something about seeing where everyone had got to, seized his cavalry cape and an old hat and bolted out of the front-door like a startled rabbit.

Having cast her net Elizabeth resolved to keep her fish firmly within it. Monopoly would be carefully rationed, and play would take place only in the afternoons on alternate days. She knew the craze could not last for ever; Tilling crazes seldom saw out the month and frequently died away within the fortnight. But she was determined to wring the last possible drop out of this one, and still be the first to drop it when it showed signs of becoming tedious. With this in her mind she had gone to the stationer's and bought up the entire stock of sets — four — to ensure that no one else could get possession of one and start up a rival school. Monopoly, she felt, must mean just that.

It had been fortunate, to say the least, that Elizabeth's finances had compelled her to select that particular hotel in Southampton while waiting to hear the worst from the garage. As an hotel it had left a lot to be desired, and her feelings on seeing their room had not been at all joyful or optimistic. There had been dust everywhere, and the thought that this might be a useful topic to pursue in the forthcoming negotiations over the bill prompted her to take a chair and examine the top of the wardrobe. There she found a red and white box, evidently left behind by some previous occupant of the room; a family, perhaps, whiling away the hours before they caught their ship. She opened it idly and almost at once realised the potential of the game. Since there was nothing else to do she sat down on the bed and laid out the board, cards and imitation money and began to study the rather complicated instructions. Major Benjy, who had been sleeping rather noisily in the chair, soon awoke. At first he pretended not to notice what she was doing, for words had passed between them at the side of the road, in the garage and in the taxi, whereas the exact opposite had been the case ever since. But the pastime looked so intriguing that his display of indifference had proved impossible to maintain. Without actually speaking, therefore, he had joined his wife and started to peruse the instructions for himself. Rather as two cats who have not been introduced will, after preliminary and hostile display, warily come to share the same hearthrug, they began to play Monopoly. So enthralling did the game turn out to be that they spoke to each other several times before they remembered their deadly enmity. They had dined that evening in silence and bad humour, but afterwards the contest had been resumed. In fact it had continued late into the night, only to be adjourned when sleep was irresistible. After a hurried (and silent) breakfast, they had set up the board again, and Elizabeth, despite being not a whit less furious with her husband than she had been beside the road, helped him set out the pieces as they had been at close of play last evening. She even found words to correct his rather faulty memory on the subject of who had finished up with Bond Street. This unspoken armistice had been dissolved by the news from the garage and the ensuing debate as to precisely who was to blame. The soldiers, so to speak, had broken off their game of football in No Man's Land and returned to their respective trenches. Nevertheless, Elizabeth reflected long and hard about the almost uncanny ability of the game to dismiss virtually everything else from the players' minds, and no doubt it was while her mind was so distracted that she inadvertently packed the Monopoly set in her suitcase, under a heavy cardigan.

It was the Wyses' turn to host the day's sitting of the Monopolists. The privilege was jealously sought after, for the host naturally had first choice of counters. Mr. Wyse had a particular fondness for the top hat, while the motor-car, appropriately enough, generally seemed to fall to Elizabeth. Georgie, as Tilling's best-dressed man, was accorded the flat-iron, Diva claimed the thimble and the Bartletts and Irene would be left to decide who got the battleship and who would be left with the boot. Since there were always fewer counters than would-be players, it had been agreed that married couples, being one in the sight of God, should also be regarded as one player for the purposes of the game. The Wyses made their decisions jointly, with the result that play was often held up for some minutes; but the Bartletts and the Mapp-Flints tended to take alternate throws. This happy device enabled the most attractive feature of Bridge, failing to understand what your partner was up to and falling out as a result, to be introduced into the game. If the required element of dissent was not forthcoming from this particular convention there were always the rules, in their splendid complexity, to fall out over.

With the set under her arm, therefore, Elizabeth rang the bell of Starling Cottage with a light heart. The door was answered by Figgis, the Wyses' grim-faced butler, and Elizabeth was ushered into the presence of her hosts. The company had long since assembled, and a buzz of tactical discussion died down; Elizabeth felt rather like a senior officer entering a briefing session, and had to restrain herself from saying 'Carry on, gentlemen.' Major Benjy would probably have done so, but she had sent him like a schoolboy unwillingly to golf, for despite his enthusiasm for the game he was at times a hindrance to her. He could never resist buying the railway stations, at whatever cost. The Great War, he would claim, was won through control of the railways; railways had hamstrung the Boers and India had been largely pacified by their construction.

The board was set out; Georgie threw highest and was thereby entitled to the first move.

'Oh look!' he exclaimed. 'I've thrown a double five. That's lucky.' He advanced the flat-iron ten places, while Mr. Wyse, as banker, counted out his initial £200. He put down his counter and his face fell. 'In jail — oh, just visiting, that's all right. Do I throw again now? Nine. Vine Street.'

'A cousin of mine lived in Vine Street once,' said Diva.

'No!' said Georgie. 'What a coincidence! I'd better buy it in that case. It must be a very select area.'

Diva did not mention that her cousin had kept an umbrella shop, and Georgie disbursed £200 into the exchequer.

Sysan Wyse was next to throw; she recorded three and landed on Whitechapel Road. 'Where,' she enquired, 'is Whitechapel Road?' Irene told her, and she decided not to buy it. As a result it went to auction and eventually was knocked down to Diva for £120. It was well known that Diva could not resist an auction with its possibilities for getting bargains, and Elizabeth exploited this weakness to the full. Elizabeth's own throw landed her on Chance, and she drew a speeding fine of £15. She regarded this as rather unjust, for she never exceeded the speed limits. . . .

Diva threw a double six and promptly bought the Electric Company. 'I can't see how that could fail to be profitable,' she said. 'I had my last quarter's bill last week. Scandalous.' She threw again and landed on Chance. Fate, merciless and arbitrary, sent her back three spaces to Vine Street. She claimed that she was only visiting her cousin, but the rules were inflexible on that point and she was separated from rent. Irene landed on Income Tax and handed over £200. She did not complain, however, for she was a good Socialist and said that she only wished there were more taxes to pay; best of all, she suggested, why not nationalise all Elizabeth's properties and build workers' co-operatives on them? The Bartletts landed on King's Cross Station, which suited them admirably.

Georgie's next throw landed him on the Water Works, and he felt obliged to buy them, for they were a public amenity and ought to be run for the good of the community. That was what Lucia would say, were she present. Mr. Wyse threw three and one which brought him to Chance. He selected a card, read it and put it down, stony-faced, on the table. Then he paid some money to the Bank. When he was not looking Georgie turned it up to see what it was. 'Drunk in Charge,' it read, 'Fine £20.' The fortunes of the Wyses did not prosper thereafter. Susan was compelled to pay super-tax, which she did with a proud flourish, and Mr. Wyse was sent to jail. Elizabeth soon gained control of all the yellow and green properties, and began buying hotels with reckless abandon, whereupon Irene called her a slum landlord and threatened her with dire punishments come the Revolution. Diva, after a great deal of tortured indecision, added the Old Kent Road to Whitechapel and built a house on each, only to be assessed for street repairs and deprived of £80. The Wyses eventually got out of jail and were promptly sent back again. The Padre, with canny Scottish good sense, gained control of all the red properties but no one landed on them, while Evie, drawing on the Community Chest, won second prize in a beauty competition.

The game was won, as usual, by Elizabeth. She seized control of London as quickly and as absolutely as she had captured Tilling, and the parallel did not go unmarked, especially at Mallards.

'I expect she'll buy Porpoise Street and West Street and Church Square,' remarked Lucia bitterly, 'and smother them in little green houses and little red hotels. Then we shall all have to throw a die in the mornings before we leave our homes. A four will permit us to go to Twemlow's; a five will entitle us to visit Mr. Worthington's and buy some meat. But should we only be vouchsafed a two, we must perforce go to Mr. Hopkins and eat fish for our supper, whether we like it or not. Should we be so fortunate as to throw a six we will be permitted to trudge out to Grebe to partake of Monopoly and potted-meat sandwiches. A throw of one —'

Georgie interrupted this fantastical monologue. 'But Lucia,' he said imploringly, 'you should join in too. It's such fun, you know, so much better than tedious old Bridge, and there's no gambling, which should appeal to your principles. I remember there was a time when you declared that gambling was at the root of half the social problems in England. And it's not just a game, it's training for commerce. It sharpens your mind. If ever I went in for property developing' (now there was a thought to conjure with!) 'I should have a very good idea of how to go about it. Buying places cheap, improving them, and then letting them at a profit. Why, it's good business practice.'

Lucia turned her head away and her eye fell on the piano. They had not played their duets together for three weeks now, what with the Tapestry and then Monopoly. She was silent for a moment and Georgie could see that a Tilling thought had struck her. When she turned back she was smiling her bright, innocent smile that generally marked the emergence of some devious strategy.

'Alas!' she exclaimed. 'My poor pianoforte. How I have neglected you — *cattiva* Lucia. No wonder my soul seems so arid and dry without sweet *Mozartino* to water it.'

Music hath charms, Georgie recalled, and he suggested that they dispel the dark clouds of discord with a little duet. But Lucia seemed strangely evasive.

'No, Georgie, not just now. I am so much out of practice. An hour tomorrow at my scales will be scarcely time enough to ease these negligent fingers.'

'But I'm just as much out of practice as you are,' Georgie protested, anxious to pin down the reason for the reluctance. 'We can get back into shape together.'

'How sweet of you, Georgie, to offer to keep me company. But I should be so ashamed to make horrible noises in your presence. You would find out what an indifferent musician I really am.'

'Oh, very well then,' he said obediently, for he was anxious to preserve this apparent reconciliation between them. He had cause to be penitent, for he had betrayed his wife and (what was surely worse) his Mayor by joining the Monopolists, and had been surprised by the overall lack of hostile reaction.

'Now *Georgino*,' crooned Lucia in her arcane dialect of baby-talk spiked with Italian, and Georgie prepared to be made to do something. 'Lucia have ickle task for clever hubby Georgie. Me so, so tired of seeing dwefful Tapestry lying about so sad and unwanted in *giardino-room*. So untidy it is, to be sure. So will'oo be kindest *Georgino* and make Tapestry into nice pair of curtains for Lucia to hang in the *fenestri*?'

'Why, of course I will!' cried Georgie, relieved and delighted. 'So sensible of you not to waste all that material. They'll do splendidly for the scullery.'

'No, *caro*, not the scullery,' continued Lucia sweetly, 'the garden-room. Those old damask curtains are so trayed at the edge that I can't bear the sight of them any longer.'

Georgie gasped. To flaunt the ruins of her great project, like a flag of surrender, in the windows of her erstwhile seat of power was a most remarkable act. And yet — it would be a subtle reproach to the weak flesh of Tilling, to pass by that reminder of dereliction of duty every day, and so reflect on what might have been.

'You're right, of course,' he said. 'Just the very thing. They could have been made for the purpose.'

That was not entirely tactful, but Lucia's demeanour did not change. 'Splendid!' she said. 'So kind of you. It shouldn't take long with Grosvenor and Foljambe to help you. And now be a dear and tell me all about Elizabeth's Monopoly this afternoon. So sorry to have been such a shrill, shrewish Lucia when you were about to tell me before.'

Curiouser and curiouser. Dimly Georgie could perceive a purpose behind this mercurial change, afar off and shrouded in mist, but his rational mind could not make out its shape, and so attributed the peripeteia to simple friendliness.

'Elizabeth won,' he said briefly. 'I didn't get much, only the Water Works and Vine Street.'

'Oh dear,' cooed his wife. 'And how exactly did Elizabeth win? It sounds like a terribly complicated game, and I've only the vaguest idea of how you play it.'

So Georgie told her all about it. He made several mistakes but Lucia did not correct him, for to do so would betray the fact that she had that morning received from a leading London toy-shop a Monopoly set and a book on tactics by the current South-Eastern Area champion, study of which had helped while away her solitary afternoon. In fact, so engrossed had she been in rehearsing the ploys and gambits suggested in the book that when Georgie had returned from the battlefield she had been compelled to find *extempore* hiding places for book and Monopoly set. The latter was under the cushion of the sofa, the former under the lid of the piano. . . .

'A strangely fascinating game,' she opined when his confused and rather inaccurate summary was concluded, 'and one with distinct possibilities for self-improvement, as you so rightly pointed out. As in Bridge the bidding helps one to learn how to communicate indirectly with one's partner, to understand without words, to tune in, so to speak, to a fellow-human's thought and feelings, so in Monopoly one learns how to plan ahead, to create a strategy far-reaching enough to ensure victory, yet flexible enough to adapt to the vicissitudes of fortune.'

'You could put it like that,' said Georgie cautiously.

'Thank you, dear. How foolish I have been,' she continued, 'how arrogant, to stand aloof so, simply because my tiresome little pet project has come to naught. How annoying it must have been for you all to be cooped up in this little room, with me being such a severe taskmistress. I see now that I took far too much for granted. I only hope I have not irretrievably alienated all my dear, dear friends. So I must try and undo some of the damage if I can. Would you be terribly sweet and ask Elizabeth for me if I could join in? I hope I have been punished enough for my wickedness by missing so much delightful entertainment.'

Georgie was dumbstruck. Had his eloquent description of the game of Monopoly so impressed his wife that she was prepared, like an Apostle, to cast away everything and follow it only? Unlikely, for he was aware that as a storyteller and narrator he lacked a certain amount of skill. Then what was behind this second, even more mercurial change? Whatever it was, it marked Lucia's return to the lists, and so it would be prudent as well as loyal to be unmistakably on her side from now on. He had no wish to share the terrible fate that must soon be inflicted on the disloyal.

In the High Street, sheltered from the rain by Twistevant's ample awning, Tilling debated Lucia's extraordinary declaration of penitence with all the gravity of an Aeschylean chorus discussing the ways of Zeus.

'She knows when she's beaten,' said Evie hesitantly.

'She never has before,' replied Georgie. 'That's why she's never been beaten. I really don't know what to make of it.'

' 'Tes a far, far better thing she does now than she has ever done before,' intoned the Padre. 'Blessed are the meek, and the peacemakers.'

'Exactly,' said Evie. 'But it's too fascinating. She was nice to Elizabeth when Elizabeth bought her motor-car, and Elizabeth was nice to her when she was doing the Tapestry. Now Lucia's being nice to Elizabeth over Monopoly and being apologetic about cooping us all up in the garden-room. It looks as though they've both turned over a new leaf.' There was a hint, more than a hint, of disappointment in Evie's voice as she said this.

'Extraordinary,' said Diva, who had heard all this as she bought her vegetables. 'Can't account for it. Must ask Elizabeth what she makes of it all. Though I don't suppose she'll tell me.'

'You make it sound as if Lucia and Elizabeth were deadly enemies,' said Georgie. 'I think they really like each other, deep down. It's just that little things come between them occasionally and they quarrel.'

The Padre muttered something under his breath about the Ninth Commandment, but Georgie chose to ignore him.

'Why else,' Georgie continued, 'should Lucia want me to turn the Tapestry into a pair of curtains for the garden-room? It means she's finished with it once and for all. She said that she'd made a mistake and taken us all too much for granted, and she's terribly sorry for being such a nuisance.'

Outside the shelter of the awnings the elements raged to mark this shattering tale. Armed men clashed in the skies and lions were seen in the streets on the night before Caesar's murder; a heavy shower was the least that Nature could do to counterpoint such an announcement.

'No!' said Evie. 'How brave of her.'

'She's up to something,' muttered Diva. 'Look forward to seeing what it turns out to be.'

Elizabeth herself, feet galoshed and basket covered from the rain, now joined the little assembly. It was not a Monopoly day today, but yesterday's excitements would no doubt be supplying the topic of this conversation.

'Good morning, Evie, Diva, Mr. Georgie — is that a new tie? — how-de-do, Padre. May I scriggle through? Nice warming vegetable soup for my Benjy and me today, I think.'

There was a silence and a slightly uncomfortable atmosphere such as one experiences when one is about to be told some bad news. Diva nudged Georgie and he spoke.

'Good morning, Elizabeth. Such a good idea, and very tasty too. I've got a message for you from Lucia.'

'And where is our dear friend today?' said Elizabeth gaily. 'So unlike her to stuff indoors in the morning. Not unwell, I hope?'

'Oh no, quite well. But she insists that she has the house to herself this morning so that I won't hear her practising the pianoforte. She says she's much too much out of practice, and she'll have to get the man from the piano shop in Hastings to come over and tune *her*.'

There was another silence, and Elizabeth cast a surreptitious eye over the sheepish faces of her friends. Georgie took a deep breath and continued.

'And she wants me to ask you if you could come to tea

and play Monopoly at Mallards one day. She — she apologises' — the word seemed as big as a turnip and Georgie could hardly force it through his lips — 'for being so stand-offish and turning down all the invitations you so kindly sent her before, when you started Monopoly, but she says she was all wrapped up in her Tapestry.'

This astounding image quite rounded off the surreal speech, and Elizabeth almost felt sorry that quaint Irene was not present. What a picture that would have made!

'But what could there possibly be to apologise for? It is we who should *apologise*' — Elizabeth evidently liked repeating the word — 'to dear Lucia for deserting our posts. Do please tell her that I will be only too delighted to bring my little *divertissement* to tea tomorrow. And how fares the dear Tapestry? We must get back to work soon, before Her Worship despairs of us altogether.'

'I'm turning it into a pair of curtains,' Georgie muttered. 'It's her idea. She said she was sorry for boring us all with it, and how kind it was of everyone to bear with her so long.'

Had Elizabeth not managed to steady herself in time she would have fallen clean through Twistevant's broad plate-glass window. As it was, she was bereft of speech and staggered without a word into the shop. The scene dissolved, and Georgie was left alone. It was all too much for him, and he must find out the truth or burst. Yet Lucia's attitude made direct questioning impossible. He had, by his own delinquency, been put in the position of being a hostile power in Mallards; inviolate and treated with almost exaggerated respect and consideration, but wholly excluded from the deliberations of the house. Even Grosvenor had taken to giving him suspicious glances as she served the soup, as if accusing him of planning to steal the spoons. And he had an idea that Foljambe didn't approve at all. . . .

'I shall ask her to her face,' he declared to the dripping canvas, and set off resolutely for home. For once his straight question received a straight answer.

'Oh, I see!' he said. 'How very clever.'

'How delightful this is,' warbled Lucia, teapot in hand. 'What a lucky woman I am to have such forgiving friends.'

Behind her was an expanse of backed hessian, like a backdrop. She had taken her place in front of those fatal curtains, and the significance of it was wasted on no one. Lucia had turned her back on the Tapestry.

'Lucia dear, I fear I must be quite stern with you.' Elizabeth apparently triumphant but inwardly somewhat nervous, although she could not for the life of her think why, smiled her best smile. 'You seem to imagine that you have offended us. It is we who have offended you. So no more apologies, you dear hypocrite. You heap coals of fire on our poor heads.'

The Padre smiled and took another sponge-finger. 'I declare that 'tes all in the past the noo,' he said warmly, 'whatever 'twas that divided us so before. Now we are all come together in the ane place, the Lord be thanked. We have beaten our swords into plough-shares, made each our own sacrifice and swallowed our pride. Now let us all partake of the guid cheer.'

This pretty speech, epitome of reconciliation, came from the heart, for the Padre had not himself been wholly untouched by suffering. *The Canterbury Tales* alone had yielded up a veritable treasury of picturesque phraseology, all of which he was prepared to forego in the interests of peace.

'Beautifully put, dear Padre,' said Lucia. 'And now let us begin. I can't wait for my first game.'

Elizabeth reached for the Monopoly set, but before she could draw it from her shopping-basket Lucia had produced, apparently from nowhere, an identical red-and-white box, and was lifting the lid clear with a practised had.

'Where did you get that from?' demanded Elizabeth hoarsely.

'I had to send away to London for it,' replied Lucia. 'I

tried to buy one at the stationer's, but, do you know, he was sold out. Apparently someone had gone in and bought four sets all at once. I wonder who on earth that could have been?'

'Mapp!' cried Irene joyfully. 'It must have been Mapp.'

'Don't be so foolish, Irene dear,' Lucia rebuked her. 'Now why on earth should Elizabeth want to have all the Monopoly sets in Tilling?'

Elizabeth flushed red and did not reply. There would be no point in answering the unspoken charge; to deny it would be fatuous, to accept it suicidal. Inside her, spreading like a cold, clammy fog, was the realisation of what Lucia's counter-stratagem was to be. She felt the urge to escape, but she could not. They had tied her to the stake, she could not fly.

As perfidious Stanley sided with the usurper at Bosworth Field, so Georgie took his place at Lucia's side, and to them, aptly enough, fell the token of the battleship. Irene was elected Banker (a *rôle* she heartily detested on moral grounds) and the Mapp-Flints, husband and trembling wife, were assigned the first move. In order to restrict the damage that the Major was capable of doing, Elizabeth had decided that they would act as a team, rather than making alternate moves, for this game was not being played for light or ludicrous prizes but for the social throne of Tilling. Grimly coy, she thrust one die into his hand and took the other herself. '*Un, deux, trois, jettons-nous!*' she shrilled, and threw her die. Her husband did likewise but not quite simultaneously.

'You're not buying, dear?' cooed Lucia. 'And so early? Such a daring tactic. I see I shall have to be ever so careful. Let me see. The space now goes to auction, does it not? Georgie, advise me. Should I bid? You think so? You're sure? Very well then.'

So shaken was Elizabeth by this praise of her daring that she joined in the auction, and finally managed to secure for £260 what she could have had for £200. Better safe, however, than sorry. . . .

In almost no time at all Lucia had secured all the yellow properties, and at once set about building houses. Her funds were almost exhausted, but behind her cries of childish delight Elizabeth could detect some awful strategy. In vain she struggled to divert it.

'Lucia darling, are you sure? You wouldn't like to reconsider that last move?' she said nervously as Lucia gobbled up Trafalgar Square. 'I'm sure that, since it's your first game, we might let you take it back.'

But Lucia was made of sterner stuff. 'So kind of you, Elizabeth,' she replied, 'but I must abide by the rules. Only by experience can I hope to learn, after all. Pain is learning, as the dear poet said.'

The dear poet was right, for Lucia had given herself a headache committing to memory the advice of the South-Eastern Area champion, and he had been most insistent on securing Trafalgar Square. Meanwhile Elizabeth found herself entertaining quite unprecedented doubts about her own hitherto unbeatable strategy, and scarcely bought anything at all. So distracted was she by her worries that the Padre landed on one of her few properties without her noticing. He was about to mention it (for he was a man of God) when his wife nudged him firmly in the ribs, and he remained silent. As Diva threw the dice Elizabeth noticed her error.

'I'm so sorry,' she exclaimed. 'Padre, you owe me some rent.'

The Padre began to count out the notes, but Lucia stopped him. 'No need, Padre. The moment has passed. You are not liable.'

'Yes he is!' cried Elizabeth.

'*Carissima*, I assure you that he isn't. Surely you recollect the ruling on this point? Let me see now, how does it go? Ah yes, I have it. "If the owner fails to ask for his rent before the next throw of the dice, no rent may be collected." And Diva has thrown. *Ecco!* So harsh, don't you think? But we must abide by the rules, as I said earlier.'

'I don't remember that rule,' said Elizabeth uneasily.

'She's right, old girl,' said Major Benjy, who had the rule-book open in front of him. 'Word for word, too, by Jove. Well remembered, Mrs. Pillson. You saved the Padre a tidy sum there, I fancy.'

Elizabeth gave Lucia such a ferocious stare that for a moment Lucia believed that her dear friend was about to strike her. Instead, she snatched the second die from her husband's hand and cast both together with the velocity of a Larwood. For all her force, the dice registered but three points; she advanced the shiny metal motor-car the required number of places and with difficulty found room for it on a square crowded with houses and hotels. Underneath the miniature tyres of the counter the space was a blaze of yellow.

The game moved remorselessly towards an inevitable conclusion. To yellow was added blue and green, and Diva was prised out of the Old Kent Road and Whitechapel (as always, her only possessions) to add brown to Lucia's kaleidoscopic empire. The moment came when the Mapp-Flints had no cash in hand, no properties to mortgage, and debts to the panchromatic Lucia of several thousand pounds. With utter disdain, Elizabeth rose from the table.

'Such a delightful game, dearest Lucia. How proficient you have become, and so quickly.'

'Beginner's luck, *carissima*, and you were most unfortunate. You always seemed to be landing on my squares.' Since Lucia had owned most of the board for most of the game, Fortune's malice was not entirely to blame.

'Nonsense, dear. Such hidden talent! I declare you'll be giving us all lessons shortly.'

This was irony, and irony was meat and drink to Lucia. 'I should be delighted to share my preliminary conclusions with you at any time,' she said innocently, 'but I'm sure you know just as much about the game as I do. I think you let me win, you kind darling.'

Elizabeth growled, and laid a hand on Major Benjy's shoulder.

73

'But you aren't thinking of leaving us already?' gasped Lucia. 'The game is not yet concluded, and anything might happen. If you like, I will gladly loan you, say five thousand more. . . .'

'Time has flown by all too swiftly,' snarled Elizabeth, 'as it always does when one is enjoying oneself so much. See, it is already seven-o'clock, and we must go home, or Withers will scold us. Let us call it a draw.'

Irene snorted at this, but Lucia ignored her. 'A draw it shall be then, between you and me. And thank you so much, Elizabeth. I have learnt a lot simply by watching you.'

'Hang on, Liz,' said Benjy, 'you ordered dinner for half-past nine. There's no need to stop just yet.'

'Benjy, you naughty one,' hissed Elizabeth, white with rage, 'dinner is at half-past seven. Come along.'

'Would you like Cadman to drive you home?' asked Lucia gently. 'I fear that we haven't seen the last of the rain, and since your motor is still being serviced. . . .'

There was a stress on the word 'still' that reminded everyone of a topic that had received too little attention of late. Elizabeth thanked Lucia for her too kind offer and stalked out of the room. As they passed by the lighted window of the garden-room on their long journey home, the Mapp-Flints paused involuntarily and gazed at its most unusual and distinctive curtains through which the light glowed warmly. They could hear a musical female voice apparently telling a humorous story, for it was frequently interrupted by joyous laughter. Unfortunately, they could not quite catch the words.

5

The new garden-room curtains soon became an object of widespread interest in Tilling. So picturesque was the town that visitors from every part of the country visited it, even in winter, and few of the eager sight-seers who brought guide-book and Kodak to bear on Mallards failed to utter some appreciative cry as the curtains caught their attention. As a result, Lucia took to keeping them drawn even during the day (for to conceal something that so obviously gave pleasure to so many would be selfishness indeed), with a consequent increase in expenditure on electric light. One American couple actually rang the front-door bell and offered Grosvenor twenty pounds for them under the impression that she was the owner of the house.

Behind these curtains, Monopoly was played every Tuesday and Friday. The games now started in the morning (at about half-past ten) and lasted most of the day, so that the town took on the melancholy appearance of Goldsmith's Deserted Village. Elizabeth had invested in a book by the North-Western Area champion on advanced tactical planning and Lucia had gone one step further by engaging in personal correspondence with the victor of the recent British Open Championship. The other players were confined to rather subsidiary *rôles* in the epic struggles that ensued, being content to watch, to wonder and, very occasionally, to assist one or other of the two Commanders in one of the secret conspiracies that gave the game its own particular spice. Thus, if Diva received, through furtive signalling, the impression that Elizabeth wanted her to buy Mayfair while she had the chance and resell it to her after a discreet interval, she would endeavour to do so; although, since she frequently failed to understand Elizabeth's necessarily perfunctory signals, the amount of assistance that she was materially able to render was limited. Nevertheless, the atmosphere of intrigue and sharp practice that such exercises bred was in itself worth its weight in hotels to the Elizabethan faction. As a result of the intensity and frequency of the contests, the two main protagonists soon achieved a mastery of the game that caused Mr. Wyse, spectator of a singularly fiercely contested encounter, to suggest that Lucia and Elizabeth should combine their formidable talents to produce a Monopoly textbook for the Badminton Library. Both parties, however, declined the suggestion with a charming display of modesty and almost at once began writing furiously, separately and in secret.

Like a forest fire which is apparently extinguished only to burst forth again in the most unexpected of places, the local history craze found a new enthusiast in the person of Major Benjy. It was universally known that he had inherited, from his poor dead friend Captain Puffin, a fine collection of notes on Tilling's past. In reality, the fine collection consisted of an Ordnance Survey map and a sixpenny guide-book, for Captain Puffin's scholarship had been an excuse for sitting up late with the newspaper and a bottle of whisky; and it must be admitted that Major Benjy's renascent fascination with the subject was largely to do with finding a pretext for getting out of the house when it was too cold or too wet to play golf. Nevertheless, the library of the Club did contain several volumes relating to local history, from which the Major would select tasty morsels to recite to his wife, thereby producing specious evidence that he was engaged in honest employment.

One miserable day, therefore, Major Benjy, having finished the crossword and replenished his glass, settled down with a large, dusty book entitled *Sussex County Families*. He was feeling unaccountably drowsy and the earnest tone of the book did little to command his attention until his eye lit upon an intriguing sub-heading:

de Map

He blinked twice and relit the cigar that had extinguished itself between his stout fingers.

de Map

Roger de Map (1004–72) received land from the Conqueror in the vicinity of modern Maidstone. Domesday Book records that his son Hugo held the same land, also a manor outside Tilling. Although Hugo's dates are lost to us. . . .

Major Benjy's eye followed the print but his mind wandered and soon he was asleep again. His fist, with the cigar gripped in it, fell across the page, which soon began to blacken and then to smoulder. Fortunately, the conflagration was short-lived; nevertheless, when he awoke he found to his annoyance that the entire entry on the de Maps had been reduced to cinders.

He cast an anxious eye round the library and soon ascertained that his incendiary activities had not been observed. He swiftly closed the book and returned it to the shelf, finished his drink and strolled innocently from the room. A final whisky-and-soda at the bar chased away the last vestiges of drowsiness and as he savoured its forbidden fruits he rehearsed to himself all he could remember of the de Map family. They had, he distinctly remembered, been given Maidstone by William the Conqueror and it said so in the Domesday Book; Roger de Map and Hugo de Map and there had been others too, whose names he could not remember.

Despite his final whisky-and-soda, he still felt slightly drowsy and on his way towards the Landgate and home, he nearly collided with Lucia and Georgie, who were taking the opportunity of a break in the weather for a gentle stroll.

'Good afternoon, Major Benjy,' said Lucia brightly. 'Good day in the library?'

'Fascinatin',' replied the historian, once he had located the source of the question. 'County families of Sussex an' all that sort of thing. Been readin' bout a fammly called de Map, marrofact, used to own all of Maidstone as far as the eye could see.' Here the Major whirled his arm around his head in a sweeping gesture and Georgie instinctively stepped a little behind Lucia as if taking cover. 'Book says they were given it by William the Conker, Conqueror. Mos' intrestin' fammly, the de Maps. Only one "p",' he added, with pride. 'You ought to read all 'bout them some day when it's too wet to play golf.' He sniggered at his own joke. 'Funny thing is, I feel mos' deuced sleepy,' he concluded, then proceeded briskly on his way, making full use of the whole of the pavement and sometimes venturing into the gutter as well.

'I think our dear Major may have been investigating something else besides the county families of Sussex,' said Lucia, sympathetically. 'How sad, Georgie.'

'He'll have sobered up by the time he gets to Grebe,' Georgie replied, emerging from behind the cover she had afforded him. 'But how interesting about the de Maps, I mean. Elizabeth's family originally came from Maidstone. I remember her telling us once.'

'No!' exclaimed Lucia. 'How fascinating! And you believe all that about William the Conqueror and owning Maidstone?'

'He generally takes a few notes to prove he's been working and not boozing,' he replied (he had seen the Major at his labours before now), 'so I suppose it could well be true. But just fancy! If Elizabeth does turn out to be descended from one of William's knights. . . .'

Lucia pondered this for a moment as they looked out from the Belvedere Platform at the great bend in the river. A huge barge was being fussed over by a small but active tug and it reminded them both irresistibly of a married couple of their acquaintance. 'It's not

78

inconceivable, I suppose,' she remarked at length. 'After all, you and I are both descended from someone or other in the Middle Ages.'

'Do you really think so?' exclaimed Georgie. 'How exciting!'

'Everyone is,' explained Lucia patiently, 'or else we wouldn't be here at all. Ultimately we are all descended from Adam and Eve, although Mr. Darwin and his followers would have us believe that Adam and Eve were no more than highly developed monkeys.'

'I suppose you're right,' said Georgie despondently. 'I thought you meant someone in particular in the Middle Ages. And I do hope I'm not descended from a monkey, however highly developed. My mother's people were Bartletts. I suppose that means I'm related to the Padre, generations and generations ago.'

'Not necessarily, *Georgino*. Many names *della famiglia* are derived from a trade or occupation: Smiths and Taylors and Farmers. I expect you'll find that a Bartlett was a mediaeval tradesman of some description.'

'That's even worse,' was Georgie's reply, 'especially if Elizabeth really does turn out to be a Norman.'

'It may be just a coincidence.'

'Unlikely, since it's not a common name and they both come from Maidstone. I do hope she isn't too tar'some about it.'

'The more I think about it,' said Lucia dreamily, 'the more likely it becomes. There was a vulgar, uncivilised streak in the Normans. They were, after all, descended from Viking raiders who seized the Normandy peninsula. Their leader — I read all this when I was researching the Tapestry — was called Rollo but his original name was Rolf the Walker.'

'Well, that sounds like Elizabeth. She walks everywhere, even though she's supposed to have that dashing little motor-car. I wonder what's become of it?'

'Do listen, Georgie. Rolf the Walker's name derived from the fact that he was so fat that no horse could bear his weight, so that he had to walk everywhere. Not that I would call Elizabeth *fat* exactly. . . .

Elizabeth knew nothing of Rolf the Walker and her delight in Major Benjy's discovery was unalloyed. She sent the Major back next day to copy out the entry in full and was most disappointed when he reported that some careless person had defaced the book in the intervening time. Nevertheless, she had no doubts at all that in the Maidstone de Maps she had identified her own progenitors. She had always wanted to know more about her ancestors, but information had been scarce. There was no family bible and apart from a few collateral branches in remote parts of the country, she was, as far as she knew, the last of her distinguished line. A determination not to be unworthy of her illustrious forebears seized her, for she was firmly of the opinion that noble birth carries with it the onerous duties of leadership. The fact that she was virtually a subject in her own rightful kingdom inspired her to seek new ways of putting Lucia firmly in her place; but how to achieve that worthy aim?

She knew all too well that her fellow-citizens were perfectly capable, if they felt so inclined, of pouring scorn on even the most justifiable pride, so she allowed the news of her new-found connections with the companions of the Conqueror to be disseminated by others. There was no shortage of willing heralds, for by the time she ventured forth into the High Street at the hour dedicated to shopping and conversation, she discovered that her news had already become common knowledge. Lucia, she was well aware, would not have broadcast the intelligence; it must have been dear Mr. Georgie. What a gossip that man was!

The enormous Rolls-Royce motor-car that daily carried the Wyses the few hundred yards from Starling Cottage to the poulterer's during the pheasant season drew up beside her. Susan Wyse, a tiny human kernel in a shell of sables, wound down the window and greeted her with more than usual warmth.

'Good morning, my dear Mrs. Mapp-Flint, although I hear that that is no longer quite correct.'

'I'm sorry?' said Elizabeth, mystified.

'My wife and I have gathered a morsel from Dame Rumour's lips,' said Mr. Wyse, craning over the sable-mountain and smiling charmingly. 'As a result, might we not expect some small alteration to that name already so highly respected in our little community?'

'Oh, I see! How naughty of your to tease me so, dear Mr. Wyse, when I have not uttered a word on the subject. Mere idle speculation on my dear husband's part, of course. He is the scholar of the household. Poor unlearned I —'

'Nevertheless,' persevered Mr. Wyse, for all that leaning across his wife was giving him cramp in his upper arm, 'I hope that I might presume to suggest an emendation to Time's poor scholarship and address you as Mrs. *de* Map-Flint in future.'

'Dear Mr. Wyse, what a suggestion! Plain Elizabeth Mapp-Flint will suffice as well today as yesterday. I would not have it otherwise, I'm sure.'

Susan, clearly deeply impressed by this monumental act of self-denial, of which she felt, had she been in Elizabeth's happy position, she would not have been capable, issued a most fervent invitation to dine the next evening — 'Just *en famille*, you understand.' Elizabeth quite understood the implication. The aristocracy should stick together. She expressed delight at the prospect and went into the shop, much to the relief of the queue of motorists that had formed behind the enormous bulk of the Royce.

Once inside, Elizabeth bought nothing grander than a boiling-fowl, for the de Maps no longer owned Maidstone and game was such a terrible price. Diva was standing at the counter, endeavouring to persuade Mr. Rice that he had a larger, plumper hare hidden away somewhere out of sight despite his protestations to the contrary.

'Are you sure that's a hare, Mr. Rice? Looks like a

large rabbit to me. Oh hello, Elizabeth. Do you think that's a hare?'

'I'm sure I don't know,' said Elizabeth brightly, 'but if Mr. Rice says so, I'm sure I believe him. It's his job to tell rabbits from hares after all, isn't it Mr. Rice? A boiling-fowl please; the Major does so like a hot curry at this time of the year.'

Diva glared at Elizabeth. It had been her duty as a friend of long standing to take her side in the hare controversy, which she now feared was at an end. So she ordered a brace of woodpigeon instead and her tone was distinctly ironical.

'Fancy boiled chicken being good enough for the de Maps of Maidstone! Partridges, I would have thought, or even a haunch of venison.'

'Dear Diva, what can you mean? I only wish I could afford to eat roast hare every day — or will you get cook to jug it? But my tastes are simple enough; plain, wholesome food and pure water to drink.'

Diva did her best to synthesise scorn. 'Ho!' she exclaimed. 'That doesn't sound fitting for the aristocracy. *Noblesse oblige*, after all. And it was a rabbit, too. You can tell by the shape of the ears.'

Thus it was that, as Elizabeth left the shop, she had food for thought in mind as well as food for dinner in her basket. Above all, she feared the acid tongue of quaint Irene Coles, dreaded mimic and fervent Socialist. As luck would have it, Irene was in the butcher's, obtaining the basic ingredients of a Stroganoff. Elizabeth could clearly make out the close-cropped head and frieze-jacketed shoulders at the counter and decided that a brisk walk in quite another direction would be good for her soul as well as her body. So she turned quickly and crossed the road to Twemlow's. Unfortunately, Diva had gone before her and they met again in the doorway.

'Here's Mrs. de Map-Flint,' cried Diva loudly (for the intervening minutes had not diminished the hurt of the presumed rabbit). 'I expect she'll be wanting one of those big tins of goose-liver *pâté*). Or do you have it sent down from London?'

Elizabeth ignored this heavy irony but could not ignore Diva's beloved Irish setter, Paddy, whose tail happened to be under her foot as she set it down. The dog howled and Elizabeth staggered, knocking over a pyramid of small tins of South African peaches.

'Now look what you've done,' said Elizabeth sharply. 'You'd better apologize to Mr. Twemlow.'

'I'll do no such thing,' retorted Diva. 'Just because your crusader ancestors went about treading on dogs. . . .'

'Why on earth should you say that?'

'On their tombs,' explained Diva, 'always got their feet up on a dog. Cruel, I call it. Come along, Paddy.'

Mr. Twemlow's assistant began the long task of rebuilding the pyramid and Elizabeth felt an obligation to buy a tin. She did not, however, want any of the tins of goose-liver *pâté* that had been brought up all the way from the basement and Mr. Twemlow muttered something under his breath about time-wasters.

Quaint Irene, it seemed, was still in the butcher's and so the way back to Grebe was still barred. Rather than go into the watchmaker's or the King's Arms, Elizabeth decided to walk up the narrow street to the Town Hall and then make her way down East Street, thereby circumventing Mr. Worthington's shop altogether. By staying under the awnings of the shops she hoped to be able to negotiate the rest of the High Street undetected and so regain the security of the Landgate. By the time she reached the foot of East Street, however, Irene had completed her meat-buying and was coming out of the shop. Elizabeth was therefore compelled to go back the way she had just come and stood outside the Town Hall counting up to fifty to give her persecutor time to move on.

When she judged the coast to be clear, she walked briskly down the cobbled street straight into the Padre and wee wifie.

'My apologies, Mistress de Map-Flint,' said the Padre lugubriously. 'I wasna' aware that you were ganging thither. I trust I havena' upset your basket o' vittles.'

'Not at all, dear Padre. And what a quaint name you choose to greet me with.'

'Eh, but it's common knowledge the noo that you've the blood of our gallant Norman forebears in your veins. 'Tes a great thing indeed to be so richly descended.'

'If I have Norman blood in my veins, dear Padre, I'm sure I didn't put it there. As you so sternly reminded us on Sunday, we must all seek to do our duty in that station of life to which it has pleased God to call us.'

'Are there any rights and privileges that you are entitled to as Lady of the Manor?' enquired Evie anxiously. 'I'm sure there must be some. So many of these delightful old traditions.'

'You must ask our dear Lucia, who is so well informed about local history. So touching, don't you think, that she, who is the most recent arrival in our beloved town, should be so careful of our heritage, while I with my roots perhaps — I say perhaps — going right back to the Conqueror should know so little. I fear I have been very idle!'

'But surely you knew all along?' demanded Evie. 'About the de Maps and so forth?'

Elizabeth smiled in a way that neither affirmed nor contradicted Evie's statement. 'As your dear fellow-country-man Burns said, dear Padre, the rank is but the penny-stamp. I am the same woman as I was yesterday and the day before.'

This Delphic comment caused the Bartletts to be silent for a moment. Then the Padre, despairing of interpreting it, said, 'Ah yes, quite so, but that doesna change the fact that ye're of the nobility. Ye've been hidin' your light under a bushel all these years.'

'Perhaps, perhaps,' Elizabeth said, without a trace of condescension in her voice, and bade them both good day. As she walked at last down through the Landgate, however, she was almost deafened by a shrill cry behind her. She turned, and with a sinking heart observed quaint Irene bearing down on her like a small but ferocious dog. Before she could even think of how she might escape, Irene was upon her.

'Death to the aristocracy!' she cried. 'Long live the Revolution!'

Elizabeth's Norman blood, or at least a fair amount of it, rushed to her cheeks. 'Don't be silly, dear,' she managed to say, although her voice was so thick with rage and embarrassment that she could hardly speak. She quickened her pace, but unfortunately Irene was just as quick and dogged her every footstep. Elizabeth looked round nervously and observed that a number of children were also following Irene with obvious enthusiasm. She broke into what she hoped was a dignified trot and, as she did so, the chicken fell from her basket. This was no bad thing, for Irene stopped to retrieve the fallen bird, which she waved round her head like a banner.

'Spoils!' she cried, 'Spoils of victory! Here,' and she thrust it at one of the children. The child inspected the chicken, discovered to its disgust that it was dead, and gave it back to Irene, who slipped it into her own basket. 'Parasite!' she bellowed after Elizabeth's fast-retreating form and returned exhausted to Taormina in pleasant anticipation of a chicken casserole.

While this deplorable scene was going on, Lucia and Georgie were sitting at the piano.

'I thought we might try a little Mozart,' suggested Georgie.

'*Caro*, on no account! We should not dare to molest the *maestro* until we have had a chance to practise after our too, too long *absentia*. Now let me see.' She leafed through the sheet-music on top of the piano. 'Here is some Grieg — strong, robust Grieg, not in the front rank of course, but a worthy craftsman nevertheless. We have much to learn from honest Grieg. Or should we venture a few pages of delicious Elgar? He is like a draught of cool spring water after heavy claret.'

Elgar always reminded Georgie of a strong cup of tea

but Elgar was not too difficult, so he made no objection. Lucia put the music on the music-rest and stretched out her hands, then checked herself, as if something were wrong. After a moment, she rose and took away the Elgar.

'It is not an Elgar sort of day,' she said sadly and returned to her search. 'But what can this be? Ah, here is that Chopin *nocturne* that you gave me for Christmas. But how negligent I am! I have not so much as glanced at it. Such ingratitude! Oo poor *Georgino*, to have such a wicked wife. So much sharper than serpent's toothy-woothy.'

This proposal seemed eminently fair to Georgie, for the choice seemed entirely fortuitous. Usually, he got the impression that Lucia forced a certain piece of music on him, as a conjuror forces a card on his victim. But unless Lucia had practised all the pieces that she had offered him, she would be as new to it as he — more so, for he had secretly run through the bass part of the Chopin a week or so ago while Lucia had been at a Council meeting.

'You take the treble, then,' he declared magnanimously. 'It looks frightfully diffy. I should be sure to make awful blunders.'

'Thank you, dear. Now then, *uno, due, TRE!*'

As they played, Georgie found that his prophecy concerning the awful blunders was coming true with a vengeance, for all that he had only meant it conditionally upon his playing the treble. Lucia, however, sailed through that difficult piece without effort; without, indeed, seeming to look at the music. 'Why, she has been practising,' he said to himself. 'How tar'some of her. Why does she do it, I wonder?' But when the piece had reached the end, both treble and bass (for the bass, rather against the composer's original intentions, finished noticeably after the treble), he said, as he always did, 'Thank you, Lucia. You never played better!'

'Don't thank me,' replied Lucia, as ever, 'thank wonderful Chopin.'

Lucia rose and went to the window, but nothing was happening out in the street, so she returned to the piano-stool. 'Ah, why do we ever distract ourselves with things temporal? What could possibly be more important than making music?'

No answer to these questions seemed to be expected, which was probably just as well. Georgie could think of lots of things — going out to tea, playing Bridge, his *bibelots* of course — in fact, most things.

'After all,' Lucia continued, 'it is in music that we find our higher being. Let there be no more words, Georgie; let us communicate henceforth only in music. Schubert for when we are happy and light-hearted; Wagner for anger and despair — those fearful chords — and Beethoven for those noble, lofty sentiments that no word can ever convey. And Mozart, Mozart for the sublime moments when the soul speaks.'

This sounded a rather impractical idea. It would mean having to take one's piano wherever one went, and how on earth could one make polite conversation, let alone ask for anything in a shop? While this lofty fit was upon her, however, it would not be advisable to raise these questions with his wife. Instead, he asked her if she would play the slow movement of the Moonlight Sonata.

'Oh, I couldn't,' replied Lucia, settling herself comfortably and reopening the lid of the piano. 'Not until I have had much, much more practice. I must work up to it again.' She paused, waiting to be remonstrated with; but Georgie was looking out of the window at Diva, who had dropped a sheet of wrapping-paper and was chasing it as it billowed in the wind. 'Perhaps a few bars then,' she relented, and extended her fingers gracefully over the keys.

At that moment, Grosvenor entered with a letter. 'By hand, madam,' she said in an awed voice. 'Sent on from the Town Hall.'

Lucia scrambled from the piano-stool and almost snatched the letter out of Grosvenor's hands. It bore a

London postmark and the address was typed. She devoured its contents eagerly.

'Georgie!' she declared. 'Listen to this! It's from the editor of *County Life*, Mr. Cuthbertson. He's planning an illustrated article on the architecture of Tilling and is writing to me as Mayor, for advice on which houses would be most appropriate and representative.'

'No!' exclaimed Georgie. 'How marvellous. What are you going to recommend?'

'Well, Mallards, of course. But what else?'

'I don't know,' confessed Georgie. 'Me must fink. But we'll have to keep this a secret or everyone will want us to recommend their houses.'

'You're right, of course,' said Lucia, but her tone of voice suggested the very opposite. 'If word of this were to leak out, I would be in the invidious position of one who has a great favour to bestow and people might try to ingratiate themselves with me in order to attempt to influence my decision, which would be too distressing. It would not be bribery exactly — none of our friends would stoop so low — but they would not be above making themselves especially pleasant to me in order to gain the recognition that they all so earnestly seek.'

'That sounds rather like fun to me,' said Georgie.

'On the contrary, Georgie, it would be pitiful. Admittedly, someone with such a high degree of moral authority could perhaps effect some useful changes in our community. The Monopoly habit, for instance — how it seems to have gripped us all of late and yet I dare say that you and I have had almost as much pleasure making music together as we would have had had we spent the time at the Monopoly table.'

'Possibly,' said Georgie.

'Of course, poor Elizabeth would not be affected by this influence. Grebe is a very fine house, in a functional way, but not historic or architecturally outstanding in any sense. On the other hand, perhaps we should suggest to Mr. Cuthbertson that his survey would not be complete without a representative of relatively modern domestic architecture.'

Georgie could take a hint, especially one this strong. He resented forever being made Lucia's mouthpiece, but consoled himself with the thought that this made him what the newspapers termed 'reliable official sources'; perhaps even 'sources close to the Mayor'. And he would at least have the satisfaction of being the first with the news.

'So, *Georgino*, not a word to anyone for the present. But we might take a stroll round the town after dinner and make a few notes. I imagine half a dozen houses will suffice for Mr. Cuthbertson's purposes.'

Lucia resumed her place on the piano-stool.

'And now, I think I might venture just a few bars of that immortal work. Shall I dare, *Georgino*?'

Georgie reassured her that she might dare as she played the First Movement of the Moonlight, he sat, chin on wrist in the approved manner, and bethought him of how he might disseminate this latest breach of confidence. Had he, he wondered, happened to catch sight of the letter lying open on Lucia's desk and cast an idle glance over its contents? Or had Lucia confided the whole story to him and confessed herself baffled as to which houses she ought to recommend? Then he would be able to play the *rôle* of the concerned husband, who, distressed at the sight of his wife's perplexity, was seeking the wise counsel of his friends.

The slow movement ended and both breathed the well-known music sigh of wistful satisfaction which Lucia had brought with her from her former domain of Riseholme, where she had ruled virtually *assoluta* before her conquest of Tilling, and which only the ill-bred would venture to associate with indigestion.

'Ah, divine Beethoven!' said Lucia, gently closing the lid of the piano. 'And now I fear I must tear myself away from these enchantments and write a brief note of acknowledgement to Mr. Cuthbertson. Such a pity I had to let Mrs. Simpson go.'

Georgie recollected Lucia's secretary and remembered that that worthy and hard-working woman had nearly exhausted Lucia's ingenuity in finding something to keep her occupied for at least an hour a day.

'So tar'some,' he said. 'You ought to learn typing yourself.'

Lucia seemed to shudder slightly at the thought. 'When would I find the time? And then I must go across to the Town Hall and see what else they have for me today. I hope I haven't kept them waiting. But everything can wait for divine Beethoven.'

Diva had chased the sheet of wrapping-paper from Church Square to the foot of West Street, only to see it go under the wheels of a motor-car and perish utterly. Irene had watched the hunt from the upstairs window of Taormina, whence she had retired after her persecution of Elizabeth, and had sought to encourage Diva with various cries from the vocabulary of *la chasse*. She now joined the baffled huntress, who was with difficulty recovering her breath.

'Gone to earth, I should say. But never mind, I've got a paper-bag at home you could put up. The wind's about nor'-nor'-east, so if we launched it from the top of Porpoise Street —'

'Very funny!' said the panting Diva. 'Cost me three-pence and now look at it.'

'Up goes half a guinea, bang goes a penny and down comes half-a-crown,' said Irene sympathetically. 'Still, it's not what you get for the carcass, it's the sport that counts. But I agree, that one's only fit for the dogs now.'

'Oh well,' said Diva obliviously, 'I'll have to get some more. Any news this morning?'

'Elizabeth a bit reluctant to talk about her Royal connections, to me at any rate. Typical Mapp! Oh yes, and Lucia's started playing the piano again. The Moonlight, I think it was.'

'I heard that too,' confirmed Diva.

'And a man from the Town Hall took a letter round to

90

Mallards. I watched him all the way. A white envelope with a stamp.'

'Golly!' exclaimed Diva. 'I wonder what that could be.'

'Another death-warrant for her to sign, of course. Mapp's, with any luck. Gosh, what a swell.'

A tall, aristocratic-looking woman had stepped out of the doorway of the King's Arms, accompanied by a massive borzoi. Suddenly, the dog stopped dead, sniffed the air noisily and then sprang forward, slipping its lead. Diva and Irene stared in astonishment as the beast sprinted past them and leapt at Susan Wyse, who had stepped down from the Royce to post a letter. The borzoi gripped Susan's enormous fur coat in its strong jaws and pulled it from her back, then stood on it and growled threateningly.

'It took Susan Wyse for a bear!' cried Irene joyfully. 'Quite an understandable mistake for a Russian dog, I suppose.'

Mr. Wyse stepped nimbly from the motor and paused for a moment as if nerving himself to confront the ferocious animal. Then it apparently occurred to him that his first duty must be to comfort his wife.

'Get that thing off my sables!' shrieked Susan, shaking her fist.

'Pray do not excite the animal, my dear, lest he do further damage to the garment. Let us await the arrival of the owner.'

The aristocratic woman was not long in coming. 'Paddy!' she commanded, and the dog reluctantly left its trophy and submitted to the lead.

'There's a coincidence!' whispered Diva.

'I am most fearfully sorry,' said the aristocratic woman in a rather beautiful voice. 'Do let me pay for the damage my wicked Paddy may have done.'

Mr. Wyse bowed from the waist and then signalled to the chauffeur to retrieve the coat. Paddy growled, causing the chauffeur to hesitate, and it was Susan Wyse who darted fearlessly forth to retrieve her beloved sables. Once reunited with them, she became calmer.

'There appears to be no damage,' said Mr. Wyse without looking. 'The borzoi is a soft-mouthed breed, is it not? Pray do not concern yourself over such a trifling incident.'

'Most kind of you,' said the aristocrat. 'But please do let me give you my card. Should there turn out to be any mark, you will of course notify me. Come along, Paddy.'

The woman departed up West Street, and Diva and Irene hurried over to the victim of the attack. She was staring with evident fascination at the card; but when she became aware of Diva and Irene she thrust it swiftly under the palm of her glove. Clearly the identity of that superior person was not to be disclosed.

'Susan dear, what a horrible adventure!' exclaimed Diva, her eyes riveted on the glove. 'Step across to Wasters and have a cup of tea. Or,' she added, for expense was unimportant at a time like this, 'a glass of sherry.'

'It was nothing, really,' said Susan. 'And it's not every day one meets —' she checked herself and then said, 'meets such a charming woman. So insistent that she should pay for any damage.'

'Who was she?' demanded Irene shamelessly. 'She looked a real toff to me. That's just like the ruling classes, setting their dogs on the proletariat.'

Both Wyses directed at Irene a glance of such pure ice that even she was cowed for a moment and mumbled, 'All right then, don't tell me.'

'Come Susan,' said Mr. Wyse stiffly. 'Good morning, Mrs. Plaistow. We meet at Mallards for Monopoly tomorrow, do we not?'

And with this alliterative dismissal, the Wyses ascended the Royce and were gone. Diva turned and shot a glance up West Street. The aristocratic woman was standing outside the garden-room inspecting the new curtains with obvious interest. Diva nudged Irene and, as they watched, the noblewoman seemed to come to a decision. She walked up to the front-door and rang the bell. Soon Grosvenor answered it and they spoke together for a while.

'Lucia's out and Georgie too,' whispered Irene. 'Will she leave a card?'

Even as she spoke, the woman took a card from her card-case and presented it to Grosvenor; then she turned and was lost to sight.

'She'll need to get some more engraved at this rate,' concluded Irene. 'Still, what fascination!'

'Our curtains,' said Diva. 'Perhaps she's a collector.'

'What's she collecting for then, the Red Cross? Or the Lifeboats? Look, there's the Padre. Hoots, mon, ye'll never guess what we've seen.'

And they scurried across to tell him.

6

Lucia made several tours of inspection in her search for houses worthy of recommendation to the editor of *County Life*; for although she knew every stick and stone of the town by now, this new responsibility seemed to demand a fresh assessment. Although only she and Georgie knew about the forthcoming visit to the town by the photographer and the journalist of that respected publication, she found to her surprise that a wave of interest in all things architectural had broken over Tilling. All her friends were able (and ready, on every possible occasion) to point out with great authority and command of really quite difficult technical terms all the many and varied peculiarities and fascinations of their respective houses. This was especially flattering for Lucia, to whom everyone brought their architectural discoveries (for how could they be aware of her brief authority in this field?) and it was clear that a hitherto undisclosed respect for her taste and judgement in matters of aesthetics was being manifested.

'As an example of the very best half-timbering,' declared Susan Wyse with a degree of passion that the subject hardly seemed to merit, 'Starling Cottage is unrivalled in Tilling. My dear Algernon and I have endeavoured to restore it to its authentic splendour by removing the blacking from the external beams — that is a West Country tradition and quite alien to the southeast coast — but in every other respect we have been the most cautious guardians of our treasured heritage.'

Lucia regarded her judicially over the rim of her coffee-cup.

'But surely,' she interposed while Susan was taking a breath, 'the old, low Tudor houses in Church Square are every bit as characteristic of the style and the period, and such delightful windows!'

Susan Wyse sniffed impatiently at this irrelevance, for the Tudor houses in Church Square belonged to no one of any importance; a dentist and a retired stock-broker, neither of them in Society. It would be a scandal if Lucia had *their* houses pictured in *County Life*.

'Chocolate-box houses!' she declared. 'Why, you could find their exact doubles in any town in England. But Starling Cottage has line, form, grace; it is virtually unique —'

'If you ask me,' interrupted Diva, 'all these Tudor houses are much of a muchness. Boxes with bits of wood stuck on them, and sometimes the walls aren't even straight. If I were writing — well, a book, say, on Tilling architecture — I'd want to mention the late seventeenth-century brick, such as Wasters, for example.'

'Or Taormina,' broke in Irene. 'Magnificent example of late seventeenth-century artisan's dwelling. That's real *Volkskunst*, and completely unspoilt.'

'I know dear,' snapped Diva. 'You're always saying you're going to have it done up properly when you've got the money, but you've never got around to it. Very fortunate, considering your latest ideas for improvements.'

Irene had planned to knock down all the internal walls and half the downstairs ceiling, replacing the stairs with a knotted rope. She made a face at Diva.

'While we're on the subject of the late seventeenth century,' said Evie quickly (for who could say when she might next be able to speak?), 'the Vicarage is of tremendous architectural interest. The chimneys, you know, and the miniature Greek metope over the doorway.'

'What's so special about your chimneys?' demanded Diva, but Lucia, observing that the debate was growing rather acrimonious, interrupted her.

'How fortunate we all are in living in such a pictur-esque town,' she said regally, 'and how fortunate am I to be the owner of what, in all honesty, I must confess to be the chief ornament of its domestic architecture. I feel I can say that without being condemned as a vain, boastful woman. I did not build Mallards — I only bought it. Its splendours, then, reflect not on me but upon the original builder whose name, alas, is lost to us. Ah, here they are at last. How you men love to tarry over your port, leaving us all alone.'

Georgie would gladly have swallowed his half-glass at a gulp, for the Padre had been giving him a lecture on the Vicarage windows and he felt that he had escaped only just in time to avoid the written test afterwards. To Georgie, a house was a simply a structure for going to tea in. His own passion was for furniture and porcelain, and *County Life* had expressed no interest in them.

'The Padre and I have been having such an interesting chat,' he nevertheless announced, for he had given his word that he would. 'All about windows. Did you know that the Vicarage —'

He was not allowed to redeem his pledge to the Padre, for the debate broke out again, all the more fiercely since windows had not been discussed before. Diva's windows, it transpired, had a discreet charm (so discreet that Diva felt compelled to spend quite five minutes pointing it out), while the windows of Taormina were the epitome of simple, functional elegance, or, as Susan Wyse rather unkindly said, square holes in the wall filled with glass. She was eloquent about the ancient leaded windows of Starling Cottage, which were not functional (little if any light ever managed to force its way through those opaque panes) but undeniably attractive. The windows of the Vicarage, however, spoke for themselves, which was just as well, for Evie, despite her best endeavours, did not get a chance to speak for them.

From windows the debate turned to roofs, about which Mr. Wyse was so exquisitely elegant that the careful listener could hear the semi-colons as he spoke them, and from roofs to doors. On this subject, too, feelings ran high, and Susan and Evie nearly came to blows before Lucia was able to restore order and change the subject.

'So disappointed that dear Elizabeth could not manage to join us this evening', she said. 'But it seems that Major Benjy was showing signs of a severe cold this morning and Elizabeth felt it would not be wise for him to venture out of doors for a day or so.'

Lucia knew, and so did everyone else, that Major Benjy's cold had not stopped him from playing golf that morning, or spending the afternoon at his historical researches, which had left him apparently incoherent with fascination, for his speech had been distinctly blurred as he greeted them all on their way to Mallards.

'Ho!' exclaimed Diva. 'I'm not so sure. Expect it's beneath her Norman dignity to dine with us. Well, we Saxons will just have to do the best we can without her.'

'Nay, Mistress Plaistow,' said the Padre severely,'you canna honestly say that Mistress Mapp-Flint's sudden revelation o' her exalted ancestry has made any difference to her demeanour. She doesna hold hersen aloof. She hasna abandoned her auld friends. She is as pleasant among us as ever she was before.'

'She wasn't particularly pleasant before,' muttered Irene. 'I'd hoped that *noblesse* might have obliged, but it hasn't. She got worse — why, she cut me dead in the street the other day when I went over to congratulate her on her news. And I won't believe in those de Maps of hers until I see some solid evidence.'

'Och awa' wi' ye, Mistress Coles!' exclaimed the Padre. 'Do ye no ken that Mistress Mapp-Flint's ane deportment, her carriage, her air are evidence enough? When a body's frae the Upper Crust' — here he looked pointedly at the Wyses — 'ye dinna need documents and certificates o' birth to prove their innate nobility. Blood will out, 'tes said, and Mistress Mapp-Flint's noble blood is plain to see. 'Tes as plain as the nose on her face.'

'Or the rest of her face for that matter,' growled Irene, who was being insufferably quaint this evening.

'What do you think, Lucia?' enquired Evie, who was largely neutral on the issue. 'Do you think Elizabeth's really descended from William the Conqueror or is it just some fairy story she's concocted?'

'Nothing would be simpler than to verify or refute the suggestion,' replied Lucia gravely. 'A little research in the Cartulary at Bodiam Castle would surely turn up the history of the de Map family. If only I could spare the time!'

'Well, one of us could go and look,' said Diva. 'It's about time that we sorted this thing out, before Elizabeth declares herself Marchioness of Tilling and starts coining money with her head on it.'

This numismatic fantasy silenced the company for some time, as they tried to picture the issues that would result. Georgie, for instance, saw Elizabeth as Britannia on the penny, with Benjy instead of a lion at her feet (or should it be a tiger-skin?); while Lucia, as befitted an antiquary, was irresistibly reminded of a Roman Victory. She pulled herself together with an effort.

'Oh, I don't think that the Cartulary is open to the general public,' she said, 'only to serious researchers who can justify their use of the facilities. I, as Mayor, could of course consult the records at any time, but I am so busy what with one thing and another. Again, Elizabeth could always go and look, since it is her own family that she is researching. In fact, I wonder why she has not already done so. There is, of course, the problem of getting to Bodiam — but I was forgetting, she has a motor now, does she not? I wonder what has become of Elizabeth's car? We do not seem to have heard very much of it of late.'

Having thus sown the seeds of doubt in everybody's mind, Lucia suggested a game of Monopoly. But the craze was already waning; not surprisingly, given that it had lasted longer than virtually any of its predecessors, and that the games themselves were always dominated by Lucia and Elizabeth. Someone — it may have been Georgie — suggested that they play Bridge instead, just for a change. Lucia smiled and agreed. The threat of Elizabethan domination through Monopoly had been well and truly defeated, and the weapon itself could now be laid aside.

After a joyfully acrimonious rubber, the guests thanked Lucia for a delightful evening and ventured out into the clear, cold night. Lucia paused for a while on the doorstep, as the Royce arrived to transport the Wyses round the corner to that apotheosis of the Elizabethan house, Starling Cottage, and wondered how she could best exploit her position. The danger was that the editor of *County Life*, and his representatives too, for that matter, had eyes of their own; they could see for themselves that Starling Cottage, with its beautiful windows and unrivalled coal-cellar, was worthy of a photograph, but that Taormina, the Vicarage and Wasters were not. It would therefore be advisable to make a virtue of necessity and recommend Starling Cottage. On the other hand, she could use the editor's decision to cover her own, and proclaim to the disappointed householders, when the Tilling edition came out and their houses were not in it, that she could not understand why Mr. Cuthbertson had seen fit to reject her suggestions and instead devote precious space to those little Tudor slums in Church Square. After all, no one could refute such a claim.

'I hope I am not being short-sighted,' she said to the stars, 'but I can't see any risks in that.'

A cloud passed over the moon as she spoke, and she paused to debate the significance of this augury. It might be an unfavourable omen; but she preferred to think that Heaven was amused by her plan and was winking its silvery eye in approbation. She nodded her head, curtsied prettily to the moon and closed the door.

Elizabeth had avoided Lucia's dinner party for two reasons. First, she knew that Grebe, for all its functional charm, would not be acceptable to the editor of *County Life* and she had no desire to witness the petty squabbles of those whose houses were more likely to recommend themselves to the vulgar taste. Secondly, she feared that Lucia might corner her with awkward questions about the three-wheeler. This difficulty would be resolved by the following noon, for the vehicle was due to be returned then by the Southampton garage, and although she did not relish the thought of writing the cheque that would complete the transaction, nevertheless she was happy at the thought of abstracting from Lucia's quiver at least one arrow of malicious enquiry.

To while away the time until mid-day, when she would once more be able to drive triumphantly into Tilling, she sat and studied a history of the town with an eye to references to Norman families. The town had been given to a French monastery by Edward the Confessor — evidently a person almost as high-handed and imperious as Lucia herself. After the Conquest, King William had granted land nearby to some of his captains, and although the name de Map was not among those listed, she drew confidence from the statement. She closed her eyes and tried to picture in her mind her warrior ancestor, but the image did not form clearly in her imagination; for if he had the distinctive Mapp ears, they would not fit inside his helmet.

It had not been her intention to make an issue of her noble descent. Others had drawn inferences from Major Benjy's rather indiscreet disclosures. But since she had been drawn into conflict, she must bear her part bravely and assemble evidence on her side. Admittedly, it was not fear of letting down the family name that troubled her; if anything, it was fear that the family name might in some way let *her* down. Still, there was a lot to be said for being of noble blood, and as she sat and read, and occasionally lifted her head to gaze out of the window at the marshes beyond, she felt a vague sense of unjustified loss. No one could be more liberal in her views than she; she was a firm believer in democracy, and honest worth must always count for more than noble blood. But the fact that Lucia — a lawyer's widow, born a Smythe and transformed by second marriage into the wife of a mere Bartlett (on his mother's side) — occupied the fine old house, the jewel of Tilling, that had been in the Mapp family for who knew how many generations (she certainly did not, which was probably just as well) pained her deeply. She had never quite forgiven Lucia, despite several attempts, for encouraging her to indulge in the Stock Market speculations that had come close to ruining her, with the result that she had been compelled to exchange her beloved Mallards for two thousand pounds and this modern and unphotogenic house on the very outskirts of town. The sudden discovery of her ancestry made this wound that had never properly healed open yet again. And now, she reflected angrily, Lucia would be photographed standing outside the de Map family home, or in the window of the Mapp garden-room and would generally take credit for a house that had been built when the Smythes, Lucia's family, were doubtless still hewers of wood and drawers of water.

Outside the window, Diva was hurrying by on her daily walk. The road that led out from Tilling towards the little village on the coast near the golf-course was one of her favourite excursions, but there was always the awkward problem of getting past Grebe. If Elizabeth were at home she would be watching at the window and would insist on her coming in for tea and a little chat. Since Elizabeth's chat, unless concerned with some object of immediate interest such as the eccentric or reprehensible behaviour of a mutual friend, tended to turn very quickly into veiled personal criticism, Diva did not relish the thought of being waylaid, and had therefore of late taken other walks, far less attractive but relatively safe. But she wanted to walk along the Military Road again and see what colour curtains people who lived along there were putting up to greet the spring, and so had resolved to take her daily exercise during the marketing hour, when Elizabeth would be sure to be in town. This meant missing the day's news, which was most unfortunate, but today, since the weather was so fine, she felt ready to make that sacrifice.

Despite her belief that Elizabeth would be in town amusing herself, no doubt at somebody else's expense,

Diva quickened her already brisk pace as she passed the windows of Grebe and could not resist a glance to make sure that Elizabeth was not at home. This was a false move, for their eyes met through the glass. Before Diva could wave cheerily and march on, Elizabeth banged on the window and motioned her to come in. Her advent, from Elizabeth's point of view, could not have been better timed. If she could delay Diva for half an hour, Elizabeth calculated that she would be returning from her walk and passing Grebe shortly after the car was delivered. She could then offer to drive Diva into town and thereby announce the continued existence of her vehicle by a medium even better than wireless telegraphy, for Diva was the worst keeper of secrets in Tilling.

'Diva, dear, what a happy coincidence!' she warbled. 'I was just about to break off my studies for a cup of coffee. You will join me, won't you?'

Diva thanked her dully and looked to be most richly railed on. Usually Elizabeth took advantage of their tête-à-têtes to pillory with oblique comment any new or distinctive article of dress she might be wearing, and it so happened that today she had put on for the first time a new and rather expensive halo hat, as worn by a certain duchess. She had told herself (several times) that it suited her very well; now, no doubt, Elizabeth would so work on her fragile confidence that she would never put on the hat again, this being Elizabeth's way of punishing her for her heretical views on the family de Map. She could not exactly recall what had sparked off this latest war between them — something, she seemed to remember, about a hare. . . .

Elizabeth rang for coffee, and, while her back was turned, Diva tore off the precious hat and sought to hide it behind her feet, whose size made them highly suitable for this purpose. Alas! she had been too late and Elizabeth was on the point of commenting on the outlandish bauble — some speculation as to how the brim had become quite so brutally distorted — when she

102

considered whether Diva might not be more use to her as an ally than merely as the unworthy victim of her wit. This thought caused her to choke back the words (which could easily be used another day) and she told herself that Diva was a grown (some might say over-grown) woman who would only learn dress sense by bitter experience.

'What a delightful hat!' she therefore trilled. 'Let me see it again.'

Diva reluctantly produced the ornament and Elizabeth inspected it with a pretty display of enthusiasm as she wondered what would be the most flattering thing she could say. She determined to seize the bull by the horns and praised the hat for the very qualities that made it most hideous.

'My dear, what a pretty brim! It suits you perfectly. If only my face were not so frightfully round I would buy one just like it.'

Diva's face was rounder than the globe itself, but Elizabeth appeared to have forgotten that. This was an olive branch, and Diva, overjoyed at the unexpected reprieve of her headdress, seized it joyfully.

'And where is dear Major Benjy today?' she enquired. 'Golf? Or research? So splendid of him to take up local history.'

'A new but most absorbing interest,' said Elizabeth. 'I believe he came across some of the papers left him by poor Captain Puffin. He felt — and I agreed with him — that it would be a pity to leave the Captain's work unfinished.'

The Captain's work, as everybody knew, had been a sustained effort to revive the Scottish distillery industry, and the only papers he had left were unpaid wine-merchants' bills. But since Elizabeth appeared to be afflicted with temporary blindness, Diva could afford temporary amnesia.

'Worthwhile,' she therefore agreed. 'Found out anything else about the de Maps? I remember how excited he was when he found the first reference.'

'Nothing specific, I fear. But he has been doing a little

work on the Conqueror's grants in this area. There were several, all to noble families. So who can say what further research might uncover? Perhaps — I say perhaps — the de Maps will turn out to be among them.'

'Sure to be. No question. But fancy you being a Norman all the time without knowing it.'

Elizabeth turned away as if to hide a blush and said nothing. The implication to be drawn from this economical gesture was clear. She *had* known all along and had kept quiet about it, for she was not the sort of woman to make a fuss about such a thing. But now that Major Benjy had stumbled across the truth, what point was there in silence? Diva, although she did not believe any of this, understood that acceptance of it was the price of peace. Compared to the price of hats, it was low enough.

'Dinner with Lucia last night. Everyone there — except you of course.'

'Poor Benjy and his cold. Men are such babies, aren't they? I almost had to thrust him from the house today. He is quite well now, however, which is the main thing. And how is dear Lucia?'

'Queening it rather,' said Diva. 'This *County Life* business. Most unsettling. Everyone wants their houses to be in it, of course.'

'Has she made her final selection? Can we breathe again?'

'No. She pretends not to know that we know about it, so we can't ask her to her face. But I believe Starling Cottage will be recommended, though I can't say anything about any of the others.'

Elizabeth would have ground her teeth had she not been afraid of damaging her new plate. She contented herself with a bitter smile.

'We cannot all afford to live in beautiful houses,' she said. 'After all, even the Wyses and Lucia are but the owners of their magnificent dwellings. They did not design them, nor did they build them with their own hands. So they have no reason to be proud.'

'That's just what Lucia says,' said Diva tactlessly.

'So pleased to hear that she appreciates the fact, though I daresay that won't stop her standing outside Mallards when they take their photographs, as if she were the ancestral owner and not some rich *parvenue*. Never mind; we know the truth, don't we?'

Elizabeth developed this theme for some time, with a number of references to shady financial deals, and then released Diva, without compelling her to witness the actuality of her motor, who went on her way thanking God that her hat had been spared her. The dispossessed one, however, sat awhile deep in thought. The iniquity gnawed at her, but she laid it down in her soul, like wine, to mature.

Lucia received a further letter from Mr. Cuthbertson. He proposed to send down his writer — no ordinary journalist, but a leading authority on the subject, a Mr. Arncott — and a specialist photographer, equipped with the latest in cameras, who would look over the houses she had recommended, namely Mallards, Starling Cottage, the two Tudor houses in Church Square and the little house at the bottom of the Mint, as well as the Church and, if space permitted, the Norman Tower. As it turned out, Lucia's choice was fully endorsed by the eminent authority, and the Bartletts watched enviously as the photographer set up his apparatus on the opposite side of the Square to their own architectural gem. But the photographer could not get the houses 'in frame' (as he called it) by standing on the pavement, and went round to the Vicarage to ask for permission to set up his tripod inside the churchyard. The Padre agreed most readily and even pointed out a low, flat tomb on which the photographer could stand so as to get the best possible result. The photographer was particularly impressed with the Church, which he considered a fine example of its very distinctive type. He also thought the same of the Padre (although he did not say so) and prevailed upon him to stand under one of the magnificent flying buttresses when he took his picture of that most outstanding feature of the edifice.

Then the Authority went to Porpoise Street, where he was virtually abducted by Susan Wyse, who called up tea and some strange-looking honey-cakes sent from Capri by the Contessa di Faraglione. She noticed — too late — that the negligent Figgis had left the lid of the box that contained her M.B.E. lying open on the table, and before she could close it the perceptive Mr. Arncott had inspected and admired it. Meanwhile, the photographer was having a wretched time trying to get his camera to stand upright on the steep slope of Porpoise Street, so Mr. Wyse sent for the Royce, in order that its ample running-board might serve as a support for one of the legs of the tripod. Having done their work, the *County Life* party declined with thanks the Wyses' generous offer of a lift down to the Mint; for it would have taken ten minutes to accomplish by motor a distance that could be walked in two, and transferred their caravanserai down the hill.

Lucia, meanwhile, had been waiting anxiously, for the light seemed to be deteriorating — there was at least one cloud in the sky and who could tell in which direction it might choose to go? — and finally came to the conclusion that the *County Life* party must have lost their way. So she sent Georgie off to look for them in the High Street, while she went to search Church Square and Curfew Street. She feared that they might have been beguiled by some other houses of interest and she did not want them to miss an opportunity of seeing Mallards at its best.

As she set off briskly towards the Church, Elizabeth, who had been furtively sketching in West Street, felt a sudden urge to take a look at her ancestral home. So she set up her easel beneath the garden-room window, selected a fresh sheet of paper, and began to sketch.

So intent upon her work must she have been that she did not notice the *County Life* photographer setting up his camera and Mr. Arncott taking out his notebook, only a few yards from where she was sitting. The photographer came over and asked her if she would mind moving just for a moment while he took his photograph.

'Delighted,' she said, 'to help a fellow-artist,' and she laughed gaily. 'Such a charming house, don't you think?'

'Remarkable,' agreed Mr. Arncott. 'One of the finest that I remember having seen. The rigid formality of the style has been fitted perfectly into a most unusual context.'

Elizabeth did not quite understand what he meant by this, but she felt sure that she agreed with it, so she nodded sagely. He wrote something in his notebook and said:

'The glorious thing is how well it has been looked after. Obviously it had suffered neglect for a while, but I think I am right in saying that a most admirable job of restoration has been done within, say, the last five or six years. So many of these houses have been spoilt recently by careless renovation.'

'Ah well,' said Elizabeth, 'our family has always been careful to preserve our precious, precious heritage. My Aunt Caroline —'

'So you are the owner? Mrs. Pillson, is it not?'

'My name is Mrs. Mapp-Flint,' said Elizabeth truthfully.

And, with a little prompting from the Authority, she told him all about Roger de Map and Hugo de Map and the Domesday Book. She did not actually assert that she was their descendant, or even that her less remote ancestors had built Mallards (for who could say what books of reference such a learned man might have access to?), but she rather feared that the Authority, who, like so many of these scholarly men, was inclined to be vague, might have formed that impression, for he asked Elizabeth if she would perhaps care to stand in front of the doorway for a moment while the photographer took a picture. The reader did so like to see what the owner of the property looked like. Elizabeth had qualms of conscience at this point, but he had not said the *present* owner and explanations would be so tiresome.

'Thank you so much,' said Mr. Arncott, 'and I do apologize for getting your name wrong. My editor informed me that the Mayor's name was Mrs. Pillson.'

'Mrs. Pillson is the Mayor,' said Elizabeth, sticking rigidly to the truth.

'She has been most helpful,' continued the Authority, 'in recommending houses for us to use in this article. She seems to be quite an accomplished scholar.'

'Which houses did she recommend?' asked Elizabeth artlessly.

'Well, your beautiful Mallards, of course, and Starling Cottage — that's in Porpoise Street, you know — a most charming couple. She is related to the European aristocracy, I believe.'

'Spanish,' said Elizabeth maliciously.

'And he was awarded the O.B.E., I think.'

'Quite.'

'I'm afraid I cannot recall their name. How awkward! I think I ought to mention it in my article.'

'Mr. and Mrs. White,' said Elizabeth innocently. 'Such delightful people and so proud of their little house.'

'And of course there were those delightful Tudor houses in Church Square — Mrs. Pillson was quite right to recommend them — and the little house at the end of the Mint. Such taste Mrs. Pillson has. Has she ever received formal architectural training, do you know? We would never have seen it had it not been for her suggestion.'

With many farewells the Authority and the photographer departed to lunch at the Traders' Arms, and Elizabeth resumed her sketching in West Street with a satisfied heart. Like all her friends in Tilling, she would await the forthcoming issue of *County Life* with great interest.

7

A week or so later, an observant person might have
noticed a small group of people hovering about near, but
not actually outside, the newsagent's shop in the High
street. The Wyses, seemingly racked with indecision as
to whether or not they should buy some stamps, went in
and out of the post-office every few minutes. Diva stood
in front of Mr. Worthington's window, apparently
studying a leg of lamb, but in fact watching the newsagent's doorway reflected in the glass. The Bartletts
stood at the Belvedere Platform, but instead of looking
out over the estuary, for the better observation of which
the platform had been constructed, they chose to face
the other way. The Mapp-Flints, meanwhile, could not
tear themselves away from contemplating something in
the jeweller's window — a bracelet, perhaps, or a
pocket-watch — and although they tried several times
to move on, they were always drawn back, as by a mag-
net. A cynic might have supposed that each of these
people was waiting for the others to go away, not
wishing to be seen to be the first to buy the latest edition
of *County Life*; but that would be an unworthy thought.

Various other inhabitants of the town had no inhibi-
tions about buying the magazine. The retired stockbroker
who lived in Church Street stepped boldly through the
door, and Diva could distinctly hear him giving his order
and just as distinctly make out the newsagent's reply,
'You're just in time, sir, we're nearly sold out.'

Diva left the leg of lamb to its fate and shot across the
street like a small cannon-ball, nearly colliding with the

Bartletts. This delay enabled the Mapp-Flints to get in first, and Susan Wyse came a close second, despite catching her heel in the hem of her sables and nearly falling. In the end, however, there were enough copies to go round and the diffident property-owners retired to their houses to inspect the Tilling article.

Lucia, being provident, had had her five copies delivered with the newspapers, and even as the Bartletts were stamping their feet and blowing on their hands on the Belvedere Platform, she was sitting sour-faced and contemplating a beautiful facsimile of Mallards, outside which (so ran the legend) stood Mrs. Elizabeth de Map-Flint, the owner of that property, whose family (of Norman descent) had lived there since the house was built. To Lucia it was no comfort that the article was a mass of factual errors, some of them almost as grave: that the brief commentary on the Church gave the Padre's name as the Reverend Mr. McBartlett, or that the owners of Starling Cottage were named as Mr. and Mrs. White, he the holder of the O.B.E., she connected to the aristocracy of Spain. There was no comfort in the fact that (to judge by the photograph) Starling Cottage was in imminent danger of falling back down on to the Mint and squashing flat the attractive little house at the foot of the hill. Although this article covered three pages and was lavishly illustrated, there was but one paragraph and one photograph that caught the attention and held it as in a vice.

'This time,' said Lucia coldly, 'she has gone too far.'

'They spelt her name right too,' said Georgie, 'or at least the Norman part of it — de Map with one "p". She must have written it down for them.'

'Surely you are mistaken, dear,' said Lucia, grim as Cromwell. 'Elizabeth's surname since her marriage has been Mapp (two "p"s)-Flint. But, then, it is such an inaccurate, carelessly researched, badly edited article that such minor errors are of no consequence.'

Georgie sought to change the subject.

'Fancy the Wyses being Spanish nobles,' he said. 'I think they call them *hidalgos*, or are those the people

110

who fight bulls? They've got their name wrong too — they won't like that, since it's such a terribly good name and whoever heard of the Whites of Whitchurch? And Mr. Wyse has been given Susan's medal, only it's grander. I bet they're furious.'

Lucia noticed that her name, in tiny italics, appeared at the bottom of the article (and nowhere else) among those thanked by the editor for their invaluable assistance in preparing the article.

'Clearly this is another of Elizabeth's insane practical jokes,' she reiterated. 'For some reason — some silly, childish reason of her own — she must have misled Mr. Arncott, who is obviously, for all his learning, not a particularly intelligent man, with deliberate falsehoods.'

'I suppose so,' said Georgie. 'But how could she manage it? And why didn't we see them taking the beastly photograph?'

'I imagine she was prowling around outside the house and, when we went off to see what had become of them, she loitered in front of the garden-room window until Mr. Arncott and the photographer — a most unprofessional photographer, by the look of it — came by. Look, she is wearing that hideous old hat that she keeps for sketching. She must have put up her easel outside. And all the time,' Lucia could not keep the emotion from her voice, 'we were wandering around the back streets looking for them in case they were lost. It's too bad of her, it really is.'

'I think we should ignore the whole thing,' said Georgie who was re-reading the passage about the Wyses.

'I agree with you, *caro*. We might possibly write a letter to the editor pointing out the strictly factual errors in the article, but beyond that it would be too humiliating to become involved directly in accusations of deception and fraud. If Elizabeth is so keen to announce to the world the depths to which she is prepared to sink, we at least should not assist her in her self-destructive mania.'

Lucia was getting excited again, and Georgie, thinking of her blood-pressure, interrupted her.

'Oh look,' he said, 'our curtains have come out terribly well. There's Brutus as clear as anything.'

'I'm surprised Elizabeth didn't claim them too. She has as much right to do so as she has to claim any connection with Mallards.' Lucia was more furious than ever and Georgie started to edge nervously from the room. 'When I think of the state this house was in when I rescued it from her! Why, if she was still the owner, there would have been nothing for her friend Mr. Arncott to see but a pile of fallen masonry.'

So quickly was Lucia speaking in her wrath that before he could attain the safety of the corridor, Georgie had to listen to a full and not particularly flattering character-study of Elizabeth, with speculation about her true ancestry and her likely ultimate fate. As he closed the door behind him, he wiped his brow with his handkerchief, for he was perspiring freely, and he noted with distress that the perspiration had made the deep auburn of his hair run a little.

'If she carries on like that,' he said to himself, 'she'll go off pop!'

The other eager readers of *County Life* had by this time reassembled in the High Street and their verdict on the article was hardly more favourable than Lucia's. Their resentment, however, was focused on another scapegoat, for they too had read the small italics at the end of the piece. Besides that, there were other well-springs of animosity.

'Gave me her word that Wasters would be in it,' said Diva, 'or as good as gave me her word. I wouldn't have minded if she hadn't gone and raised my hopes.'

'Why, she virtually promised me that the Vicarage windows would be prominently featured,' said Evie. 'She thought that the sills alone —'

'Currying favour,' replied Diva. 'Now I suppose she'll blame poor Mr. Arncott and say that he ignored her recommendations. Won't believe a word of it. Bet *she* suggested that hovel in Church Square. Why, it's no bigger than my scullery.'

'Why on earth she made all those promises when she knew she'd be found out, I really can't imagine. But that's so like Lucia. She must have everyone looking up to her and saying how clever she is.'

'She can't be all that clever,' broke in Susan Wyse, 'or she'd know my name by now. And what on earth possessed her to say that I was related to the Spanish aristocracy?'

'Come now, Susan, my dear,' said Mr. Wyse, although he knew in his heart that the devil whose advocate he was merited no defence, 'we have no conclusive evidence that it was Mrs. Pillson who so misled those journalists.'

'Yes we have!' cried Diva. 'It's there at the bottom of the third page, in black and white. Thanks Mrs. Pillson for her invaluable assistance. Fancy that! And calling the Padre Mr. McBartlett. I call that downright disrespectful to a clergyman, but I suppose it's her idea of a joke.'

'There's something that puzzles me,' said Evie darkly. 'Why did she say that Mallards belonged to Elizabeth and had been in her family since the Norman Conquest or whatever it was? And all that stuff about Hugo de Map and the Domesday Book? *That's* not like Lucia.'

'Easy,' said Diva, who had puzzled long and hard over an explanation for this inconsistency. '*She* didn't tell them that. Must've found it out for themselves. Looked up the history of the area, I shouldn't wonder. Which only goes to show that what Elizabeth's been saying all this time is perfectly true. Confirmed by Mr. Arncott no less. In black and white,' she added, for she was fond of the phrase.

The word 'white' made Mr. Wyse wince. 'It is some small consolation,' he said, 'that our dear friend Mrs. de Map-Flint's noble lineage has been independently researched and confirmed. I thought that Mrs. Pillson had been unnecessarily sceptical on the subject.'

Thus the battle-lines were drawn, and it became necessary to believe in Elizabeth's ancestry if one was against Lucia and her trickery. Irene, who had been to

113

the Public Library to consult the copy of _County Life_ available there (all the others having by now been sold), came running down the street grinning broadly. Thus it is that Fate seals our dooms, for her intervention at this point made Lucia's condemnation irrevocable.

At the sight of the Wyses, she stopped and bowed gravely. Having greeted Mr. Wyse as Don Alhernon and Susan as Mrs. White, she proceeded to advance a theory accounting for what had happened, a theory that was precisely correct. However, since it was she who had suggested it, if was, of course, dismissed at once as a tissue of malicious lies, and Irene was received in silence and cold disdain.

'Oh, please yourselves,' she said equably. 'But, if I were you, I'd get an architect to look over Starling Cottage. Judging by that photograph, I don't think it's terribly safe. Did you see how it was leaning over backwards? _Olé._'

She departed as quickly as she had come and raced off towards Mallards to comfort Lucia. In fact, she did not have very far to go, for she met her outside Mr. Hopkins's shop, where Lucia had paused to buy some turbot and to summon up her courage before facing the High Street.

'Don't worry,' said Irene. 'It's an awful score for Mapp, of course, but I'll put her in her place all right, you just wait and see. I've scrapped my painting of the storm, by the way, and started a new one. You'll like it. It's the Battle of Hastings, only you're William and Mapp is Harold — which is logical; since she's not a Norman she's got to be a Saxon, hasn't she? And she's got an arrow in her eye, and Major Benjy is standing beside her with a gonfalon tied to his golf-club and a bottle of whisky. Come across and have a look.'

'Sweet of you, dear,' said Lucia. 'I must come and see it, but not just now. Shopping first.'

'I should get the car out and go into Hastings for your shopping,' said Irene. 'They're frightfully cross with you at the moment. They think _you_ told all those fibs — it was Mapp, of course, but do you think they'd believe me?

I think they got the impression that you promised to recommend their mouldy houses and then went back on your word. Utter rubbish, of course. You never promised anything.'

'I most certainly did not!' snapped Lucia, and that was true enough.

'Well, take care,' said Irene, and she darted across into Taormina to start the work of changing the faces of the Saxon dead to resemble the Wyses, the Bartletts and Diva.

It had been one of the lowest troughs of Lucia's career. To be snubbed en bloc by the whole of Tilling, to see them all cross the street at her approach to fawn on Elizabeth and compliment her on her excellent likeness in the photograph; to hear Evie Bartlett, the mouse-like, the insignificant, saying quite loudly, 'Of course, Elizabeth dear, it's appropriate really. And the rest of it was quite correct. In your family for generations'; it was a bitter blow, and Lucia seemed for a moment to be bowed by it. But she was Lucia yet, and Mayor of Tilling. It was horribly unjust to be blamed for Elizabeth's forgeries. Of course, she had herself trodden dangerous ground by seeming to make promises that she could not and had not intended to keep. We learn by our mistakes, and Lucia had learnt from this disaster; now there was lost ground to be made up and mutiny to be suppressed. If she could engineer her own release from excommunication, she felt confident that she could deal with Elizabeth without too much difficulty, for Elizabeth had a delightful knack of making trouble for herself. But how was she to overcome this excommunication? Tilling had turned its back on her, and with those who will not hear, who can reason? Although she was sure that tea was still drunk and Bridge played in the town, she had received no invitations and her own had been declined with a cold formality that would have pleased Lord Chesterfield. She was under embargo; she did not exist.

Meanwhile Georgie, usually so resolute and unflinching (when properly handled), had refused to be her *agens in rebus.* He still existed in the eyes of Tilling, but his existence had from time to time been called into question by some of the more extreme agnostics, especially if he mentioned his wife or recounted her views on a subject. Then a sort of deafness afflicted his listeners, or else his voice became suddenly inaudible, for the conversation would continue as if he had not spoken. Indeed, if the house in which they were gathered had gone up in flames and he had said, 'The house is on fire, as Lucia would have pointed out if she were here,' he was sure that they would have stayed where they were and been burnt to death rather than acknowledge his words.

'You've offended them,' he said, on his return from a particularly enjoyable tea party at which Lucia's name had not been mentioned once. 'And so they've cut you out. I think they think they've proved that they can do without you perfectly well.'

Lucia received this message in stoical silence. She knew the difficulties that faced her; she also knew that if she had not existed, it would have been necessary to invent her. She rose from her place in front of the curtains, where she had been dividing the afternoon between Sallust's *Jugurtha* and a report from the Municipal Refuse Disposal Committee, and went to the piano.

'Dear Irene called while you were out,' she said absently. 'Such a delightful chat — Art, Philosophy, municipal affairs. I feel that much could be made of Irene if her eccentricities could be ironed out — for she has a Brain, no question about that. I wish you could have been here. So rare in the hurly-burly of social and political life to find time to pause, or reflect, with one or two good friends.' She opened the lid of the piano and her fingers strayed idly over the keys. 'That is why I do not resent this foolish, spiteful ostracism. I welcome it. So distracting, the ebb and flow of human interaction. How does that magnificent savage Wagner put it in his *Siegfried*? *"Männertaten undämmern mir den Mut"* — human actions cloud my mind.'

116

Georgie regarded her nervously, for Wagner was very much the heavy artillery of her intellectual armoury. That she should be using it now on him was rather alarming. So like a kitten which, when frightened, rolls on its back and purrs defensively (but with eyes open and ears back), he decided to be cautiously jocund.

'I do believe that you've been practising some of our little duets while my back has been turned,' he said tentatively. 'I know you, *cattiva* Lucia, polishing up the treble so as to be oh so much better that your *Georgino* when we play together.'

'Me innocent Lucia,' she replied, 'only play tiresome old scales all day long, like going up and down stairs.'

'I don't believe you,' said Georgie. 'You'd better play me something and then I'll know if you've been practising or not.'

So Lucia played the slow movement of the Moonlight Sonata; and, after the requisite sigh, Lucia said that it proved that she hadn't been practising and Georgie said that, on the contrary, it proved that she had.

'So many unbearable errors,' she said sadly, ignoring him. 'My point, I think, is proved. I do need a break, *Georgino*, a holiday if you like, to sharpen up my blunt soul. Tilling has kept me from my studies, my music, my interests, with its incessant demands upon me. Now that it tells me that it needs me no more, I can resume my own life. I shall take this opportunity to retire from the world, and if the world ever wants me back it had better ask me very politely.'

'That's the spirit,' said Georgie, stifling a yawn. 'That'll show them.'

This was not quite the reaction Lucia had been looking for, but since Georgie's reactions were not of the least importance, she was not unduly disappointed. The coming days and weeks would try her patience severely, but she knew in her heart that Tilling could not give her up, any more than a nicotine addict could give up smoking.

* * *

Lucia would have been reassured on this point had she been outside Twistevant's the next morning when Susan Wyse's market-basket happened to collide with Evie Bartlett's.

'So sorry,' said Evie. 'Clumsy of me. I could have upset something. No motor today?'

'A punctured tyre, I believe. But chauffeur assures me that it will soon be repaired.'

'And where is Mr. Wyse today?'

'A slight headache, nothing to be concerned about. But I insisted that he stay indoors. Any news?'

'None at all,' said Evie sadly. 'Everything seems quite dead without —' She paused, like a philosopher who has just stumbled across a new concept for which no name as yet exists.

'Without Lucia, you mean?' said Susan, almost in a whisper.

Thus, in the third week, the vague possibility of Lucia's existence began to take more concrete form, rather as a photograph slowly begins to take shape in the developer's tray; first a blurred outline, then a recognisable shape, then finally the complete picture. There was resentment enough even now, but curiosity is stronger than wrath; like Charity it suffereth long and is not afraid. Tilling had discovered that it could not give up the Lucia habit and was curious to know how Lucia had managed to do without Tilling for so long. It was true that Lucia had her books and her Council and the piano had been tinkling away in the garden-room at all hours of the day, but surely a meagre diet was not enough to sustain life. Was it?

On the way from Grebe, where tea and Bridge had been a rather subdued affair (for Lucia, like Banquo's ghost, had somehow seemed to be present at the table, displacing the mirth), Diva asked Georgie as they walked together back to town how Lucia had been filling her time. She almost said 'filling her time since she stopped being invited anywhere', but she didn't quite like to, even to Georgie, who understood.

'Oh, she's been as busy as anything,' said Georgie truthfully. 'There's all her official work and her being a J.P., and the Council is considering where they should put the new rubbish dump, and she's very concerned with *that*. And the rest of the time she reads or plays the piano — she's playing much better than she has for a long time now — and when it's fine she does her exercises. And sometimes we go for drives in the motor and sketch old castles and manor-houses, which makes a nice change from drawing the same old houses over and over again. And this morning she was talking of popping up to London for a week or so — *The Magic Flute* at Covent Garden and the new production of *Othello* — and then perhaps going on to Cannes for a month.'

It all sounded so pleasant and relaxing that Diva almost wished that she could be excommunicated too. It had not occurred to her that anyone could have so much fun outside Society, or be so busy. And London, and quite possibly Cannes after that — suppose Lucia decided that she preferred being an outcast and went away for ever and ever, leaving them all at the mercy of Elizabeth? That would be terrible.

'So she's not too miserable then?'

'Well, she misses all her friends, of course,' Georgie nerved himself to ask the important question, for he still did not know for certain (although he could guess) why the excommunication had come about in the first place. 'And she always asks me what the news is.'

Diva was slightly comforted by this, although the fear of Lucia seceding, which would be no more than Tilling deserved, had begun to sink into her heart.

'Everyone is still angry with her, of course,' she declared. 'Deeply offended. She should have known better.'

'But what did she actually *do*?' demanded Georgie, for he could delay no longer.

'Why, saying that she was going to put all our houses in *County Life* and then recommending those others.'

'She didn't actually say that,' said Georgie judicially.

119

'P'raps not, but she implied it. Still, *that* wasn't so bad.'

'Wasn't it?' said Georgie mystified.

'Oh no, it was all those other things. All those fibs about the Padre and the Wyses — telling that writer that the Wyses were the Whites and —'

'But that wasn't Lucia,' said Georgie. 'We didn't even speak to Mr. Arncott. We missed him.'

'No! Then who told him all those stories?'

'I don't know,' Georgie confessed. 'Perhaps he just got it all down wrong in his notebook or couldn't read his own writing. That's happened to me before now. I've made a list of things I want from the draper's and by the time I get there the list looks like something quite other, and I don't remember what I really wanted until I get home.'

Georgie was silent for a moment, as if recalling some forgotten grief. Diva, however, had weighed up the likelihood of his suggestion and found it wanting.

'But it says at the bottom,' she wailed, 'that Mrs. Pillson had given invaluable assistance or something. Surely that was —'

'That was just for recommending the houses and saying when the streets were likely not to be too crowded. I don't think she told them anything else, for she read me the letter she wrote to Mr. Cuthbertson, the editor.'

'How fascinating,' said Diva. 'But she did recommend those houses in Church Square and not the Vicarage and Wasters.'

'Yes, that's true enough. But she never actually promised that she would recommend the Vicarage and Wasters. After all, you weren't supposed to know about it, so how could she?'

'Well, Elizabeth said that Mr. Arncott told her —' She stopped dead in her tracks, her brain working furiously. Georgie, not noticing that she had stopped, walked on a few paces alone, then realised his mistake and went back.

'What is it?' he demanded. 'You've thought of something. I can tell.'

'Well,' said Diva, 'it's like this. If Lucia didn't speak to Mr. Arncott and Elizabeth did. . . .'

By the time they reached the Landgate they were both utterly confused and if anyone had stopped them at that point and asked for a brief summary of their findings, they would have been hard put to it even to agree with each other. Nevertheless, the charge of practical joking was all but lifted from Lucia's shoulders and was, so to speak, circling slowly before swooping down on Elizabeth. Try as they might they could not quite fit together the pieces of the immense jigsaw of evidence that they had compiled and deduced, but both were convinced that a logical explanation could not be far away.

'Does that mean that you'll start talking to her again?' asked Georgie as they stopped outside Wasters.

'I suppose so. I'm terribly muddled, though.'

'So am I. Should I tell her she's forgiven?'

'No, don't do that. In fact, don't do anything yet. Oh, how worrying it all is. I'm sure I don't know what we ought to do for the best. And what *will* Lucia think of us all? And what will Elizabeth do when we all start talking to Lucia again? And should we all stop speaking to Elizabeth? I shan't get a wink of sleep tonight. Come in for a sherry?'

Georgie very much wanted to continue the discussion, but it was dark and he was a married man. Besides, rather than become any more confused he wanted to go home and get Lucia to explain it all to him. So he said it was getting late and went on his way. For her part, Diva let herself into the house and sat down dejectedly on a straight-backed chair.

'Oh dear,' she wailed aloud, 'how terribly complicated! Now, if Elizabeth told Mr. Arncott. . . .'

But the more she thought about it the more difficult it became, and she poured herself a glass of sherry to calm her nerves. Janet, her maid, asked her what she wanted for dinner, but she had no appetite for mere food and bespoke nothing but an omelette. Should she go and confer with the Bartletts? Or should she telephone Lucia?

She had already picked up the receiver when she thought of the awkwardness (and the cost) of such a call, and put it down again. Then she thought of the Wyses. They might be able to cast some light on the matter, but she could not now remember all the ins and outs of the argument herself. In the end she ate her omelette and went to bed. After lying awake for several hours, she fell into a troubled sleep and dreams — the product of worry and the slice of strong cheddar cheese she had eaten after her omelette (for man cannot live by thought alone) — fluttered around her head all night; conspiracies, cabals, lies and false witness, all of which were entirely her fault. Finally she dreamt that she was brought to trial at the Old Bailey on a charge of perjury, where Lucia, resplendent in her red Mayoral robes and a black cap, to which was pinned a most elegant little cameo brooch, sentenced her to be transported to Cannes for the rest of her natural life. . . . She awoke with a start and lay still for a while, trembling slightly. Then something became transparently clear in her mind.

'Of course!' she cried. 'That's it! Why didn't I think of it before? Just wait till I tell —'

Then she went back to sleep.

8

The next morning historical interest seemed to be at a peak in Tilling. Major Benjy, on his way to the Club to resume his studies, passed Lucia's motor-car as he went through the Landgate. He was on foot and the front wheel of Lucia's Rolls-Royce, going through a puddle, sprayed him with water. At once the motor stopped and Lucia got down. The Major was in a quandary. Lucia did not exist; on the other hand, her motor quite palpably did, and even a non-existent motorist must be allowed to apologise for inflicting puddle-water on an innocent pedestrian. It would have been easier, reflected Major Benjy, if Cadman, the actual driver of the vehicle, had got down to apologise, but that, in strict terms, would have been rather impolite. The Major resolved on a compromise. He would speak to Lucia if necessary, but he would not, if he could possibly help it, remember her name.

'My dear Major Mapp-Flint!' cried Lucia, and her respectful use of his rank and full surname seemed to strike exactly the right note. 'I am most terribly sorry. Are they wet through?

Such politeness and sincere concern was most disarming and the Major suddenly found that he could remember that her name was Mrs. Pillson.

'Not at all, Mrs. Pillson,' he said loftily, 'a mere splash, that's all.'

'But it was too careless of Cadman. He shall be fully reprimanded; and your poor trousers! Do have them cleaned and send me the bill.'

That sounded, or could be made to sound, as if the Major's trousers never saw the inside of a cleaner's from one year to the next, but he let it pass. He found it hard to be rude to such a polite and charming lady as Lucia was making herself this morning.

'No need, I assure you. Fine day,' he added sociably.

'It is indeed. Are you off to your admirable studies? How diligent! And I am about the same business, in a way.'

'Really?' Was she, too, off to indulge in secret drinking? He doubted it.

'I am going to the Cartulary — the depository of ancient manuscripts — oh, of course you must know that already — at Bodiam Castle. No doubt you have used it yourself. No? You must. Invaluable documents, sources, original papers. I must get them to send you one of their Catalogues of Manuscripts. So sorry about the trousers.'

She waved gaily and returned to her vehicle. The Major, a damper but scarcely a wiser man, continued on his way. The High Street was unusually busy today and shoppers were swarming like excited bees from group to group. Cries of 'No!' and 'Oh, how fascinating!' echoed between the buildings, betokening some news or other, and the Major resolved to find out what was going on.

'Good morning,' he boomed, advancing on Diva and the Wyses and raising his hat. 'Bit of a respite from the rain, eh? Any news?'

Diva, for some unexplained reason, flushed a deep red. Mr. Wyse fidgeted with his ebony cane, while Susan Wyse picked nervously at one of her gloves.

'Nothing in particular,' said Diva. 'Should there be?'

'I read in the newspapers,' said Mr. Wyse abruptly, 'that the Duchess of Westminster has joined a party at the Lido in Venice. The news from Abyssinia, however, remains discouraging.'

'Oh,' replied the nonplussed Major. 'Well, I must get on, don't you know. Good day to you, Mr. Wyse, Mrs. Wyse, Mrs. Plaistow.'

As he moved on, hurried whispers seemed to break out behind his back, but he did not turn. He was a soldier with a certain dignity to maintain. He next greeted the Bartletts, who were deep in discussion with Irene, whose tone was unusually moderate.

'God gi' ye good den, Major,' exclaimed the Padre, and his voice was rather strained. ''Tes a bonny morning for the time o' year, is it not? All the pretty flowers an' a'.'

'Splendid, splendid, splendid,' said the Major cautiously. 'Any news?'

There was a distinctly awkward silence. Evie looked at Irene, who made a great pantomime of knocking out her pipe on the heel of her boot and refilling it with what looked like wet leaves from a battered sealskin pouch.

'Nothing much,' said Evie at last, 'Oh, there was something that might interest you, wasn't there, Kenneth?'

'I read in *The Times*,' said the Padre (and a slight Midlands inflection clouded the limpid pool of his Caledonian dialect), 'that the Pathans have retreated in the face of our latest punitive expedition. Such gallantry, especially on the part of one o' our bonny Highland regiments. The Seaforth Highlanders, was it not, wifie?'

Evie looked a little nervously at her husband, as if deciding whether or not he needed to be rescued.

'Were you ever on the frontier, Major?' she gabbled. 'It must be a dreadfully unfriendly place.'

'Briefly,' said the Major. 'Shot a tiger there once. Place called Fort Everett.'

'I didn't know there were any tigers —' Evie stopped herself abruptly and smiled a brittle smile. 'How thrilling! Is that one of the tiger-skins in the drawing-room at Grebe! You must point it out to me if ever — I mean, when we next come to tea.'

Irene was having trouble with her pipe, for a puff of smoke seemed to go down the wrong way. She spluttered, said 'Excuse me,' and dashed off. The Major raised his hat again, bade the Bartletts good morning, and walked swiftly to the Club.

He was extremely befogged and felt in need of a stiff measure of local history, possibly without the customary soda. Having obtained it, he took his place in his favourite chair with his glass and some old book or other. From this vantage point he could look down through the window on the street, although he usually tended to lean back rather, to avoid being seen himself.

The little knots of shoppers were still engaged in most animated conversation; evidently they found the activities of the Duchess of Westminster and the Seaforth Highlanders rather more fascinating than he did. He took a sip from his glass and opened the book, but his eye kept on straying down into the street. Georgie, his black cape and broad-brimmed hat identifiable across great distances, was hastening to join the throng and both groups with one accord surged to meet him. Was he the bearer of fresh tidings of the retreat of the Pathans? He could only wish that his own discourses on the military situation in India were greeted with such enthusiasm. Or perhaps the Duchess of Westminster had fallen into the Grand Canal? The notion pleased him and he ordered another drink.

Elizabeth had been down to the garage whence the three-wheeler had been obtained. She had shown the obdurate man the bills from Southampton — garage repairs, hotel expenses and so on; she had related all that had been said about the condition of the vehicle; she had insisted, pleaded and threatened, all to no avail. Apparently she had bought the vehicle 'as seen', and not even Solomon, Minos and Judge Jeffreys sitting in conclave could award her a penny of compensation. She had, she was informed, got the machine cheap, and although she was sure she had not encountered this meaning of the word before (perhaps it was a dialect usage meaning 'expensive'), she was urged to understand that in this wicked world one generally gets only what one pays for. Cheap, the man had said, and cheerful, that little Beezer had been. Now, if she was interested in something with a bit of quality. . . .

'My husband shall hear of this!' she cried, and with this awful threat hanging in the air like smoke, she ascended the motor and was gone. The further she went, however, the more unlikely she thought it that her husband should hear anything of what had transpired. Let alone anyone else, for a certain loss of prestige must attend such a disclosure. Better, perhaps, to forget all about it, at least for the present. In her fury she was driving perhaps a little too fast and when the corner of the road at which the Mint became the High Street suddenly leapt at her, she was compelled to brake rather fiercely and swing the wheel right round. But it appeared that the manufacturers of her motor had thought of the brakes only in an ornamental or ceremonial capacity and the car did not actually stop until it was within inches of the wall. Fortunately, the only witnesses to this regrettable incident were a few tradespeople who would keep their mouths shut if they wanted their exorbitant bills settled promptly, and Elizabeth was eventually able to continue on her way, albeit at a more sedate pace.

She returned to Grebe, took off her motoring hat and gloves and called savagely for tea. When it arrived, Withers informed her that Mrs. Pillson had telephoned shortly after she had left for town. She would be out until late afternoon, but could Mrs. Mapp-Flint kindly return her call at, say, half-past five?

Elizabeth snorted. Lucia was in no position to telephone anybody, let alone demand that they telephone her. If Lucia were to call again she might speak to her. Then again, she might be out or in the garden or simply, crushingly, unavailable. She took up her crochet work — she was making a pair of cuffs — and worked grimly for a while, but the annoyance of her interview with the garage-owner weighed heavily on her mind and she sought to purge her irritation by some more energetic pursuit. It was then that she realised that she had omitted to do her marketing, so she took up her basket and changed into a pair of walking shoes, for motoring had temporarily lost its charms, and prepared to walk into town. The exercise would do her good.

Just then the second post arrived (late as usual). There was only one letter, written in Lucia's unmistakable hand. She put down her basket, removed her hat and contemplated the document. Had she not been alone it would have gone straight onto the fire, but there was no one to see; besides, she was curious. She opened the envelope. 'My dear Mrs. Mapp-Flint,' she read:

First, I feel I must apologise to you as much as to everyone else, for my entirely reprehensible conduct in connection with the article in *County Life*. I am most truly sorry and I feel I must give some solid token of repentance to those I have offended.

Extraordinary, thought Elizabeth. Why should Lucia be so terribly apologetic when she had, in truth, committed no actual crime beyond the customary misdemeanour of *suggestio falsi*? Was she so crushed under the burden of her exile that she was prepared to confess to crimes that she had not committed simply in order to be admitted back into Society? Possibly, but quite unlike Lucia.

Would you, then, be tremendously forgiving and dine with me on Thursday night? All our friends (if I may still count them as friends after my foolish deceptions) have done me the honour of consenting to be present to hear my act of contrition; yet it is your forgiveness and that of your dear husband that would mean the most to me.

Yours sincerely,
Emmeline Pillson.

It was many years since Lucia had signed a letter with her rather commonplace baptismal name and the humility inherent in the fact was as conspicuous as the tone of the epistle itself. What on earth could it mean? She read it again; it was as good as a signed confession. 'Entirely reprehensible', 'foolish deceptions'. Elizabeth groped in the recesses of her mind for some explanation of these phrases with all the zeal of one who regularly inspects the teeth of gift-horses.

Perhaps Lucia had seen a vision of angels and had decided to renounce the devil and all his pomps. She had read of the religious mania that sometimes seizes rather unstable middle-aged women. Had Lucia, as the vulgar expression put it, 'got religion'? Then again, there were people who, as a result of some mental disturbance, went about confessing to crimes of which they were entirely innocent and could not conceivably have committed, either to purge some deep-rooted sense of guilt or to gain the brief notoriety of the Police Reports. Lucia, she knew, adored to be conspicuous and she had plenty to feel guilty about, but such a drastic change of character was quite remarkable. Then again, this strange letter might be some sort of snare, the bait of some Machiavellian trap (Lucia with her professed love of all things Italian might well be familiar with the philosophy of the Father of Deceits). But how could that be? She herself was not, so far as she knew, vulnerable on any point: she had told no lies, deceived nobody, unless the trifling fibs she had told Mr. Arncott might be included under that heading. But unless he had told anyone (which was unlikely), how could such things be known, or at least proved? She searched her conscience but found it bare. The people of Tilling were on her side and surely if anyone were to be trapped Lucia would need popular support and assistance. Unless she had resolved, like Lucrezia Borgia (the Italian *motif* again), to poison them all at one fell swoop, there was no way in which she could make herself in any way formidable.

Curiosity, that bane of all things feline, overrode her doubts and fears and she telephoned Mallards. Georgie was brought to the receiver and acknowledged her acceptance of the invitation. She could get nothing else out of him, however, and she put the instrument down unsatisfied. She would have to wait until Thursday

129

night. She looked at the calendar. Thursday was the fifteenth: the Ides of March.

'And was it?' demanded Georgie, as soon as Lucia came through the door.

'Of course,' she replied. 'Just as I expected.'

'Well, you are clever!' cried her husband. 'I would never have noticed.'

'It was simple,' said Lucia. 'Now all we have to do is get Elizabeth to accept the invitation.'

'She already has,' said Georgie. 'She telephoned just before lunch. I hope I didn't give anything away.'

'Splendid. And now, perhaps, a cup of tea, and then a little cleansing *Mozartino*; Lucia so tired.'

The Ides of March had come (but not yet gone) and by a strange coincidence the *Hastings Chronicle* carried a report of an unusually large jet-black herring caught by a Tilling trawler. Had Elizabeth been more attuned to omens she would have been a little more wary (for when beggars die there are no black herrings seen). As it was, she went blithely to Mallards for her dinner. Over the sherry Lucia had made a short but eloquent speech, fully admitting that some remarks she had made might well have given the false impression that she had recommended certain houses to the editor of *County Life*. But there was little sweetness in this for Elizabeth for the injured parties were only too ready to declare that they had received no such impression — that the first they knew about the visit was when Mr. Arncott arrived in the town. Then the subject was changed, changed utterly.

It was a spectacular meal and its centrepiece was that celebrated dish, lobster *à la Riseholme*, for the recipe of which Elizabeth had once gone to sea on a kitchen-table. Rarely if ever had the dish been served in Tilling since that time, for so colourful and poignant were its associations that neither Lucia nor Elizabeth felt it tactful to produce it. It was, however, greeted on this occasion not with embarrassment but with rapturous applause. Lucia's cook had made of it a master-piece such as only a Midlander, born as far from the sea as is possible in the British Isles, can make of shellfish.

When all was eaten and Major Benjy had been separated from the port, the company gathered in the garden-room for coffee and Bridge. On the table under the window, where hung the celebrated curtains, were a pile of ancient, leather-bound books. They were all to do with local history: Bryant's *Prosopography of Mediaeval Sussex*, Vaill's *A Sussex Antiquarian* and other standard works, as well as a number whose Latin titles and roughly cut pages were unfamiliar even to the most erudite. Among them, largest and most magnificently bound, was that rare and noble monument to a great scholar, Pasmore's *Sussex County Families*. It was on this volume that Lucia laid her hand, rather as a learned judge might lay his hand on the law-reports.

'Major Benjy,' she said in a loud but clear voice, 'perhaps some of these books might prove helpful to you in your researches. Bryant and Vaill you will of course be familiar with. . . .'

'Exactly. Bryant and — ah — Vaill,' said Major Benjy hesitantly.

'These are from my collection,' went on Lucia, 'these are from the County Library, and these from the London Library. Oh yes, and here is my copy of Pasmore, in case you do not have one of your own.'

The name seemed vaguely familiar to Major Benjy and he took a surreptitious glance at the title.

'Ah yes,' he said confidently. 'I read that one. Got a copy at the Club, don't you know.'

Elizabeth felt her hand shaking, so that her coffee-cup rattled on the saucer. This ferocious collection of books had not come together by chance. What exactly *had* Lucia been occupying her time with during her exile? Could it by any chance have been local history, with possibly even special attention to the Norman era? Something inside her warned of a terrible danger, but what could she do?

'And you must go over to the Cartulary at Bodiam Castle,' Lucia went on remorselessly. 'The manuscript collection — quite magnificent. The papers of several important local families are lodged there. I spent an enthralling morning — such a helpful librarian — and you might like to cast an eye over some of the notes that I made.'

As if on cue, Susan Wyse interrupted her, asking if during the course of her own studies Lucia had come across any references to the de Map family. Elizabeth, said Susan, would be sure to be interested, as would they all.

'But of course,' said Lucia. 'The name de Map is writ large across the pages of the history of the south coast. But I am sure you are familiar with the chief authorities.'

'We aren't,' said Diva, perhaps a shade abruptly. 'Elizabeth is far too modest to tell us anything. Won't you tell us, Lucia?'

'Shall I? Have I your permission, Elizabeth? Very well then.'

Lucia leaned forward and opened some of the books at previously marked pages and as she spoke she pointed out the passages she referred to with a little lecturer's baton which she had taken from the desk.

'We start with Hugo de Map, who was descended from Eric the Fat, a prominent Norwegian Viking. He received land from William the Conqueror, his patron, in the vicinity of Maidstone; this was Hugo's reward for services to the King before the Conquest —'

'Before?' queried Diva.

'Before,' confirmed Lucia. 'Sir Hugo was unfortunately indisposed during the Conquest itself. His son, Roger, was given a manor near Tilling, to which was added, in the time of his grandson, also called Hugo, the substantial property of Udimore. But the family — too distressing! — fell upon hard times. In the unhappy civil strife that so disfigured the reign of King Stephen' (here Lucia pointed to a wholly incomprehensible piece of Latin) 'the de Maps made the mistake of siding with that formidable woman Queen Matilda, and on her defeat were stripped of all their possessions in the south of England. They migrated', continued Lucia, without the slightest hint of triumph in her voice, 'to the then wild and uncivilised region of Northumberland, where they had a few windswept acres. Their fortunes continued to decline until the reign of Elizabeth' (a muffled snigger from Evie and a loud 'Shush!' from Diva) 'when Lambert Map — the "de" had by then been dropped — and a band of outlaws terrorised the neighbourhood of Penrith and were hunted down and destroyed by a local levy led by Lord Percy. Lambert's only son, Perkin — the last surviving member of the de Map family — followed his ill-starred father to the gallows in 1602, having been convicted of stealing a sheep. Such a dreadful story, is it not, of the decline of a once powerful and noble house, and such a tragic end to your namesake family, dear Elizabeth. I have compiled what I think is an exhaustive list of references should you wish to check the story for yourself. Now, shall we have a *piccolo* rubber of Bridge?'

Lucia perched at her desk in the telephone-room, a pencil placed clerkwise behind her ear, and studied a volume of ancient manuscript. Her recent studies had given her a taste for the placid occupation of the antiquary and the revelation that ancient books can bring forth information capable of being put to good use in the present had not failed to make its impression on her. Therefore her bright, bespectacled eyes were picking out, although with some difficulty, the spidery and heavily abbreviated script of a venerable old parchment, while her fascination with its contents made her entirely oblivious to its difficulties. For the text she was reading was a centuries-old compilation of the duties and privileges of the Mayors of Tilling, 'used thereof from time out of mind, which Men's mind cannot think the contrary'.

Many of the duties had been repealed or discontinued, but of the privileges she could find no mention in subsequent legislation; so perhaps she was still entitled to some of them, if they were worth having. As she read, she wrote a simple but faithful translation in modern English, which, when the work was done, she would have privately printed and distributed among her friends.

'If the Mayor should refuse,' she read, 'and if the Mayor, so chosen and elected, will not take the charge but refuse it, all the whole commons together shall go sit beneath his house and entreat until such time as he come forth. . . .'

Lucia could picture the scene: the Wyses and Diva

134

and Elizabeth (as Mayoress) filling the narrow street, beseeching her to come out and assume her responsibilities. Herself in the garden-room, all blushes, the unwilling choice of an adoring commons; 'How you all work me, you dear people! Very well then, just for an hour or so.' It would make a pretty piece of ceremonial, if people could be induced to be present, and the visitors to the town would flock to see it. It was passing fine to be a Mayor, but it would be better still if a little more notice were taken.

Nevertheless, March had turned out to be a pleasant month; she had resumed her rightful place in Society and her return had been marked by a sort of general amnesty. Elizabeth, for example, had not been punished for her petty deceptions, since the view was generally taken that at times the poor woman was not wholly responsible for her actions. Her tyranny having been overthrown, she was not granted the dignity of persecution. In the *Jugurtha*, which Lucia had just finished, she had read of how the strife of Marius and Sulla had brought untold hardship upon the people of Rome. There was a lesson to be learnt from that; oppressing a fallen rival tended to invite reprisal; far better to forgive and forget — or, at any rate, forgive.

As she sat in rapt concentration, Georgie tiptoed down the stairs and crept out into the garden. He had no wish to be observed, for his hair and beard, which had long needed retouching, were still glistening with wet dye. He had intended to carry out the necessary repairs that morning, but Lucia had dragged him off to the shops (she wanted his advice on a new hat) and in the afternoon they had been promised forth to tea. He had therefore, on their return, developed a tactical headache; and since it was generally unnecessary to have more than something on a tray for dinner after filling up with cake and muffins at tea-time, he had demanded privacy and seclusion for the evening.

Unfortunately, uncharacteristic negligence on the part of the hairdresser had compelled him to use a new preparation for his process of rejuvenation and, although the colour matched perfectly, it took rather longer to dry than the old one, as well as giving off rather unpleasant fumes. Wherefore, he decided to risk slipping out into the garden to see if the fresh air would dry it off more quickly and help dispel the unpleasant chemical smell. It was a clear night with only an occasional cloud disturbing the brilliance of the moon, but still quite chilly; so he slipped on his long, dark cape with the fur collar. The last thing he wanted to do was catch a chill by going outside with wet hair. He sat down in the *giardino segreto*, where he ought to be out of sight of the house, and waited for chemistry to take its course.

Suddenly the green-room doors opened and Lucia appeared, walking leisurely across to the garden-room. The light went on, revealing her taking her place behind her desk; she was probably settling down to read for an hour or so. This meant that Georgie was trapped. He could not move for fear of being seen with his hair still wet, but he could not safely stay where he was for the same reason. It was getting colder and he felt a sneeze coming on, yet to stifle it would require movement and movement would betray him. What if Lucia saw him and took him for a burglar? To the best of his knowledge, she did not own a gun of any sort, for the sharpness of her mind and of her tongue were all the armoury she needed, but she might scream and call the police. The moon, emerging from behind a cloud, was bathing the entire garden in silvery-grey light, making the shadows stand out sharp and clear and causing Georgie to feel distinctly uncomfortable.

Lucia had gone out to the garden-room to check a rather fanciful story told in her *Legends of Old Sussex*, a book she had bought only recently and found enthralling. As she glanced at the list of contents her eye fell on a chapter entitled 'The Ghosts of Tilling'. This she could not resist. Apparently, the town was a centre of supernatural activity. A nun who had been deceived by a priest stalked through Church Square on Christmas Eve.

136

A phantom coach with a headless coachman and four coal-black horses rattled down the High Street on stormy nights, occasionally stopping while the coachman hammered on the doors of the houses (which reminded Lucia of Susan Wyse doing her shopping in the Royce), while gangs of spectral pirates and smugglers rehearsed the crimes they had committed during their lives the length and breadth of Porpoise Street. There were other spirits too, less well attested but recorded here nonetheless: the grey lady of West Street; a new-born baby walled up in Curfew Street and, of course, the notorious Black Spaniard of Mallards. . . .

Lucia nearly dropped the book. A Spanish merchant, so legend had it, had been invited to show his wares to the owner of Mallards House ('a large Queen Anne mansion between Church Square and West Street; see plan at end of chapter'). He had been seen going in with a bale of fine cloth under his arm, but no one ever saw him leave; and his ghost, a tall, dark figure in a black cloak with flashing eyes and ghastly, phosphorescent hair, had on several occasions been seen about the house and grounds in early spring.

She read the story five times, then closed the book with a snap. She had long felt the want of a ghost at Mallards, to complete the otherwise comprehensive attractions of the house. Although her sceptical, scientific mind did not accept foolish tales of tormented spirits bound to earth by crime or guilt, she did believe that some sort of spiritual emanation, what the old Romans called Numen, could cling to the scene of violent or significant action, such as a battlefield or a house where murder had been done. It might be that some form of psychic energy was released, leaving behind some trace which, lingering for centuries, might be noticed by the perceptive. Of all forms of such spiritual energy, of course, an elegant Spaniard in a black mantle was one of the best. She rose and silently opened the door.

Georgie was bitterly cold and a moth had taken an interest in his moustache. He felt the urge to sneeze growing steadily stronger, until he could hardly keep it at bay; but the night was so utterly still and quiet that a sneeze must inevitably be heard. He resolved to take a chance and escape to the warmth and comfort of the house. The moon was vanishing behind a cloud and he need only traverse a small patch of moonlight on his way; most of his flight would be hidden in shadows. Noiselessly, he rose to his feet and tiptoed across the lawn and into the house. Then he ran upstairs to his dressing-room and locked the door.

As she looked out of the doorway of the garden-room, Lucia could see only darkness, and she was on the point of turning back when she saw something that nearly caused her heart to stop beating. A dark figure flitted across the lawn, coming from nowhere and vanishing in a second. But, although she saw it only for a moment, the image burned itself on to her optic nerve. A tall man, dressed entirely in black with a long cloak, piercing eyes, and hair and pointed Spanish beard that glowed an unearthly colour in the surrounding darkness, had moved noiselessly across the grass and disappeared through the wall of the house.

Georgie put on his dressing-gown and examined his hair and beard in the mirror. They were both now quite dry, but the chemical shine still lingered. That, however, could easily be removed by vigorous towelling, and he was soon restored to his normal appearance. A few minutes with a comb completed the process and he inspected his handiwork with satisfaction. It was almost a pity that it was such a deadly secret, for he was quite an artist in his way and his work merited congratulation.

'One thing I'm good at,' he moaned, 'and I can't tell anyone.'

Finally, he replaced his *toupée* and combed the hair round it to shape. There was now no evidence whatsoever of his transformation, and so confident was he in the subtlety of his skill that he decided that his headache was much better and he could go downstairs for an hour or so. There would be a good fire in the drawing-room and he still felt decidedly cold.

138

Lucia was standing in front of the fire and she turned towards him as he entered. She was as white as paper and her eyes wide open.

'Lucia!' he exclaimed. 'Why, what on earth's the matter? You look as if you had seen a ghost!'

'I have,' she replied. 'Out in the garden.'

A chill ran down Georgie's spine. 'No!' he exclaimed, for he was terrified of ghosts, being by nature very superstitious.

'A tall man in a black cloak, with burning eyes and — oh Georgie, it was too awful! His head glowed in the dark, like sulphur.'

Georgie turned quite pale, for he had been outside too, with luminous spectres roaming about all around him. For all he knew, the beastly thing might have been standing over him and grinning. A dark phantom with a glowing head sounded most unpleasant.

'I was just coming out of the garden-room,' continued Lucia, 'and there it was. It walked straight across the lawn and then right through — *through*, Georgie — the wall of the house. And do you know, as it went by, I felt a distinct drop in temperature. In fact, it was as cold as ice.'

No wonder I felt cold, said Georgie to himself. 'Straight through the wall?' he asked, terrified. 'You mean the horrid thing is in here somewhere? Wandering about?'

'Unlikely, Georgie. It has probably departed, who can say whither?' Lucia was feeling better now and her face had taken on a tranquil appearance.

'Well, if you think I'm going to spend another night under this roof, you're very much mistaken.' Georgie was not feeling in the least better.

'The Black Spaniard is only seen very occasionally. So we are safe from visitation for tonight at least!'

'So you knew about it all along and you never said anything? Oh, how could you, Lucia!'

'I never gave the old legend any credence,' said Lucia smoothly. 'You know my views on superstitious beliefs. But having seen it with my own eyes, I fear that I must modify my sceptical opinions.' Unwise, she thought, to mention what she had just been reading; she knew what she had seen, but others might whisper darkly of auto-suggestion. 'Besides, I do not believe that it is a malevolent spirit. In fact, I'm sure there's no such thing: only the echo of discharges of psychic energy, given off by violent emotions in the past. Calm yourself, *caro*. There's nothing to fear.'

Nevertheless, Georgie went uneasily to bed and did not sleep. The room seemed to be full of strange shapes and noises; of dark shadows that moved as soon as you took your eye off them. He switched on his bedside lamp and started to read a book, over which he soon fell asleep. Lucia, on the other hand, took her camera up to her room with her, with its diaphragm fully open, just in case the vision should reappear. The next time, she would be prepared.

Elizabeth's sleep was not troubled by phantoms, for Grebe was rather too modern to be haunted. But she had felt a sort of presence looming over her recently; no Black Spaniard but Lucia, who stood between her and the sun.

Lucia had not been unduly oppressive after her rather cheap victory over the de Maps. She had permitted her conquered foe to enjoy liberty and freedom of associa-tion, if not of expression. Yet there was always the threat of tactless reference to be feared; should Elizabeth venture to criticise some article of furniture, the reply (not only from Lucia but from anyone else — for the weapon was common to all) would be that, ugly as it was, it had been in the family for generations. If her partner at Bridge found herself heavily overbid, she could still all Elizabeth's reproaches simply by say-ing that she might as well be hung for a sheep as a lamb. . . .

As well as this cruel treatment at the hands of those she had thought of as her friends, there was the com-plete loss, at a stroke, of all those sweet dreams of ancient lineage and noble blood that Elizabeth had so briefly entertained. Even now, she believed that there might be something behind the idea. She had, of course, followed up Lucia's list of references, scavenging scraps of school-room Latin from the sides and corners of her mind to battle her way through chronicles and annals, and had found neither falsification nor error in that diligent woman's account. With Perkin Map the line had perished; of that there could be no doubt. Yet something seemed to tell her that this could not be true; that somehow there was some evidence, perhaps as yet undiscovered, that might turn the whole tale on its head. It could not, of course, ameliorate such embarrassments as Eric the Fat; the brigandage in Cumbria; or Perkin's life of crime and distasteful punishment; but Norman blood is Norman blood and any ancestor, however disreputable, is better than none at all.

She had taken her researches further, therefore, and obtained books from distant libraries, on which she had expended many hours of uncomfortable and fruitless labour. As if to mock her, the sun had shone brightly while she ground her way through the scholars' impassable prose. Some promising clues had been revealed. She read, for instance, that a large number of Huguenots had settled in the area, and the thought that she might be a descendant of one of those romantic refugees had crossed her mind. But Huguenots were poor things to one who had been promised Normans; and besides, they had been in Trade, which would never do. There had been a certain Robert de Map, in the time of the first Henry, who was not strictly accounted for; he had supposedly been eaten by a wolf, but his head was never found. It was a possibility, but only a remote one. If only she could uncover some stronger link. . . .

As they ate breakfast together, Major Benjy, if he was in a good mood, would read out snippets from the newspapers that might amuse his wife. On that particular morning, he was in a very cheerful frame of mind, for his wife's sudden immersion in historical study had meant that she had little time to spare in which she could persecute him. Therefore he was studying the *Hastings Chronicle* for something of interest.

'Here, listen to this,' he said. 'There's going to be a house-sale at Breakspear Hall, near Tilling, Sussex, on Tuesday, the twelfth of April. The entire contents, too, not just the expensive stuff. D'you fancy going to that, old girl?'

Elizabeth considered the idea for a moment. She enjoyed house-sales, with their unique licence for poking round other people's houses and disparaging their possessions in a loud voice. And there was no need to buy anything. Besides, it would be a rather distinguished occasion, with all the county families (the phrase, with its unpleasant associations, made her shudder) present in full strength. Breakspear Hall was not very far away; they could drive out in the motor without overtaxing that unreliable vehicle and, on the whole, she was inclined to favour the idea. On the other hand, Major Benjy had been too much at liberty of late and there was the risk that, grown overconfident because of this, he might seek to elude her and start bidding for things: golf-clubs; tiger-skins, perhaps even cases of wine. Auction sales brought out the very worst in her husband; there had been a most awkward moment at the last sale they had been to. She had been compelled to inform the auctioneer (fortunately a most understanding man) that her husband, as a result of a wound received in the service of his country, suffered from a nervous tic that some might interpret as attempts at bidding. This slight untruth had saved the Mapp-Flint family exchequer nearly forty pounds and spared the attic of Grebe from housing still more relics of colonial life. On that occasion, however, the Major's excessive recklessness had been directly due to the agent, who had mistaken him for someone else and given him four large glasses of whisky before Elizabeth could undeceive him. She was certain that she could ensure that there would be no repetition of that sort of thing, and for herself she knew that her own iron will-power would be proof against even the heady temptations of sale by auction.

'I think it might be rather fun,' she therefore replied. 'Morning or afternoon?'

'Eleven-o'clock sharp. Catalogues from Woolgar and Pipstow, two shillings.'

'Oh, we shan't need a catalogue,' said Elizabeth firmly. 'We're only going to have a look. Now then, dear, what are you going to do today? Off to the golf-course again, you idle one?'

Major Benjy had found it politic to abandon his own local historical research, yielding place to his wife. Since then, the Major had returned to his first love, golf, and endured even the most inclement weather in the pursuit of excellence and exercise, either on the course or (more frequently) in the club-house. Thus it was that, despite a sharp wind and the threat of April showers, Benjy caught the eleven-o'clock tram to the links.

The Padre was his companion today, for he devoted every Monday morning to the national sport of his adopted country. They shared the first hole and, on the second, simple faith was worth more than Norman blood (or the lack of it). The third was marred by an unseemly quarrel about a supposedly lost ball in which the Padre's cloth did not protect him from aspersions on his complete honesty; and the fact that the ball was found, after a long search, under the Padre's foot did not strike the Major as the modern miracle that the Padre immediately proclaimed. The hole was ultimately shared and this dispute seemed to inspire both men, so that the game took on the appearance of a mediaeval ordeal by combat. At the half-way stage, however, Heaven had not made up its mind who should have had the third hole, for the match was all square and the two combatants, exhausted by their own unwonted virtuosity, decided to rest for a while.

They sought shelter from the wind in the large bunker and the Major spent a frustrating five minutes trying to light an oily Indian cheroot. When all his matches were used up and still Prometheus' gift had not been imparted to the recalcitrant tobacco, he gave it up.

'After all,' said the Padre, ''tes an Indian weed, not used to our wintry climate. 'Tes no wonder it willna burn.'

The Major did not take this comment kindly; perhaps he thought it savoured somewhat of irony. Therefore he resumed the debate on the third hole.

'I still find it remarkable that you didn't feel the ball through the sole of your boot. A golf-ball is not so small, after all.'

'Och, man, I tell ye I took it for a stone, and I'll swear that it was stone when I put my foot on it. These things are not for us to rationalize; if the Lord wishes to replace a stone with a golf-ball —'

'Nevertheless —' Benjy checked himself, for it was unseemly to wrangle with a man of God about what might be a spiritual manifestation, especially within earshot of the President of the Club and two members of the Committee. 'Oh well, never mind, then,' he declared magnanimously. 'There are more things in Heaven and Earth, especially Heaven. And if you can't believe a clergyman, who can you believe?'

'That's very sporting o' ye, Major, and also very pious. And since the hole was shared, let us say no more about it.'

'But if it was a miracle —'

'Then we were fortunate indeed to be the observers of it and we should keep it to ourselves. Can I no offer you a match for your cheroot?'

The wind abated as he spoke — surely another miracle — and the Major succeeded in lighting his tobacco. A mood of reconciliation fell over the two men and they sat a while in silence.

'So ye've discontinued your researches for the time being?' said the Padre. ''Tes a pity to be sure.'

'Well, after that de Map business. . . .'

'Och, it was a mistake that anyone could have made.

144

No, ye should continue with it. Scholarship is a service to the community. Indeed, it is God's work. The ancient monks of Iona kept Learning alive in the dark days o' the heathen. The Christian Church —'

Major Benjy had heard the Padre's excellent summary of the subject only yesterday, in church, and had taken the opportunity to rest his eyes. He had no desire to hear it all again.

'Yes, yes, Padre, just as you said. Excellent sermon that was. But my Liz has taken against me doing any more research now that she's started, and she's far better at it than me.'

'Well, I'm sorry tae hear it, Major. Can ye no continue the work without her knowing?'

'Difficult. My wife is a fine woman, Padre. Takes an interest in everything I do. In fact, that can be rather wearing at times, though I dare say it's with the best of intentions. Never mind.'

A golf-ball came sailing into the bunker and landed at the Padre's feet. It was followed a moment later by Mr. Phillipson, the President of the Club.

'Good morning, Major,' he said. 'Didn't see you there.'

'Don't worry,' replied the Major. 'I say, that's fearfully bad luck. Dreadfully difficult to get out of, this bunker.'

'I know,' said Mr. Phillipson ruefully. 'Good morning, Vicar. Fine Sermon, that, all about the Picts and so on. Oh, by the way, did you hear? Braithwaite's leaving us at the end of the month. Being transferred back to Ullapool.'

Mr. Phillipson gave his ball a mighty blow, which sent it vertically up in the air. It landed on the edge of the bunker, wobbled indecisively and fell back to its original position.

'Is that so?' said the Major, casually. 'So there'll be a vacancy on the — ah — Committee?'

'That's right,' said Mr. Phillipson, rather red in the face. 'You didn't see that last shot of mine, did you?'

'Me? Of course not,' said the Major sympathetically.

Mr. Phillipson leant on his club and studied the ball as a cat studies a distant sparrow. 'Were you thinking of putting your name forward for that vacant place on the Committee?' he asked.

'I might,' said Benjy nonchalantly. 'Don't know if I can spare the time. Other commitments, you know. Still, if you think the Committee might look favourably. . . .'

'Ah, yes,' said Mr. Phillipson. 'I heard you had taken up local history or something of the sort. Well, if you want us to consider you for that seat, let me know. No other applicants as yet. Apathy, I call it.' He hit the ball again: again it soared up into the air, but this time cleared the lip of the bunker by a good four inches. 'That's better. Well, cheerio for now.'

Major Benjy had often yearned to be on the Committee of the club he had for so long graced with his membership; he had once gone so far as to stand for election, but had received only one vote (his own). Now here was another opportunity and a better one; he did not wish to expose himself to the humiliation of another ballot, but co-option might well prove a feasible course. He felt reluctant to let this opportunity slip by. But how to manage it?

'Well then, Padre,' he said, 'shall we continue our match?'

His mind was not on the game as they flailed their way round the remaining holes, with the result that he beat the Padre easily and separated him from two shillings. That was a good omen in itself. He was silent in the tram back to Tilling, giving the Padre another chance to air his views on scholarship in early Christian Britain. Benjy wanted to find some tactic, some ploy that would guarantee him that longed-for seat on the Committee, and, as they drew into the Tilling terminus, an idea came to him. For the tram came in sight of the Cricket Club pavilion, which was being roused from its hibernation by the flannelled fools of the town. Lucia, he recalled, had secured for herself the presidency of that unlikely organization simply by presenting them with a new pavilion and a new roller. Could he use such a scheme to win himself the far nobler prize of a Golf Club Committee seat? He could not, of course, afford to equip the club with a new club-house, and besides, the old one had just been renovated. But a small, unostentatious gift might cause the membership to think more highly of him. A trophy of some sort; the Flint Shield for mixed four-somes, perhaps, might be competed for and the competi-tors must inevitably think kindly of the man who had instituted the noble prize. Instead of walking straight home, therefore, he stopped off at the jeweller's and made enquiries about the price of a presentation silver tray. The jeweller told him.

'How much?' he exclaimed, horrified. 'Oh well, forget it.'

Then he walked home.

Lucia thought it advisable not to release the news of her encounter with the Black Spaniard. Anything that savoured of a stunt would be hazardous at present and even at the best of times a reputation for seeing things could be a mixed blessing, if not a positive handicap. On the other hand, it was perfectly safe to pass on the various stories recounted in *Legends of Old Sussex*, and she found that the topic was of interest to all her friends. Susan Wyse was by nature inclined towards Spiritual-ism and firmly believed that the departed could return. She preferred to contact them through *séance* or Ouija-board, rather than have them drop in on her uninvited and was in two minds whether she liked the thought of living in a street haunted by the shades of smugglers and such disreputable persons; nevertheless, she did not allow her reservations about the suitability of such ghosts as her neighbours to disturb her belief in the existence of the Spirit World. Diva, who had lived in the High Street for many years without ever seeing or hear-ing a phantom coach, suddenly became terribly aware of any noises after dark and had extra shutters put on all her windows. Irene, who was a neighbour of the Grey Lady, set about the secret construction of a shapeless grey garment in which to imitate the spectre under Mr.

147

Hopkins's window (for that blameless tradesman had complained about her playing of the ukelele late into the night); while the Padre refreshed his memory of the Service of Exorcism and sent to a specialist ecclesiastical supplier in London for a selection of exorcising bells on approval. The Black Spaniard was, of course, the best of all the ghosts in Tilling and it seemed only fitting that Lucia should have the use of it, so to speak. When asked if she had ever seen it herself, she would shudder, smile a brittle smile and change the subject, so that everyone was left in no doubt that she had.

Elizabeth, not unnaturally, resented this and set about quizzing her neighbours and their servants and gardeners for any mythological reminiscences concerning Grebe. When she had almost given up hope of ever finding anything, she happened to fall into conversation with a gnarled old man who delivered the coal. He was not prepared to commit himself on the subject, but he seemed to remember that his grandfather, who had been one of the men who had worked on the construction of Grebe, had spoken of rumours of a French sea-captain who might have haunted the area before the house was built. Elizabeth toyed with this legend for a while and practised shuddering and changing the subject; but the connection was too tenuous and her recent immersion in the habits of scholars caused her to place no reliance on an unsupported oral tradition, especially since Lucia might be irritated by her French sea-captain and start her own researches into the story. So Elizabeth decided to outflank Lucia and annex the Black Spaniard. She declared, therefore, that she had known about that distinguished ghost since her childhood; Aunt Caroline had seen him so often that she stopped noticing him, and she herself was virtually on first-name terms. Certainly, she could not understand what all the fuss was about; a ghost was only a ghost after all.

Supernatural visitations apart, Elizabeth had other things on her mind. For a start, there was the matter of ensuring that Major Benjy was co-opted on to the

Committee of the Golf Club. Her canvassing had been discreet at first. She had taken a sprained wrist to Dr. Dobbie, as prominent in golfing circles as in medicine, and had done her best to drop hints; but that grim man had resolutely failed to notice them. She had called at Woolgar and Pipstow to enquire whether it would be worthwhile letting Grebe for the summer; but Mr. Woolgar, the Secretary of the Club, was out and Mr. Pipstow had nearly turned her out of her own house before she was able to escape. Finally, she had gone to see the dentist in his pretty little cottage in Church Square, for he was a highly respected golfer. But she made the tactical error of allowing him to remove her plate for examination, with the result that she could not make herself understood.

Having suffered all these reverses, Elizabeth was thrown back upon Benjy's original idea of a Challenge Trophy. She quickly overcame the major obstacle, that of expense, by suggesting that they look out for some reasonably priced article of silverware at the sale at Breakspear Hall. A relatively cheap piece could be bought and engraved for a fraction of the cost of a new one. Not that expense was an overriding consideration in this case; she was prepared to go as high as six pounds for a suitable specimen, since she had long felt that it was high time that the Major's golf should be put to some sort of social use. Further urgency was added by the rumour that Dr. Dobbie and Mr. Phillipson were considering asking the dentist whether he might be interested in the vacant seat, Major Benjy being as yet the only candidate.

On the appointed day, therefore, Elizabeth and the Major set off in the motor for Breakspear Hall. Their journey was uneventful (except that a herd of cows delayed them for quite ten minutes and one beast tried to eat the spare wheel) and they arrived with three-quarters of an hour in hand. Elizabeth spent the time in making a rigorous examination of the property, pointing out numerous patches of damp to her husband and

149

detecting several areas of quite deep dust on some pieces of furniture. She also formed a very low opinion of the taste of the late owner, taking especial exception to a rather gaudy painting of the martyrdom of St. Sebastian on the ceiling of the dining-room, which her guide-book later informed her was by Angelica Kauffmann. Major Benjy expressed an interest in a set of steel-shafted drivers and some split-cane fishing-rods, which Elizabeth was quick to discourage. She pointed out that he already had more than enough golf-clubs and he never went fishing — to which he replied that he could hardly go fishing without any rods.

The discussion that ensued filled up most of the remaining time, so that there were only a few minutes to go when Elizabeth noticed a small, flat, tarnished silver tray which, together with a huge, drab urn and a rather ugly oil-painting, comprised the thirtieth lot.

'There!' she exclaimed. 'That would do splendidly for your Challenge Trophy. Look, no dents or scratches to speak of. All it needs is a good polish.'

She bent over the tray and examined it closely as the auctioneer, young Mr. Pipstow, entered the room. There was a rather florid coat of arms (but that was of no consequence) and a name inscribed on the bottom, just to the left of the gummed label showing the lot number. She peered at the name and the shock of recognition nearly made her lose her balance. As young Mr. Pipstow requested everyone to take their seats for the beginning of the sale, Elizabeth distinctly made out, in small but clear-cut letters, her own surname.

10

The sight of the three-wheeler returning, heavily laden, from Breakspear Hall was witnessed only by the lamplighter, and, since he was a naturally morose and untalkative man, he held his peace on the subject. This was probably just as well, for the spectacle of Major Benjy with a tarnished silver tray under one arm, a dull-framed portrait on his knees and an enormous porcelain urn clasped to his bosom would have provided men and women of ill-will with great scope for sardonic comment.

Elizabeth gave little or no thought to appearances as she drove the vehicle down the Military Road in the gathering darkness, for her thoughts were divided between two subjects, one deeply troublesome, one so inviting as to be scarcely fit to be considered for fear of tempting providence.

The cause of concern was the fifteen pounds which she had been compelled to pay to secure the three rather unattractive objects that filled her little car to overflowing. The bidding had started at four pounds ten shillings and Elizabeth had indicated that she thought this a reasonable price by waving her glove. The hall had been silent, except for the passionate eloquence of young Mr. Pipstow. The lot had been offered — once, twice — and then a little man in an old overcoat, who kept a small second-hand furniture shop in the town, had offered five pounds. Elizabeth had responded at once by offering another ten shillings, but the little man had met her bid and surpassed it, and, before she knew where she was, Elizabeth had found herself promising twelve pounds for the lot. That had silenced her rival, but an elderly lady with a *lorgnette*, who had up till then been asleep, had ventured twelve pounds ten shillings and had refused to let go, like the bulldog she so much resembled, until the price had risen to fourteen pounds. Just as the sale seemed as good as made, a young man with a pencil moustache had, probably just to be awkward broken in with fourteen pounds ten shillings and Elizabeth was forced once again to wave her glove.

Yet the thought that in the silver tray Elizabeth had secured evidence of the survival of the family de Map, whose florid crest surely occupied the surface area of the tray, made even fifteen pounds seem irrelevant. Furthermore, the tray had come from no less a place than Breakspear Hall, and unless the occupants of that magnificent dwelling were in the habit of purchasing their silver second-hand, it could only mean that between herself and the Perowne family (now all sadly deceased, hence the sale) there must be ties of blood.

The likeliest explanation was that a Miss Mapp of some preceeding generation had married a Mr. Perowne. Thus the silver tray was all that remained of an apparently lavish dowry. What had become of the rest of it was not her business and the thought that she might conceivably stand to inherit at least part of the considerable wealth of the Perownes only fleetingly crossed her mind. What mattered most was that she had found the vital piece of evidence that she had known must exist somewhere. What could all Lucia's Latin manuscripts avail her now?

The motor was parked, the trophies were transferred to the dining-room of Grebe, Major Benjy had been cast forth. With a little silver polish and a soft, clean cloth, Elizabeth sat down and began to work. Under her fingers details began to emerge of the coat of arms. It was, to say the least, distinctive. A shield on which crossed keys were quartered with what looked like dolphins was supported by two fishermen in quaint but unmistakable apparel. The piscatorial theme was confirmed by a large crowned lobster that surmounted the shield and she deduced that the dolphins were in all probability cod, and that the crossed keys signified St. Peter as patron saint of fisher-folk. This maritime symbolism seemed faintly out of place in the arms of a family as distinguished as the de Maps, and it was with mounting curiosity that she clarified the motto. Her recently sharpened Latin enabled her to translate it, but she could not quite comprehend why her family should have chosen the well-known text 'I shall make you fishers of men'.

She had cleaned the coat of arms first simply in order to delay the moment of truth when she must investigate the name at the bottom. It still read Mapp, just as clearly as it had under the unique chandeliers of Breakspear Hall. She polished round it, the letters did not change. With tentative fingers she picked off the gummed label that showed the lot number . . .

Major Benjy, taking a surreptitious gulp of sherry from the decanter in the dining-room (he had drunk straight from the decanter to eliminate the necessity of washing out a glass in secret), heard a sound like a gong, struck hard, and what could well have been a cry of rage and despair. His first thought was of the French sea-captain, whose ghost might possibly be haunting the house. But if the oath had been an oath (and the Major had been a soldier long enough to recognise an oath when he heard one), why should a Frenchman, no matter how long he had been haunting an English house, swear in anything other than his native tongue?

Elizabeth may have lost her self-control for a fraction of a second — who would not have done so in her position? — but she had regained it almost at once. It was unfortunate, to say the very least, that the inscription, once the gummed label had been removed, had proved not to read simply Mapp but Mappin and Webb; nevertheless, she was an Englishwoman and could disguise her feelings. She picked up the tray from the floor and tried to comfort herself with the reflection that she had

153

picked up the Mapp-Flint Challenge Shield (by a very good silversmith, too) for a mere five pounds, that being one-third of the total price she had paid for all three items. Then her eye fell upon the hideous porcelain urn and the disreputable-looking oil-painting and comfort eluded her. For if she had paid a mere five pounds for the tray, she had paid an exorbitant five pounds apiece for the other two monstrosities. With the presence of mind that remained to her even in this shipwreck of her hopes, she replaced the gummed label over the superfluous letters in the silversmith's name and set the offending article down in an inconspicuous corner. On top of it she placed a dried-flower arrangement and a small china figurine of an owl that she had been given many years ago and had never liked, and tried to dismiss the whole business from her mind.

Try as she might, she could not. The tray, to be sure, was as good as forgotten. But the urn and the painting were far too visible to be so lightly disposed of. The urn especially seemed to follow her about the room, so that wherever she turned her eyes she saw it. She inspected it for any slight sign of merit, but this search proved entirely fruitless, and so she turned her attention to the painting in the hope that it might serve as some sort of counter-irritant.

Despite the recent tendency to over-value any work of art painted in the late eighteenth century, it was all too obvious that five pounds was far too much to pay for such a hideous daub. The subject was a stout woman in early middle-age, with a startlingly pink face and a deformed-looking dog on her lap, so wretched-looking that Elizabeth thought it cruel to have kept it alive and not have had it put out of its misery. Through the ill-proportioned window in front of which the subject sat, or more properly was positioned (for no human being could sit in that particular attitude without breaking a leg) was visible a blank green expanse and in the distance a travestied depiction of the town of Tilling, which resembled a pile of children's bricks knocked over by a violent blow. The piece was covered in a thick layer of grime and discolouration which served to obscure the ferocity of the colours; Time, who makes the grass grow again even on the bloodiest battlefield, had begun the work of salvage.

The painting told its own story; a portrait had been commissioned, had not pleased, and had been put away, most probably in the bedroom of the humblest kitchen-maid, there to await the Day of Judgement. Elizabeth sat quietly and reconstructed this tale of human guilt and suffering, and as she gazed she noticed first the signature (Antonio Pedretti), and then the name of the grossly misrepresented subject, Miss Lydia. . . . Elizabeth blinked and rubbed her eyes. So turbulent was her soul within her that she could not distinguish what was real with what seemed to be. Yet, by the dim light of the standard-lamp, she thought that the name of the woman in the picture, as written below, was Miss Lydia Mapp.

To be first elated, then cast down, then suddenly swept back up to the very pinnacle of hope, all in the space of a single day, is exhausting work. For a moment, therefore, Elizabeth was stunned; nor was it the thought that the hideous creature depicted on the dingy canvas was a relation that deprived her of speech. Indeed, under the fouling that over-laid the entire surface, she could just detect, despite Signor Pedretti's best efforts, the Mapp chin, the Mapp ears. The eyes, as far as she could judge, were as brown as her own; the hair was her colour. Under the exaggerated signature, she could clearly read the date: 1768. Fully five generations separated her from this Lydia Mapp, and indeed she stood almost exactly half-way between the death of Perkin Map and Elizabeth's own nativity. Here, then, was proof positive that the family had survived, and survived not in the Northumbrian wastes but here in Sussex — for what else could the depiction of Tilling signify, if not that? The setting of the portrait exuded wealth and position; the curtains around the window were deep, red velvet, the chair was richly carved. Once again she could not help but remember whence the painting had come. Even if the Perownes had bought their silver second-hand, no one in the world would willingly buy this terrible icon unless some family connection compelled it. For all its aesthetic shortcomings, the portrait was better proof than the tray could ever have been that the line of Hugo de Map had not ended with Perkin dancing on the gallows-tree.

She propped the portrait against the urn and stood back to take a longer view. From a distance it looked far better. From a distance . . . the name, which had taken her so much by surprise, was flanked by a deep patch of fouling. She knew, before her moistened handkerchief had cleared it away, what lay beneath the grime. Fate had stabbed once again, and she bore the blow not with fury or anger but as the ox bows to the slaughter. It had long been considered a remarkable coincidence that a small neighbourhood should contain two families with such similar names; the Mapps, who lived in the town, and the Mapperleys, who lived in the big house on the coast. Miss Lydia Mapperley was the name that emerged, just as Elizabeth had expected.

She shook her head sadly and turned away. All the fight had gone out of her; and into that vacuum an evil spirit, sent from who can say what malign power, slipped in and took possession of the shrine. It whispered something very quietly, and her better nature, so weary after the onslaught of disappointment, could not drown the terrible words.

As she stood and was silent an idea came to her. She did not care whether she was descended from Hugo and Robert and Lambert or not. Rank was of no importance to her and, besides, there was no title to which she might lay claim. She knew that she was descended from the noblest of all ancestors, namely Adam and Eve. That was irrelevant. What concerned her was the fact that Lucia needed to be taught a lesson, and if Fortune could not supply the means of chastisement, she must manufacture her own. She had spent fifteen pounds on the instruments of correction, and she was determined to get value for her money. If she had not been able, at first glance, to decipher the true name on the portrait, who else could? Particularly if she took the watercolours she knew so well how to mix and made a slight — ever so slight — alteration? Miss Lydia Mapperley could scarcely mind if this libel was removed from her name. As for Signor Pedretti, what concern could it be of his? This pitiful work would, at last, find some useful purpose. Most of all, the thought of the public service that she was about to perform for Tilling, namely the destruction of Lucia's reputation for infallibility, steeled her to what amounted to an act of deliberate forgery. Finally, she recollected that she had bought and paid for this painting; it was her property and she could do with it what she chose. As for fear of detection, the painting itself would remove any suspicions, for who would claim for herself such an unsightly ancestress?

With black she mixed a little slate grey; to this she added burnt umber and painted away the superfluous letters. When this was dry, she took a little lard, mixed it with dust, which she found on a shelf of the book-case (Withers would hear of that) and a tiny quantity of poster white, and smeared the compound very lightly over her delicate work. As a final test, she dabbed at it with a corner of her handkerchief. The forgery was undetectable and permanent. She packed up her paint-box, returned the lard to the kitchen and admired her work. Then she called Major Benjy.

'Just look,' she cried, with girlish excitement, 'what I've found.'

The Mallards ghost, and all the other disembodied spirits of Tilling, were maintaining an infuriating silence. An observer from the Psychical Research Society in London had been approached and had declared he would be only too willing to come down and inspect whatever manifestations the townsfolk cared to show him as long as they could vouch for punctual appearance. But he was not prepared to 'turn out on the off-chance', as he put it; he was a busy man, the Society's resources were over-stretched at the best of times, and especially at this time of the year. There was also a brief flutter of correspondence concerning who was to pay his expenses, should a reliable spectre be located.

This slight discouragement had only a minimal effect on the high degree of interest that the subject had aroused in the town. Lucia had received a representative of a firm of specialist photographic suppliers, who retailed a camera that was activated by sudden falls in temperature or unusual electrical discharges. The apparatus was set up in the drawing-room for a trial period of a week, at the end of which time it was found to have taken seven exposures. Lucia had the film developed at once, only to find seven rather blurred photographs of Foljambe opening the windows each morning to air the room. Since the apparatus was priced at well over forty pounds, Lucia sent it back.

'It's most frustrating,' she exclaimed to Georgie, as they strolled back to Mallards after tea at the Vicarage. 'But I suppose these things cannot be rushed. The spectre will reappear in its own good time.'

'I hope not,' said Georgie, who had not had a good night's sleep since the apparition's visit. 'I hope that tar' some camera thing has scared it away.'

'There is that possibility,' Lucia conceded. 'But I seem to feel its presence all the time; there is a sort of chill in the air. . . .'

'That reminds me,' said Georgie, 'we ought to order some more coal.'

'And besides the physical effects, I sense a kind of numinous aura, like the god in the woods in Vergil's *Aeneid*. A feeling that we are not alone. Almost a brooding vigilance.'

'You mean it's hiding somewhere all the time?' cried Georgie. 'And watching us, without our being able to see it?' He blushed deeply. 'But that's unspeakable. We must get the Padre to exorcise it at once!'

As he spoke, Lucia seemed to sense something else; not so much a numinous aura as a feeling that she had made a very foolish mistake. She could not, however, isolate the reason for this sensation until they arrived at the front-door. It was quite dark by then and under the lamplight she noticed with a rather sickening feeling of recognition that Georgie was wearing his black cape. There was something all too familiar about his appearance as he stood silhouetted against the wall. A flash of intuition passed through her active and perceptive mind and, when they were sitting in front of the drawing-room fire, she asked him as casually as he could whether he had been out in the garden on the night of the haunting.

'Yes,' he replied, rather startled. 'Why do you ask?'

'My dear, I cannot say,' she answered, fixing him with her bright, bird-like eye, and he writhed like a whelk on a pin. 'It suddenly entered my mind that you might have been. Quite clairvoyant of me, don't you think? I cannot imagine why I thought of it, I just did. What were you doing out there?'

Georgie, had he not been guarding a guilty secret, would have resented this questioning, more suited to a police inspector than a wife; as it was, he was saved from embarrassing revelations by a sudden flash of inspiration.

'After my headache got better, I washed my hair and towelling it dry sometimes makes me feel dizzy, so I went out into the garden to let the fresh air dry it,' he said triumphantly. 'Why do you ask?'

Lucia buried her head in her book to hide her shame and disappointment. The spectre's dark cape and Spanish beard had first roused her suspicions this evening; its luminous hair confirmed them. At least she had been right about one thing: she had indeed been conscious of the spectre's constant presence in the house, for here he was now, sitting by the fire embroidering a small woollen purse. How foolish she had been!

'I've been thinking, *caro*,' she said, when she had recovered her composure. 'You're quite right about

159

having the ghost exorcised. We should not allow ourselves to become victims of the dangerous fascination of
the occult. Who knows what perils we might be incur-
ring, sharing our house with a dead person! In fact I
shall telephone the Padre at once. I'm not sure how long
it takes to arrange a ceremony of exorcism, and I do
want to be rid of the thing as quickly as possible.'

Georgie was overjoyed. 'I can't wait,' he said. 'It's
been preying on my mind ever since you saw it. I believe
it's a rather fascinating ceremony, almost unchanged
since the Middle Ages. I don't know when it was last
performed in Tilling. The Padre's been looking forward
to it, he says. I wonder if he wears special robes or just
the ordinary ones? And do you think the local papers
might want to send a few photographers along?'

That night as Georgie disrobed and got into bed, he
felt as if some terrible load had been lifted from his
shoulders. He could put away the ornate Venetian
paper-knife which he had placed by his bed for use as a
last resort, and perhaps he could get some sleep for a
change. As he turned out the light, however, and drifted
into that curious state, half waking and half sleeping,
during which unexpected insights occasionally manifest
themselves and apparently insoluble problems suddenly
melt away, he made the connection between the decision to do away with the Black Spaniard and Lucia's
burning desire to know his movements on that particular evening. He sat up with a jolt.

'It was me all the time,' he said angrily. 'Oh, how could
she think that!'

Then he went to sleep.

The next morning brought fresh excitement. Everyone
had received an invitation to dine at Grebe — an
unusual thing in itself, for Elizabeth rarely took it upon
herself to feed all of Tilling Society at a sitting. Such
Homeric gestures, she reasoned, were best left to Lucia
and the Wyses. More fascinating still was the handwritten post-script to each invitation: 'Do, please, try to

come if you can, as I have something interesting to tell you all.'

'That's typical of Elizabeth,' said Evie to Diva. 'A great deal of mystery and suspense and all it will turn out to be is a new hat, or Benjy-boy managing the fifth hole in less than twelve! How she loves to dramatize everything!'

'Perhaps,' said Diva. 'Or maybe she has got some news. She's been very quiet of late. All she's really done is try and steal Lucia's ghost.'

This unfortunate choice of words conjured up a strange picture in the minds of both of them; Evie seemed to see Elizabeth engaged in some hideous necromantic rite, in which she sought to capture Lucia's spirit, while Diva, whose imagination was rather more mundane, pictured Elizabeth laying a trial of aniseed from Mallards to Grebe. They freed themselves from these strange imaginings.

'That'll be it, then. She'll have found a ghost for Grebe. Or perhaps she's having one sent down from London in a hamper. Talking of ghosts, by the way, Lucia has asked Kenneth to exorcise the Black Spaniard. As quietly as possible, she said.'

'How thrilling!' cried Diva. 'But why? She was as keen as anything on having a ghost before. What can have changed her mind?'

'No idea. But Kenneth is terribly excited. He's been studying the service and he's written to the Bishop for advice. He's never been asked to perform an exorcism before.'

The Wyses, passing by in the Royce, stopped for a moment to ascertain indirectly whether Elizabeth's hospitality had been extended to all or simply to themselves alone. They too were fascinated to hear of the Black Spaniard's imminent demise. Susan, with her keen interest in Spiritualism, was particularly interested in the ghost's well-being.

'I do hope the dear Padre will use a humane form of exorcism,' she said. 'Some of the forms and procedures for driving out spirits are rather brutal and I would hate to think of the poor thing's suffering. Is it over quickly, Evie dear, or does the ghost linger on for some minutes?'

'I can't say for sure,' said Evie, who had not considered this aspect of the matter. 'I know Kenneth has to ring a little bell and call it all sorts of names. I don't think he actually kills it, though.'

'He couldn't kill it,' said Susan. 'It is a spirit and therefore immortal.'

'You mean it'll be wandering around looking for somewhere to go?' asked Diva excitedly. She had already thought of offering it a home at Wasters, should it require one. But she could not see how she might make her house especially attractive for the spirit. One could not put out bowls of bread and milk as one did for hedgehogs.

'The ejected spirit, unless it be malign, which in this case seems unlikely, will probably find release from its earthly bonds and be translated to the Other Side,' explained Susan loftily.

'Oh, I see,' said Diva sadly. 'What a pity. It seems such a waste.'

Elizabeth, meanwhile, was preoccupied with other matters, to wit, her dinner party and the triumphant exhibition of Miss Lydia Mapp. Major Benjy's inspection of the (altered) portrait had been enough to convince her that no one would be able to detect her slight emendations. He had peered at the name for quite three minutes and pronounced it genuine in reply to her anxious query of 'Oh Benjy, do you think it can really say that?' In fact, Benjy had gone rather further: he had at once inspected the silver tray and she rather feared that he gained the erroneous impression that it said 'Mapp' too. But it would be too complicated to explain all that and, since his subsequent scrutiny of the porcelain urn had proved fruitless, she let the matter rest. She was preparing to go into town when Benjy, rather red-faced, stopped her.

'You were — um — thinking of driving in?' he asked cautiously.

'Yes, why? Has that wretched car broken down again?'

'In the motor, you mean?'

This was a foolish question, more foolish than she would have expected even from the Major, and it put her on her guard.

'Is there something the matter with the motor?' she reiterated.

'No, nothing at all. But — well, you can't drive it, I'm afraid. Not just now anyway.'

'What can you mean, you obscure one? Of course I can. I've been driving it for months.'

'Well, old girl, it's like this.' The Major swallowed hard. 'I was chattin' with the bobby just now — or, rather, he called specially. Asked if you had a Driving Licence.'

'A *what*, dear?' demanded Elizabeth sharply.

'Some damn' Government thing. Apparently you have to have one, and to get one nowadays you have to pass some sort of test. Just come in, apparently. Otherwise you can't drive a motor on the road. It's illegal.'

'But Benjy, this is absurd. Apart from the sheer tyranny of it, how on earth can one learn to drive and so pass this test if one is not allowed to drive without a licence?'

'Oh, you can drive without passing the test if someone who has a licence is with you.'

Elizabeth relaxed and said patiently, as if to a small child, 'That's all right, then. You can accompany me until I pass this test and obtain my licence. I presume it will be just a formality.'

'Not exactly, Liz,' said the Major uncomfortably. 'You see, I haven't got a licence either. Didn't really know you had to have one.' He shut his eyes as a man will do before an explosion. 'It's only been the law for a little while,' he said pleadingly.

'You mean that for that *little* while,' said Elizabeth aghast, 'we've been regularly and systematically breaking the law? Ever since you persuaded me — against my better judgment, let me say — to pay good money for that — that wretched thing? And I could have been

163

arrested? And taken to court?' The horror of this struck Elizabeth like a hammer, for she knew only too well that Lucia was a magistrate. Her heart nearly stopped beating as images of a packed court and Lucia in a black cap flashed across her mind. Had she been apprehended and brought before the Mayor in her wrath, who could doubt that she would have gone the way of Perkin Map?

'Oh, Benjy,' she gasped, 'how could you have been so utterly stupid? Get rid of it at once, do you hear? I never want to set eyes on it again.'

'But Liz,' pleaded the Major, 'it's only a matter of passing the test. I'm sure we could get someone to sit in the car with you until you're ready.'

'Whom, for instance?'

'Well, if we were to ask her, Lucia might let us have Cadman for a day or so each week. If we paid his wages, of course.'

That, as far as Elizabeth was concerned, was that. Rather than subject herself to such an indignity, she would prefer to crawl about on her knees for the rest of her days. With a terrible cry, therefore, she drove the Major from her presence, and, going out into the garden, vented her fury on the rose-bushes (which had already been thoroughly pruned) until sweet thoughts of Miss Lydia Mapp restored her equilibrium.

For his part, Major Benjy could bear the loss with a degree of equanimity. He had scarcely ever been able to get the machine to himself and it had been rather shaming to be driven everywhere by his wife, with her incessant cries of 'Do move your knee, dear, I'm trying to change gear!' In fact, it was this humiliation rather than dire threats from officers of the law that had led him, on finding out about the new motoring regulations from an acquaintance at the Golf Club, to concoct that mythical meeting with the policeman. If someone in the Mapp-Flint household had been going to learn to drive, he knew for certain that it would not have been him. He would have been condemned to eternal passengerhood, with all its attendant ignominy. His tale, with the threat of the magistrates' court and the suggestion — calculated to inspire rage — that she should take lessons from Cadman, had produced the desired result. All rather neat, especially since his golfing friend, informed of his difficulties, had offered to take the three-wheeler off his hands for seventy pounds. He toyed with the idea of concealing the true sum from Elizabeth and converting the difference to his own use, but that would be fraught with danger. . . . He drove the machine, for the first and last time, down to the links, handed it over as arranged, and stayed to drink a whisky-and-soda until the tram left to take him back to Tilling.

The mellowing fumes of the whisky softened his heart, already light with the successful conclusion of his strategy, and he began to find himself feeling a little sorry for his wife. It must have been a distinct disappointment to her to lose her motor in this way and he felt it would be a kindly gesture if he looked about him for some small, unostentatious and preferably cheap token of his affection. As he reflected on this and a second glass of whisky, a rather splendid idea formed in his mind, not the first that he had had during the last few days. In fact, it was becoming something of a habit.

11

It was a long-standing problem to the organisers of social events in Tilling that, when Society met in full conclave, there was always one individual left out after the two Bridge-tables had been assembled. Generally, it would be incumbent upon the host or hostess to yield place to a guest; but Elizabeth found this ideal of behaviour difficult to achieve when she entertained at Grebe. If she deselected herself, she was excluded from the one occupation that she enjoyed above all others; if she dismissed her husband, there was no knowing what he might get up to while her attention was given over to the fascinations of Bridge. As a result, the first rubber of the evening at Grebe was always preceded by the ritual of cutting the cards to see who was to be excluded. The victim of this ostracism had the right to a place in the next rubber (if time permitted), but during the course of the game itself was condemned to sit and watch without being able to participate in any way. During the actual playing of the hand, the outcast could always chat to the player who had gone dummy; during the auction, however, there was nothing to do but listen, observe and reflect on how much better the entire hand could have been played had the outcast had some *rôle* in it. Elizabeth, by some infuriating chance, often tended to find herself cast out by her own procedure and on these occasions had been known to pace up and down like a caged animal. Lucia, on the other hand, would sit like an enraptured disciple at the feet of his master, watching every move and occasionally making notes in her pocket-book, so as to be able to contribute an independent commentary to the storm of recrimination and self-congratulation that followed every rubber. She could, if the need arose, sit opposite Elizabeth by the hour, watching in the strictest silence and without making the slightest movement (no one could accuse her of trying to distract Elizabeth's attention), and thus scarcely needing to resort to the faint quiver of an eyebrow or heavily muffled intake of breath to destroy Elizabeth's confidence at some crucial stage of the game.

It was this difficulty that occupied Elizabeth's mind as she made her final preparations for the great dinner party at which Miss Lydia Mapp was to make her *début*. Everything else had been so finely scheduled and organised as to admit of no possibility of disturbance. She had personally supervised the preparation of the meal (mock-turtle soup, lemon sole, roast lamb, sherry trifle) and had stood over the cook during the genesis of the trifle to ensure that all the worthy woman's diligence was directed to perfecting that safe and reliable delicacy. She had likewise invigilated Withers' treatment of the wine and gone to great lengths to make certain that the coffee would be hot and strong. She had inspected all the plates and cutlery as rigorously as in days gone by Major Benjy had inspected his troops; minutely examined the tablecloth and observed implacably while the napkins were folded. She had checked every surface in the house for dust and found none; she had evicted the more disreputable of the tiger-skins; and so great was the moral force that she had by this stage generated that she was able to persuade the Major that one of this trophies of native weapons, that had long been unchallenged in the dining-room, would look far better in the coal-shed. In any of these areas, she felt, Fate could not hurt her.

So to the drawing-room, where Miss Lydia Mapp, (*née* Mapperley) was so placed that she seemed to fill the room. Her portrait was framed by two enormous pot-plants and the coffee-tray would come to rest beneath

167

her patrician nose. There too she placed the plate of nougat chocolates; Diva, at least, should have no excuse for not seeing the portrait. Conscience being in all of us an ever-pricking thorn, she examined the portrait under the piercing glare of a table-lamp; the forgery (or restoration, as she preferred to think of it) was undetectable. As if to emphasize, indeed to celebrate this, she left the lamp there, like the light in a shrine, and very pleasing it looked too. The silver tray and the urn she had banished to a dark, crowded place beneath the stairs, so the only novelty would be the portrait, and Elizabeth had sorely misjudged her friends if she thought that they would not notice at once any new thing, however trivial. Diva had been known to comment on a new stair-rod.

There remained nothing to do but rehearse in her mind the words she would use to dismiss, lightly and modestly, the apologies that would be rained upon her by all who had doubted her word. How, she repeated to herself, could they possibly have known? She had not been aware of it herself; indeed, nobody, not even Lucia's grave scholars, had been aware of it. Above all, dear Lucia had no call to reproach herself for introducing the red herring of Perkin Map and his disreputable fate. What she had said had been the truth, if not exactly the whole truth. . . .

Much had been happening in the world while Elizabeth had been thus occupied in elaborate preparation. The Padre had received a long and rather unfriendly letter from the Bishop's chaplain in reply to his request for advice on the ceremony of exorcism. The policy of the diocese, said the Bishop's chaplain, was to exorcise only in the last resort. Had the alleged ghost been observed frequently? How many people had seen it? Was the nuisance it caused sufficiently troublesome to justify exorcism? Could the Reverend Bartlett honestly say that the presence of this reported apparition was causing a spiritual danger to his parishioners?

There followed an ominously worded paragraph about the need to minimize ritual for ritual's sake, to avoid the active pursuit of spectacle and melodramatic effect, with several minatory hints that excessive interest in the more arcane functions of the Church might imply a sub-conscious leaning towards a 'certain Italian city'.

Then there had been the bombshell, lobbed almost absent-mindedly into a crowded High Street by an obviously preoccupied Elizabeth, of the news of the departure of the three-wheeler. Diva, approaching Mr. Hopkins's shop, had met the erstwhile motorist.

'No motor this morning?' she had enquired.

'Motor?' asked Elizabeth, as if the concept was foreign to her. 'Oh, I see what you mean. No, dear, I've sold it. Do you think these herrings are properly fresh?'

'Sold it? Why? What's happened? Did it break down?'

'We didn't really need it,' replied Elizabeth, as if the topic bored her. 'After all, what does anyone need a motor for in Tilling? The wretched machines do nothing but congest the streets and spoil their appearance. If I were Mayor, I would prohibit their use within the town.'

'But the day before yesterday you were saying —' Diva shouted, but too late. Elizabeth had vanished into Mr. Hopkins's shop and was lost to communication, for Diva had quarrelled with that worthy fishmonger recently over the definition of *fruits de mer* and had vowed never to cross his threshold again. Elizabeth, so Diva reflected, had the useful knack of appearing to move more slowly than she actually did. Major Benjy, however, moved much more predictably, and was thus more easily waylaid. Confirmation of the story was extracted from him. He stated (as previously instructed) that Elizabeth had read in the papers of the damage done to historic buildings by the exhaust fumes of motor-vehicles, and had decided to set an example.

'Well, that's what he said,' Diva reported to the Bartletts over tea at Wasters. 'That and the vibration of heavy traffic, which is supposed to damage foundations, or something of the sort.'

'Do you think that's the announcement she was going

to make this evening?' demanded Evie, hastily swallowing a mouthful of seed cake. 'It's certainly interesting enough.'

'I don't think it can be,' Diva replied. 'She gave the impression that it wasn't in the least important. Quite off-hand about it, in fact.'

'Well, if the Excitement is more interesting still, I can't wait to find out what it's going to be.'

'I haven't the faintest idea. What do you think, Padre?'

But the Padre was morose and untalkative, as he had been all day. The Bishop's chaplain's letter had scarred his soul and beside the terrible affront to his dignity and integrity even the final departure of the three-wheeler seemed trivial.

'I dinna ken, I'm sure,' he growled. ' 'Tes bound to be some new prate or idolatry. I'm no concerned about Mistress Mapp-Flint's wondrous disclosure.'

This was an ideally suitable cue for reopening the scarce-healed wound of the letter and the Padre spoke warmly for some time about what he considered to be dangerous new trends in the higher echelons of the clergy, tantamount in some cases to Methodism. After delivering himself of a veiled but fearsome attack on the Bishop's views, as recently printed in a national newspaper, on Lot's wife and naturally occurring salt deposits in the Holy Land, he rose abruptly and announced that he had a confirmation class to give.

'Though why I bother to teach the True Faith in this diocese,' he snarled, 'I dinna ken. 'Tes all in vain the way things are going.'

With that, he was gone, leaving behind him an awkward atmosphere, heavy with Doubt and Schism. To dispel these dark clouds, Diva returned to the subject of Elizabeth's forthcoming revelations.

'I suppose it might be something to do with Benjy and the Golf Club,' she said.

'Hadn't you heard?' cried Evie, delighted to find that she was not, as she had previously thought, the last to hear the news. 'Benjy didn't get on to the Committee after all and his offer of a prize for a mixed-doubles tournament was rejected.'

'No!' exclaimed Diva, Schism completely forgotten. 'What happened?'

'Well, Kenneth told me that he and Benjy were playing a round of golf together and Benjy hit a most glorious drive, much further than he's ever hit one before, right on to the green.'

'That's the bit where the hole is, isn't it?' asked Diva.

'I think so. But Benjy hadn't expected it to go that far — usually his shots go right up in the air and land a few yards away — and he hadn't bothered to call out — what is that word they use?'

'I can't imagine,' said Diva, who could easily imagine the sort of word the Major might use, if provoked.

'Fore! That's it. The Major hadn't called out "Fore" and the ball went down very fast and hit Mr. Phillipson — he's the Chairman or the President or something — right on the nose, just when he was putting to win the match. Of course, he missed his putt and that made him absolutely furious. Kenneth suspects he had a wager on it. Meanwhile, Benjy was angry too because it was the best stroke he's ever played and he kept saying that, if Mr. Phillipson hadn't been in the way, the ball would have gone down the hole and been a starling, or whatever it is they call it.'

'I know that one,' said Diva. 'It's a birdie. Go on.'

'And then the Major accused Mr. Phillipson of sabotage and Mr. Phillipson did the same and then they had words. And the Major had already bought the plate he was going to present as a prize. It's very sad.'

This epic tale seemed to deprive both of them of speech for a while.

'He could still present the plate,' said Diva.

'I think he offered, but Mr. Phillipson was very rude to him and so he said he would report Mr. Phillipson to the Committee. I don't think that was very tactful of him in the circumstances.'

Evie finished her seed-cake and took her leave, for it would soon be time to dress, and set off for Grebe. The Wyses and Lucia had offered to provide transport, but Diva began to feel rather concerned about whether she should accept or not, in the light of Elizabeth's pronouncement. What if the passage of the Royce along the High Street, with her and the Wyses in it, should cause Wasters to collapse? As a householder, she felt that she ought to refuse the offer. On the other hand, it was a long way to Grebe and it looked as if it might rain. Diva sat worrying about this for some minutes, until it was nearly too late to dress and walk to Grebe (that is, if she was going to walk). She got up and then sat down again.

'Oh, why is everything so difficult?' she wailed.

Lucia and Georgie (it went without saying) were the last to arrive at Grebe.

'So sorry,' trilled Lucia, as they were shown into the morning-room, 'but official business held me up. One is hardly able to call one's evenings one's own. But my police inspector had some warrants for me to sign.'

'Never mind,' said Elizabeth, 'you're here now.'

'One of them — a most unfortunate case — Mr. Archer's son. You know Mr. Archer, don't you, Major?'

Mr. Archer was the man to whom the Major had sold the three-wheeler. For a moment, the Major felt a little uncomfortable, but Lucia had said that it was his son that was in trouble, not Mr. Archer himself. He steadied himself with a sip of sherry from Georgie's glass.

'The prosecution alleges,' Lucia continued, 'that young Archer borrowed his father's car — a new one he had bought only recently — to drive into Hastings with some friends. He was stopped on the main road and his headlights and back tyre were found to be in an unfit condition. There was only one — the vehicle was a three-wheeler. As if that were not bad enough, the prosecution also alleges that the young man had no licence to drive the aforesaid vehicle. If the case is proven I shall have no alternative but to fine the young man heavily.

Such a shame — the boy is about to go back to Cambridge
for his final examinations. I do hope the college authorities will not be too hard on him'.

'A most shocking case,' said Elizabeth firmly. 'Such
people are a menace to society. Another glass of sherry,
Mr. Georgie?'

Mr. Wyse had knitted his eyebrows during this narra-
tion and something was plainly troubling him. 'Mrs.
Pillson,' he said at length, 'you spoke of a licence to
drive. Pray enlighten me as to the nature of this licence.'

Lucia did so and Mr. Wyse thanked her. 'Remind me,
Susan dear,' he said to his wife, 'to ascertain whether
our chauffeur has one of these licences. If not, we must
insist that he obtain one as quickly as possible.

Elizabeth, who had gone a strange colour, interrupted
Mr. Wyse at this moment and began to praise the rather
magnificent cummerbund he was wearing, which it
seemed she had only just noticed (although she had been
sitting opposite him for quite some time). Such a beautiful shade of purple, or should she say claret? And such
material!

'A present from my dear wife,' said Mr. Wyse, rather
indistinctly.

'And this is, so to speak, its *début*?' enquired
Elizabeth sweetly.

'Indeed, yes,' replied Mr. Wyse, whose normally
impassive face was turning almost the same colour as
his cummerbund. The significance of this was wasted on
nobody; a present, at this unseasonable time of the year,
must mark the anniversary either of a birth or of a
marriage, and everyone knew when Mr. Wyse had been
married. What they had never been able to ascertain,
however, despite their very best endeavours, was when
Mr. Wyse's birthday was, let alone how many birthdays
he had celebrated. This evidence of the cummerbund
had narrowed the search down to April. Was this, Diva
wondered, the interesting item of news for which they
had been assembled? It was certainly interesting
enough.

'Charming,' said Elizabeth, 'quite charming.'

'Tell me,' Lucia persisted, 'what has become of your motor? I did not see it outside in its usual place when I arrived just now. No trouble with it, I hope?'

Elizabeth laughed gaily. 'Trouble? It was trouble incarnate. Such a bore, Lucia dear, quite like a little child with all its tiresome requirements. No, I think I shall be much better off without it. Benjy-boy and I were beginning to miss our lovely walk into town — quite stout we were both becoming, I dare say. And so anti-social, with its fearful noise and its awful fumes. And all the damage it must have been doing to our beautiful town.'

'Damage?' asked Lucia, unwittingly.

'Did you know that motor-vehicles are threatening to undermine our oldest and most historic buildings? Their incessant vibrations and the noxious chemicals in their exhaust emissions. A study has recently been published. You ought to get a copy.'

'How terrible,' observed Lucia calmly. 'I must look into this. We cannot have our buildings put at risk.'

'Quite so,' said Elizabeth, 'for a start —'

'In fact,' continued Lucia, 'as Mayor I should say I had a duty to take official notice of this study. I must obtain a copy, as you suggest.'

'Splendid,' said Elizabeth. 'If I were you —'

'Depending on what the study had to say,' Lucia said, her voice rising serenely over Elizabeth's interruptions, 'I think I might recommend that the Council take some action. . . . A ban on motor traffic, let us say, through the old town, except for vehicles collecting or delivering goods. That ought to alleviate the problem to some extent, although it would of course cause some consider-able hardship to some members of the community.'

The Wyses were nodding their heads; it would cause them more than mere hardship. But Elizabeth had not noticed them. She therefore said:

'My dear, you should not concern yourself with the worries of a few selfish individuals. Let them walk.

174

What really matters is the preservation of our wonderful heritage.'

At these words, a strangled cry burst from Mr. Wyse's lips, and Elizabeth, turning round, was confronted by a fierce scowl of rage from Susan and a look of great sadness from her husband. At once, Elizabeth realised that she had been led into a trap. Before she could say anything, however, Lucia had started again.

'Of course,' she drawled, in her most infuriating tone, 'some of these studies are based on the flimsiest of evidence. Should this study turn out to be of such a nature, no action will be required. I wonder if that will be the case. It really doesn't do, I always find, to make up one's mind before one has had a chance to examine all the evidence and to take every factor and viewpoint into consideration. What new evidence did you say was contained in this particular study, Elizabeth?'

Elizabeth was forced to confess that she had not actually read the study, only a brief summary of it in the newspaper. Mr. Wyse seemed visibly relieved, while Susan, who had been clutching his arm as if in need of protection, released it and gave Elizabeth a look of concentrated hatred.

'I see,' said Lucia judicially, 'you have not actually read the study, yet the brief account of its findings in the paper was enough to make you sell your car at once. That was most public-spirited, dear, but perhaps a trifle hasty.'

Elizabeth felt herself concerned and for a moment knew not which way to turn. Then inspiration came to her and she turned, without replying to Lucia, and addressed the Padre.

'So sorry to hear that the Bishop is being so difficult about the exorcism,' she said. 'So foolish and uncooperative, too. What possible harm could it do? Not to mention all the benefits. Now I confess that, while I lived at Mallards, I found the ghost was no trouble at all — company for me, in fact — but to those of a nervous disposition —'

"'Tes enough to make one despair o' the Kirk of England,' muttered the Padre ferociously. 'Why, the service is there in the prayer-book. How dare they say I canna perform it in my own parish.'

Georgie stirred uncomfortably in his chair. He had been secretly glad when he heard that the service had been forbidden, for he was dreadfully afraid that, as the object of the exorcism, he would be affected in some way. He had no wish to be exorcised.

'But it's such a tar'some business,' he burst out, 'and so unkind to the poor ghost. And besides, it sounds awfully messy — all that water being splashed about and candle-wax dripping on to the furniture. And suppose my *bibelots* got wet?'

'You wouldna like it if a poltergeist got into your collection,' said the Padre angrily. 'Just think of the harm that it might do. It would hurl your snuff-boxes about the room and shatter your Venetian glass!'

Georgie was struck dumb at this horrible thought. Could one do anything to prevent a poltergeist getting into the house? He had an idea that garlic was supposed to keep them away (or was that only for vampires?).

'For my part,' said Susan Wyse, 'I am quite relieved that this proposed ceremony will not be taking place. Not,' she added hastily, 'for the quite absurd reasons put forward by the Bishop's chaplain, which I am sure are not the views of the Bishop himself. It is, however, my firm belief that genuine ghosts are rare enough as it is. Why, it would be comparable to pulling down an historic building, or killing some endangered species of animal. It takes hundreds of years to build up the psychic energy required to manifest an apparition.'

The debate could have raged further, for all had their own contribution to make on this topic. Major Benjy could have spoken about devil-worship in the East, while Diva was convinced that she had once seen a friend's gardener coming out of a public-house in Hastings when he should have been at work in Tilling, although when questioned later he gave his word that he had been in

Tilling all day — clearly a case of a psychic phenomenon. However, this valuable evidence was not heard,
for Withers announced that dinner was ready, and
everyone went into the dining-room. Conversation during the meal was confined to more or less neutral topics,
for it is hard to participate fully in a discussion if one's
mouth is full of lemon sole, especially if the lemon sole
is unusually palatable. Even Lucia was forced to admit
to herself that Elizabeth's cook had produced edible
food on this occasion: and since the shortcomings of
Elizabeth's table were generally to be attributed not to
the cook's incompetence but to Elizabeth's excessive
frugality in the obtaining of the ingredients, Lucia
wondered why Elizabeth had chosen on this occasion to
spend money on ingredients of reasonable quality.
Indeed, Diva was moved to describe the sherry trifle as
'luxurious'.

'I quite agree with you, Diva dear,' said Lucia. 'Con-
gratulations to cook, Elizabeth, and tell her how well
she's mastered my recipe.'

'Your recipe?' cried Elizabeth, nearly choking. She
would have developed this theme further had she not
recalled, in a sudden access of memory, that the recipe
was indeed one of Lucia's, sent as a peace-offering after
a long-forgotten period of civil war. So she was forced to
smile and say, 'Of course, I remember now. But I think
that cook has found a way to improve on your perfection,
dear friend. A little less cream, so as not to mask the
flavour.'

'I thought I detected a slight — how shall I put it? Not
blandness exactly, but a mildness to which I am not
accustomed. But I agree with you, an improvement. No
great loss of flavour; and cream is so expensive nowadays, isn't it?'

Elizabeth could not help but admire, purely as one
craftswoman admires the work of another, the skill
with which Lucia made it seem as if she had interfered
with the recipe simply in order to save a few pennies.
She made no reply, but instead resolved to make Lucia's

forthcoming humiliation all the more severe. Hitherto she had not planned to make it sound as if Lucia had deliberately concealed evidence of the survival of the de Maps. After this latest sally, however, she began to compose the form of words that she would use to cast the aspersion. As soon as it was feasible to do so, she proposed that the men be abandoned to the mercy of the port and ushered her female guests into the drawing-room.

It was Diva, quick of eye and incurably inquisitive, who first took notice of Miss Lydia Mapp, glorious in her shrine of pot-plants.

'That's new,' she cried, and, scuttling across the room like a circular Jack Russell chasing a rabbit down a hole, she thrust her head through the surrounding foliage. 'Who's it meant to be?'

Elizabeth did not reply; indeed, she averted her head and chattered gaily to Susan Wyse. It would be only a matter of time before Diva's investigative powers answered her question for her.

'Miss Lydia Mapp,' Diva spelled out. 'Any relation?'

'What was that, Diva dear? Oh, you've found my little discovery, have you?'

Diva's eyes were glued to the canvas, for she had seen the date and was making rapid mathematical calculations in her head.

'Benjy and I went to the sale at Breakspear Hall. So sad, all those lovely things being sold off. Those terrible death-duties — so morbid, don't you think? And there it was.'

'But the date says 1768,' said Diva, in an awed voice.

'That is my interpretation, certainly.'

'So what was it doing at Breakspear Hall?' demanded Evie, manners wholly forgotten.

'How I racked my brains, dear Evie! I can only conclude that this Miss Mapp later became a Mrs. Perowne — the family at the Hall, you know — and that her future husband requested her portrait as a token of love. So romantic, don't you think?'

Susan Wyse, though not by nature easily manoeuvrable, had gained her feet and almost jostled Diva out of the way.

'But my dear, this is most thrilling!' she exclaimed. 'Such a find!'

'Why dear?' asked Elizabeth innocently. Far better to have the explanation given by an independent source.

'It's obvious,' said Susan impatiently. 'It means that your distinguished ancestors, the de Maps, could not have died out in the seventeenth century, as some people', and she gave Lucia a pointed look, 'have led us to believe. They were obviously a family of great prestige in the eighteenth century, if a Miss Mapp was a suitable match for one of the Perownes.'

Elizabeth's expression, one of pleasant unconcern, did not change at these words, although in her heart she was deeply relieved. It had suddenly struck her that she ought perhaps to have restored away the second 'p' of Mapp, to ensure that the link might be easily made. But Susan Wyse had grasped it at once — she who was not, perhaps, the most brilliant mind in Tilling. It had worked.

'Why, that seems logical enough,' said Evie. 'Fancy! But Lucia said. . . .' She fell silent and gave Lucia a suspicious glance. Why had that account of the de Maps been so categorical, she wondered? Either Lucia's scholarship or her veracity was at fault, it seemed. To put it bluntly, had Lucia told a deliberate untruth? Evie did not appear to be alone in her doubts, for Diva and Susan were quiet also.

'Wouldn't it be pleasant if it were so! exclaimed Elizabeth. 'And mine is not a common name. But of course there is no way of proving it. I'm afraid the Perowne papers were all dispersed at the sale, some to a private collector, some, I recall, to an American university. So now we will never know the truth.'

'The portrait is evidence enough, surely,' said Susan, her eyes fixed on the canvas.

'Kenneth will be fascinated when he sees it,' said Evie,

and who could fail to detect the significance of the words? Susan nodded her agreement, for Kenneth would not be nearly as interested as Algernon would be, except perhaps in his professional *rôle* as guardian of truth and enemy of falsehoods.

Lucia recognised their mood and a sick feeling of panic surged briefly inside her. 'May I?' she asked, and stepped in front of the painting. Style, date and signature were all above suspicion and despite (or perhaps because of) Signor Pedretti's lack of skill, she was certain that she could detect a likeness; look thou upon this picture and on this, as it were. The ears, in particular, were most distinctive.

'There is a strong resemblance, don't you think?' said Evie to Lucia, acidly (for already in her mind she had convicted Lucia of *suppressio veri*).

'Remarkable!' said Diva. 'Quite remarkable!'

'So it was not just my idle fancy,' cooed Elizabeth. 'I was most forcefully reminded of my Aunt Caroline as she was when I first knew her. In fact, the resemblance is quite startling. Almost a photograph.'

At this point, the men entered the room, and were at once pressed to inspect the Discovery. Georgie quite failed to grasp its unfortunate implications and repeatedly expressed the opinion that the likeness was beyond dispute.

'Why, Elizabeth, you might almost be sisters,' he said, and Elizabeth, although pleased by this enthusiasm, could not help but feel a little annoyed. The painting was, after all, extremely ugly. Mr. Wyse also pronounced the likeness to be uncanny and pointed out the town of Tilling, which none of the other observers, for all their acuteness, had so far noticed. Then there was a renewed crush to see the picture. If, as seemed highly likely, the house through whose window Tilling was to be seen was that of Miss Lydia Mapp's father, then surely it must be possible to identify, by the angle from which the town was seen, roughly where the ancestral home of the de Maps (and therefore of Elizabeth) must be. A hubbub of speculation followed, much to Elizabeth's alarm, for if the house were successfully pinpointed, might not exposure follow? As it turned out, however, the painter's lack of skill came once again to her aid; for it was finally agreed that such a view of the town could only be obtained from the middle of the English Channel, through a telescope and not allowing for the curvature of the earth. Mr. Wyse therefore declared it to be 'stylised' and the matter was dropped.

After such commotions, Bridge seemed quite unbearably mundane and Mr. Wyse had no objection at all when Fate dictated that he should be the one to be excluded from the two tables.

'The time shall slip away in contemplation of your divine painting,' he exclaimed with a charming bow. Elizabeth, who had taken such pains to render her forgery undetectable, waved gaily at him and started to deal the cards. Soon she was upbraiding her partner for not supporting her bid and quite unconscious of Mr. Wyse whose delighted fascination had not been exaggerated.

Mr. Wyse knew how to look at pictures. First he stood about seven feet away and allowed his sub-conscious mind to drink in all the hidden depths and subtleties of the work. This process, however, took rather less time than he had expected and he stepped closer to the canvas and inspected it in detail. His generous soul found much to admire in the vigorous, almost impressionistic brushwork (years ahead of its time), the daring manipulation of form and proportion that seemed almost to break the rules of composition, of anatomy itself, in its efforts to express the artist's intentions.

Having satisfied himself that he had done the aesthetic side of the painting full justice, he turned his mind to contemplation of the portrait as a piece of historical evidence, and determined to extract from it every last scrap of information that it contained. He correctly placed the period from the style of the interior furnishings, identified to a nicety the breed of the lapdog and amply justified his opinion of the subject's social position from her dress and manner of arranging her hair. He also noted an engagement ring on her finger — more evidence, if any were needed, to support his hypothesis. Finally, when all was apparently noted, he observed what appeared to be some heraldic device on the table-cloth on which the subject's hand was resting. But it was partly covered by the signature of the artist and further obscured by a dark smear of discolouration around the subject's name. Nevertheless, Mr. Wyse's excellent education in the fine and liberal arts had prepared him for this eventuality. He knew that the best way of removing such marks without any risk at all to the canvas was to moisten the tip of one's finger (not a handkerchief, which might scratch) with one's tongue and rub gently but vigorously until the marks were removed. Having made certain that he was unobserved (for he had no desire to offend anyone by sticking out his tongue while they were watching), he moistened his finger in the approved manner and began to rub. The stain came away as easily as if it had been water-colour and the heraldic device became steadily clearer. He remoistened his finger and rubbed until it began to ache, for the device was one that he thought he recognised. As he did so, he saw, to his utter amazement, lettering beginning to appear under his finger-tip, just to the right of the subject's name. He returned to his task with renewed diligence, careless now of observation in the excitement of his discovery, and scarcely heard Elizabeth's hoarse cry of 'Leave my painting alone!' For, when all the discolouration was swept away, the name was clearly not Mapp but Mapperley, as in Mapperley House, near Tilling, Sussex.

'I am convinced,' said Mr. Wyse, as he stood next morning outside the post-office, waiting for his wife to post her letter, 'that the remainder of the name was simply obscured by the discolouration and that Mrs. Mapp-Flint was the victim of a genuine misapprehension.'

182

'Fiddlesticks!' cried Evie. 'It was forgery, plain and simple. Why, you said last night as we drove home that the stuff on your fingers looked rather like water-colour. She just painted over the rest of the letters. Typical!'

Mr. Wyse shook his head sadly. Try as he might he could not account for it otherwise. He knew that public opinion was against his view. Even Susan Wyse had thought as much — had written as much in her letter to the Contessa di Faraglione, hurriedly composed upon their return to Starling Cottage last night. He even believed it himself; but, as author of Elizabeth's downfall, he felt that he owed it to his victim to give her the benefit of such little doubt as still remained.

'We should not be too hasty,' was all that he could find to say.

Evie would have remonstrated with him further had she not caught sight of Major Benjy walking out towards Grebe with a parcel under his arm. The Major was feeling rather out of sorts, for Elizabeth had been in a frightful temper ever since Mr. Wyse had interfered, as she put it, with her painting. What he could not understand was why Elizabeth, her ancestry once more put in doubt by Mr. Wyse's revelations, had not produced the silver tray as evidence. The tray, with its name and spectacular crest, was just as good as the painting — as things had turned out, better — but Elizabeth had not mentioned it and, when he had tried to raise the subject, she had trodden on his foot. Whatever the matter was, he felt sure that the thoughtful gift he was taking home to her would cheer her up no end.

He had taken a rubbing of the crest on the tray — the de Map family crest — and ordered a year's supply of writing-paper with the crest at the top. This inspiration had come upon him out of the blue and the thought of his own kindness and cleverness warmed him inside almost as much as a whisky-and-soda would have done, had he had access to that desirable commodity. Elizabeth loved that sort of thing. All the way back to Grebe he tried to picture her face. She wasn't such a bad old soul, after all, and it was a husband's duty to perform these small acts of kindness.

Arriving at Grebe he went straight to his wife and asked her how she was feeling. Elizabeth did not reply. She had hardly stirred all morning, for images of the nightmare of the last evening had come upon her in a constant stream and her head still echoed with the mocking condolences of her friends. It had been Major Benjy who had first uttered the word 'forgery' and his foolish question, 'Now who would want to do a thing like that?', had been answered only by Evie's foolish squeaking and Susan's embarrassed chatter. She would not forgive him for that as long as she lived. As if all that had not been enough, there was a monstrous bill from Mr. Hopkins for lemon sole — at least double what she really owed him — which she would of course resist with the last fibre of her being, and if necessary take to the House of Lords. But there was another aspect of the bill that worried her, although she could not think what it was.

'Buck up, old girl,' said the Major, as he placed the parcel before her. 'Take a look at this. It'll cheer you up, you see if it doesn't.'

Dully, Elizabeth opened the parcel, which at first sight seemed to contain writing-paper with a gaudy crest on it.

'What's this?' she asked sourly.

'Writing-paper, Liz. With your family arms on it. I took a rubbing off that tray of yours.'

At first, Elizabeth thought this was some terrible practical joke. Then, as she stared at the crest, she recognised it as the embellishment on the tray — and as something more.

'That's not my crest,' she began to explain, but as she looked at it something seemed to connect in her brain and she scrabbled furiously for Mr. Hopkins's bill.

'The chap at the stationer's was most co-operative,' said the Major, blithely. 'He said there was no difficulty at all reproducing *that* particular crest. He made some joke about not knowing that we were setting up in the wet-fish business; I s'pose that's to do with the fish on the crest.'

'I'm not surprised,' snarled Elizabeth, 'it's the crest of the Rother Fishmongers' Association.' And she pointed, white with rage, to the letterhead of Mr. Hopkins's bill. There was the same crest, with the explanatory legend printed beneath it and the date of its foundation, 1770.

Thus it was that Diva, taking her favourite walk past Grebe, secure in the knowledge that she was unlikely to be waylaid, noticed an unusually thick column of smoke proceeding from the chimney.

'It's almost as if they were burning paper,' she said to herself. 'Well, they'd better be careful if they don't want to set the chimney on fire. Paddy! Leave that cat alone!'

12

When May came to Tilling, bringing with it new flowers and seasonal excitements, the inhabitants of the town seemed surprised to find that the year was still so young. Since Christmas there had been a quite extraordinary amount of activity in one way or another and Easter had slipped by almost unnoticed. There had been the Tapestry and then Monopoly; first Lucia and then Elizabeth had held a position almost akin to social dictatorship; then Lucia had ousted Elizabeth again, only to overreach herself with the business of the *County Life* article and to fall headlong into the shadows for nearly a month of exile. The precedent of that excommunication had cast a shadow over the town, for who could say, now that the weapon of total exclusion had, so to speak, been forged, on whose neck its blade might fall next? As a result everyone seemed to realise that we are put on this earth to love our neighbour, not to quarrel with him. Thus it was that Elizabeth's subsequent disasters had been treated almost mildly, as if such things as deceit and malice no longer mattered and could be lightly overlooked.

Now, with the first mellowing signs of summer to be seen, all those temporary furies were but as the memory of a dream. Peace had broken out and, although the atmosphere of stability and reconciliation that blossomed in the little town was scarcely mirrored in the world outside, the pace of life had slowed down to that of a pleasant Sunday afternoon stroll. With the return of the sun and the longer evenings, there no longer seemed to be the need for frenzied activity just to keep the elements at bay.

There were summer outfits to be planned, patterns and materials to be chosen, with all the care and effort that must attend such crucial decisions. It was also advisable to plan well in advance the celebrations that would attend the advent of the strawberry and those other seasonal delicacies that provide us with the framework of our summer life. There was the Produce Show to consider and the Summer Exhibition. Georgie had already chosen his subject for this — a view of the Norman Tower and the Gun Garden, with the river in the distance, all framed by the small arch. With such an ambitious project in mind, he rather feared that he had left himself too little time. The distractions of the season were countless and when Lucia deployed his long-neglected croquet-hoops on the lawn and thereby set off a minor craze for the game, he nearly cried out in despair; another afternoon a week, at the very least, must be sacrificed — as if he were not busy enough already.

Lucia, on the other hand, seemed to be having difficulty in filling up the extended hours of daylight, for she was, like the Athenians, forever searching after some new thing, rather as if she wished the hectic pace of the past few months to continue, or even increase. Above all, her mind had become set on the idea of reviving the Tilling Festival, to consist of a week or, better still, a fortnight of artistic activity and celebration. There would have to be, she insisted, at least two *premières* of important plays by promising young authors, two concerts (at least) by a leading orchestra, and although she felt that she had left it too late to commission any new works, she must not be so negligent in the future. Then there would be exhibitions by exciting contemporary artists, poetry recitals and a civic parade.

'The advantages to all the parties concerned are stupendous,' she said for the umpteenth time as she and Georgie played croquet together. 'The town, the artists, the nation as a whole stand to benefit from such a project.'

187

'Quite so,' said Georgie, knitting his brows. He had found that if you tapped the ball not in the centre but near the top, it rolled rather further and rather straighter than usual and didn't veer off quite so much to one side. But if you hit it in the wrong place, it hardly moved at all, or else went up in the air like one of Major Benjy's drives at golf.

'First, the advantages to the artists.' Lucia stooped to address her ball, talking all the while. 'They would have a unique forum — through that hoop there did you say? Thank you — for *premières* and previews. Critical and public attention would be focused upon them and they would not have to take their chances with the London reviewers. You object' — Georgie had done no such thing, but he let it pass — 'that we cannot afford to finance whole new productions by unknown playwrights — an agent's objection if I may say so, and indicative of the attitude that is strangling artistic progress in this country. Very well then, we will have readings, in costume or if necessary in plain evening-dress, like a concert performance, by the celebrated actors who are present to perform in the major productions brought down from London. They would be delighted, I am sure, to contribute a few hours of their precious time to such a worthy enterprise. Think of the benefits, Georgie. Suppose I had written a play — oh, is it my turn now? There! Straight through the darling little hoop — and I wanted someone to produce it for me —'

'That was very clever,' said Georgie bitterly. Lucia had pulled off a tremendously difficult shot and she had hardly looked at the ball. He got the impression that she was not interested in the game, and as a result was playing superbly. The voice continued, as jarring and irritating as the sound of a distant motor-cycle at a summer picnic.

'And then there are the advantages to the town,' buzzed the voice. 'As I intend to say to my Council, people would come from all over the country and perhaps from overseas as well. Oh, bad luck, Georgie, you usually have no trouble at all with that sort of stroke. That is why we must be sure to get lots of famous people, to make sure that lots of people come, to provide an audience for the new works we are assisting, if you see what I mean; the young, talented artists who have never been able to get a commercial production. The visitors would bring so much money to the town. . . .'

Georgie tried to shut out the voice and concentrate on his next shot, for he had already heard a great deal about the visitors and their money. Yet try as he might, he could not help but listen and his ball went straight into the leg of the hoop, nearly knocking it out of the ground.

'We've been over all this before, Lucia,' he said snappishly, 'and I think it's a splendid idea. But you must have a little rest now — you've been thinking about it for days and you'll tire yourself out.' He racked his brain for some snippet of Tilling news that might distract her from her theme, but could think of nothing. While he was silent, Lucia started speaking again.

'But I *am* resting, *Georgino*. What could be more relaxing than a quiet game of croquet? Now, the money that we get from the visitors — think of all the wonderful things we could do for the town with all that extra revenue! There are the drains, for example — simply falling to pieces, so they tell me, and in most urgent need of renovation. With this extra income we could repair them. Fancy that, Georgie! Art subsidising Sanitation.'

Georgie did not fancy it at all. Nor did he much like the situation he had got into with his last shot. Lucia, on the other hand was miles ahead, and although she seemed hardly to be looking at the ball, it skimmed through the hoops as if it were a performing animal. Soon the game was over and Lucia had won overwhelmingly.

'So glad we've had this little chat,' she said, as they collected up the balls. 'Since neither of us seems to have any major reservations about the ideas I have outlined to you, I think I might start writing my letters now.' She stopped, and a troubled look crossed her face. 'And yet I cannot help thinking that we have forgotten something, you know. It's as if we need some spearhead, some catalyst, a gentle push to set the ship off on its long voyage of adventure. Well, I must give it some more thought. Thank you so much for the game. I was terribly lucky, wasn't I?'

'Yes,' thought Georgie savagely. But he simply smiled and Lucia went into the house. Georgie, however, set the balls out once more and played a game against himself. As he thought, all the shots he had missed when he was playing against Lucia worked perfectly in her absence, even the trickiest ones which he rarely if ever attempted.

'Isn't that always the way?' he reflected morosely, and gathered up the balls once again.

Diva stood outside the draper's shop and tried frantically to come to some definite decision. It was not fair, she considered, that the *Ladies' Home Journal* should be so insistent on Marina blue this summer, when *Woman and Beauty* had so firmly declared that any other colours but orange and fawn would be unthinkable. As if that were not enough, whereas both of these august publications had stated unequivocally that navy and white court shoes were to be worn as long as the sun shone and the railways ran according to the summer schedules, *Woman's Journal* spoke unsettlingly of straps, while *Vogue* thundered Delphic riddles about lizard and buckskin. As a result, Diva was thoroughly confused and not a little angry. Government action, she felt, might be called for if some degree of concord could not be reached by voluntary agreement.

She resolved to leave the question to be decided by omens. If the next motor to pass her was going up the street, it would be Marina blue; if it was going down the street, *Woman and Beauty* would prevail, and orange and fawn would be preferred. Unfortunately, two motors came almost simultaneously from opposite directions and passed each other at her feet. The only possible conclusion to be drawn from that was that the Fates were mocking her and she resolved, impulsively, on Marina blue.

The sight of Elizabeth emerging from the shop shattered her resolution, for everything would depend on what Elizabeth had chosen. And should she follow Elizabeth's lead or try to be different?

'Good morning, dear,' said Elizabeth. 'Ah, the sun!'

Diva ignored these pleasantries.

'Which one have you chosen?' she demanded sternly.

'I'm sorry, dear?' asked Elizabeth, slightly puzzled.

'Orange and fawn or Marina blue? I can't make up my mind at all.'

Elizabeth had made her decision, but Diva was not to know what it was. Far better for her to be forced to make her own choice; it would be character-forming for her.

'I only popped in for some button-thread,' she therefore replied. 'Besides, it doesn't do to believe everything you read.'

With this devastating comment, she continued blithely on her way, leaving Diva a prey to all sorts of desperate worries. What did Elizabeth know that she did not? Had both alternatives been left behind by the remorseless progress of fashion? Pulling herself together with an effort, Diva resolved firmly to put the decision off for another day and buy some cream wool for a pullover. On *that* topic all the recognised authorities were agreed, and, although it was scarcely exciting, it was at least safe.

Evie Bartlett was the next to emerge. She seemed rather secretive, as well she might, for she was conspiring with draper and dressmaker to bring about a pongee tennis-coat that ought to have a devastating effect upon the other ladies of Tilling, scattering them in the imagination of their hearts.

'Good morning, Diva,' she said bravely, determined to sell her life before her secret.

'What did Elizabeth order?' demanded Diva anxiously. 'Did you manage to see?'

'Macclesfield silk,' said Evie reverently. 'I didn't gather which colours. The assistant said "What sort of silk, madam?" and Elizabeth said "Macclesfield" and then I think she saw me because she lowered her voice. But I think it's having to be ordered specially; I saw the assistant writing something down in a book.'

'That's stripes,' said Diva enviously. Why hadn't she thought of that?

To Irene, these matters were of purely academic interest, for she tended to buy her clothes from the ships' chandlers down by the harbour. Nevertheless, her interest in academic matters was sufficiently strong to cause her to pause for a moment in the doorway of the newsagent's shop and listen to this sartorial debate. Having satisfied herself on the salient points, she filled her pipe and strolled across to join Diva and Evie.

'What ho!' she exclaimed boisterously. 'Getting ready for the summer season, are we? Such a worry, isn't it? Should I wear my blue pea-jacket with my moleskin breeches, and, if so, would black or brown ammunition boots be appropriate?'

She struck a match and endeavoured to light her pipe; but, since clay pipes were being smoked short in the stem that year, she succeeded only in singeing the tip of her nose.

'Bother this dratted tobacco; I suppose they make it fire-proof in case the warehouse it's stored in burns down. For persons of generous build, I believe Vogue recommends tarpaulins, or, for summer wear, dust-sheets.'

This low sarcasm was all that could be expected from Irene, and so Diva was able to rise above it (for she had had plenty of practice over the years). There was still the serious problem of Elizabeth's Macclesfield silk to be considered. She gave a brief summary of her opinion on the subject to Evie and, when she looked round, Irene had disappeared. She had, in fact, slipped into the shop, where the draper, who knew her only by sight, asked her if there were anything he could do for her.

'Yes,' she said promptly. 'You know that Macclesfield silk that Mrs. Mapp-Flint ordered just now?'

'Ah, yes, madam. Grey and white stripes, I recall.'

'Well, she's changed her mind. Seen something in a magazine, I think. Anyway,' said Irene unblushingly, 'have you got any sateen in Marina blue?'

'Sateen,' said the draper with distaste, 'and in Marina blue. Well, that's something we don't usually stock, especially in what you might call fashion colours. It seems a funny thing to be making a frock out of. I could order some, but it would probably have to be specially dyed and that would make it expensive for what it is.'

'Splendid!' said Irene. 'How soon can you get it?'

The draper did a few calculations and said it would take about a week. Irene said that if that was as long as it took, that would have to do.

'Are you *sure* she said sateen?' persisted the draper, as she turned to go.

'Positive,' replied Irene. 'Goodbye.'

Counting on her fingers, she worked out that if the material were ready in a week and Elizabeth took it straight round to the dressmaker without opening it, ten days would elapse before she discovered what had happened. Say another week before the Macclesfield silk had arrived and been made up — then Elizabeth would be a fortnight behind everyone else with her summer outfit, which would make her absolutely furious. She smiled angelically, turned the bowl of her pipe at an angle to light it, and went demurely on her way.

Georgie had decided that his summer suit was to be a light-grey worsted, with a new plum-coloured waistcoat and dark-blue socks. He also had dreams of a single-breasted blazer and a straw boater. A quick glance at his financial situation dictated a choice between the boater and the waistcoat. After much indecision he decided that the waistcoat would be rather too daring and dismissed it from his mind. As he did so he reflected sadly on the missed opportunities that Fate offers us, to haunt the reflection of our later years, and it was in a sombre mood that he stepped into the hatter's to be measured. Perhaps it was this preoccupation that drove from his mind the important point that he had overlooked, for it was not until the hatter asked him what sort of ribbon he wanted round the boater that the concept of attaching such a ribbon occurred to him.

'Perhaps in your school colours, sir? Or your college?'

Georgie flushed and explained that he had been privately educated. Nor could he think of any club or society whose cause he espoused. When the hatter asked him which side he supported in the Boat Race, he said Cambridge, and so the hatter suggested light-blue. Georgie, relieved, agreed to this, and it was only when he was half-way back to Mallards that he remembered the dark-blue socks.

'How tar'some!' he exclaimed bitterly. 'They will have to be altered now.'

As he entered the house, however, he became aware of a strange atmosphere, as if some visitation or spiritual phenomenon had taken place there. He remembered what Lucia had said about the Black Spaniard, about the aura left behind by momentous events, and deduced that something had been going on while he was out.

'Good morning, Georgino,' said his wife. 'Been shopping?'

'I've been planning my summer wardrobe,' he replied. 'But it's no use your trying to find out what it's going to be. It's a surprise.'

'Whatever you've chosen will, I'm sure, be absolutely right,' replied Lucia absently. She seemed rather preoccupied with something and it was a little humiliating to have no interest taken in his summer clothes. Perhaps she was sulking because he had shown no interest in her wretched festival that morning; but the preoccupation suggested something else. Georgie sat down and took up his embroidery — the long-forgotten hassocks for the Church. After a while, he asked carelessly:

'Any news?'

'As a matter of fact,' Lucia drawled, 'there was something.' Her façade of relaxed indifference crumbled quite suddenly and her voice became quick and excited. 'Guess what! Queen Mary wants to visit Tilling!'

'No!' gasped Georgie. 'How exciting!'

'It's true. And she's coming very soon, and it was just a whim of hers. Do you remember that superior-looking woman who came and peered at our curtains and rang the bell and asked about them?'

'The one whose dog thought Susan Wyse was a bear?' hazarded Georgie.

'The very same. Well, she was none other than Lady Jane Hall, who is, as you know, an old friend of Her Majesty and one of her Ladies in Waiting. She happened to be staying in Tilling —'

'How do you know all this?' interrupted Georgie.

'A letter. Anyway, she was staying in Tilling on her way to somewhere and she liked it so much that she told the Queen, and Her Majesty liked the sound of it and now she wants to come here herself. Now, what do you think of that?'

'Let me see the letter,' demanded Georgie, rather in the manner of the disciple also named Didymus.

So Georgie read the letter and believed, and gave it back to Lucia.

'Well,' he said, 'I suppose it is reasonable enough. After all, Tilling is Tilling, and if she hasn't seen it before. . . .'

A great wave of pity washed over his heart, as it always did when he thought of the millions of people who did not live in Tilling, and of those even more unfortunate, of whom there must be hundreds of thousands, who had never even seen it. He shook his head sadly, for there is such hardship in the world, and then asked Lucia if she thought Lady Jane had mentioned their curtains to the Queen.

'Certainly, dear,' replied Lucia. 'Lady Jane was most specific on that point. Her Majesty, you will remember, is President of the Needlewomen's Guild, and so she has a special interest in such things. Anyway, we must start right away, for there are a hundred and one things to be done before the town is ready for the visit.'

Suddenly Georgie realised what this meant. Lucia, as Mayor of Tilling, would meet Her Majesty at the station, with a brass band and the rest of the Corporation, and drive with her all round the town pointing out objects of interest. Perhaps the Queen might even take tea at Mallards (glorious prospect!). If the weather continued fine and the sun warm, they might have their tea in the garden — perhaps even in the *giardino segreto*. Georgie scarcely dared to voice these hopes, but Lucia was less superstitious.

'After the reception and the tour,' she said, 'I feel sure that Her Majesty might be prevailed upon to take tea with us here — in the garden if the weather is fine. I have been thinking for some time of renaming the *giardino segreto* Queen Mary's Garden; it must have been an omen —'

'Goodness,' said Georgie suddenly, 'I've just ordered my summer suit. Boring light-grey worsted. I can't wear that in front of Her Majesty. How long before the visit?'

'Just over a week,' replied Lucia. 'Plenty of time to get another suit made up.'

'But what can I wear?' Georgie wailed. 'I can't think of anything at all. Oh, how terrible!'

'Cream barathea and crocodile shoes,' said Lucia serenely, for she had anticipated this difficulty. 'And you shall have it as your birthday present from me. Now don't you worry; I telephoned the tailor while you were out and he has exactly the right material in stock and he's sure he can do it in time because he's got your measurements already. I, of course, will be wearing my Mayoral robes. . . .'

But Georgie had gone. With a quick 'Bless you!', he had leapt to his feet and run hatless down the street to the tailor's shop to give him, immediately, the design for this wonderful apparel. But when he got there the shop was closed for lunch. He was tempted to wait until it reopened, but that would not be until two-o'clock. On the way back to Mallards he met Elizabeth and was on the point of telling her the news when it occurred to him that Lucia might not want the visit announced just yet, so he said nothing, but simply waved his hand.

'They were shut,' he told Lucia on his return. 'What are we going to tell everyone?'

'Everything, of course. There is no need of secrecy, and, besides, we shall all have to pull together if the town is to be presentable in time.'

Grosvenor announced that lunch was ready and, although she presented them with the first asparagus of the season, they heeded it not. Lunch was quickly eaten and then the planning began.

The Tilling Brass Band must be engaged and Lucia said that she had better supervise their rehearsals herself. Elgar's Pomp and Circumstance would follow God Save the Queen as the Queen arrived, and a selection from *The Yeomen of the Guard* (Lucia's lip curled as she spoke the words, for she detested Sullivan) to see her on her way; such simple, reliable music ought not to be beyond even the rude mechanicals of Tilling. Then the police must be organised to prevent the crowds from pressing too close in their enthusiasm; Lucia decided that she had better see the Inspector personally, for there must be no mistake. Then there was the cleaning of the streets and the closing of the necessary roads — could she leave all that to the Town Clerk, or must she see to that herself? On balance, better to do it herself, to ensure that it was done properly. Also she must take personal charge of the decorations. Then there was the problem of selecting a suitable child to present the Queen with a bouquet of flowers; there was the risk that if the task were left to fellow School Governors, they might be swayed by affection for their own offspring, with the result that one of them would be chosen regardless of suitability. Therefore, it was best that she exercised her own powers, as Chairman of the Governors of the school, to make the choice herself. The flowers would, of course, have to be supplied by the Parks Department, and the head gardener, for all his skill in growing flowers, had quite appalling taste, so it rather looked as if she must do that too. Finally, the Mayoral motor was handsome enough, to be sure, but the upholstery was a trifle worn in places, for it seemed extravagant to spend public money on refurbishing it when only Lucia herself saw it. Now, as it happened, she had a vehicle of the same make, only rather more modern, that might be pressed into service instead; and Cadman was a far better driver than the official chauffeur, who was also caretaker of the Town Hall and who tended to brake violently when anything, however distant, crossed his path.

Lucia consulted the list that she had drawn up and noted with apparent surprise that she would have to do everything herself. But that, she said, was what being a public servant meant.

The first and greatest task would be to draw up an itinerary. There was so much to see: the Landgate, the Norman Tower, the Museum, the Church . . . how could so much be fitted into an afternoon? She felt sorely tempted, she said, to leave it to someone else. But there was, as the saying went, only one woman's hand on the lonely plough, and so she sent out for town maps, red pencils and rulers and set about calculating the best possible route.

'And what can I do?' asked Georgie hopefully.

'Why, tell everyone, of course.'

This was exactly what he wanted her to say, for to be first with news of this sort was a great privilege. But first, before doing anything else, he ordered his cream barathea suit.

13

Georgie's announcement caused a minor panic, for it was obvious that outfits that had been ordered for the summer would be far too plain for a Royal visit. It was the civic duty of each citizen to look respectable, for what would the Queen think if she only saw dowdy, depressed-looking women in the streets of the town? She might get the impression that Tilling was a miserable place, and that would never do.

So there was a great changing of orders and insisting upon rare and exotic colours and fabrics, and the draper began to fear for his sanity. Where orange had previously sufficed, there must now be tangerine; mere fawn was no longer acceptable, *café au lait* was the only conceivable shade. Mrs. Bartlett, who had before wanted plain blue poplin, now insisted upon navy *foulard* with a small spot, and Mrs. Plaistow's urgent request for tea-rose georgette quite spoilt his afternoon. However, he was a conscientious man and all these extraordinary stuffs were obtained and supplied. Yet from the one person he had expected to change her mind, Mrs. Mapp-Flint, he heard nothing at all, which worried him intensely.

Lucia, meanwhile, seemed to have been transformed into a small hurricane, so quickly and furiously did she sweep about the town. Georgie saw her rarely between breakfast and dinner, and then it was only to be quizzed about the whereabouts of this or that sheaf of papers that had mysteriously vanished, or to hear some unintelligible complaint against the stupidity and stubbornness of some minor functionary. When she returned, exhausted but still talking, in the evening, she would recite an epic of the day's complaints, for which Georgie was made to feel in some inexplicable way vaguely responsible. When he asked if there were anything he could do to help, Lucia would reply that only she could hope to bring any sort of order to the chaos that was Tilling (for, according to what Lucia had to say, there was open Bolshevism afoot, especially among the staff of the Parks Department) and that she would be perfectly capable of achieving this aim if only people were not so difficult. Georgie, who had found people difficult all his life, could sympathize with this, but he rather resented being implicitly counted as one of them. When their joyless meals were concluded in the evening, he would often go straight to bed, bewildered and bad-tempered, while Lucia worked on late into the night, surrounded by charts, routes, diagrams, proposed schedules and sketch-maps of the sort usually appended to histories of military campaigns.

The barathea suit helped Georgie to console himself during this hectic period, for it had to be fitted several times. Just when it seemed almost complete, inspiration came to him in a dream and he insisted on a third button for the jacket. The eloquence and passion with which he argued his case made him feel quite magnificent afterwards, especially since he had heard those words he had never expected to hear from a tailor, 'Perhaps you are right, sir. I never thought of it like that.' But the news that Mr. Wyse had commissioned a black frock-coat and a new top hat gave him several sleepless nights. Would it not, after all, have been better to have insisted upon absolute formality? Suppose the Queen thought he was not taking her visit seriously, and that he had turned out in the first suit that had come to hand? But a careful study of the Society papers reassured him that no possible exception could be taken to his choice of costume, and that Mr. Wyse would, if anything, be a trifle overdressed. It was, however, too late to warn him, and impossible to let him know without breaking the confidentiality of the fitting-room. As to his other competitors in the field of male elegance, Georgie felt secure from challenge. The Padre would be bound to wear his clerical weeds and Major Benjy, having been dissuaded by his wife from resurrecting his old uniform, was sulking and had declared that his Sunday suit was good enough for the House of God and therefore must be good enough for the Queen of England.

Even more important than costume was actual location. There was no point in being dressed well if the Tillingites were in the wrong place, unable to see or to be seen. Georgie was unable to tell them what the proposed itinerary was to be; he tried to explain that even Lucia did not know yet, for the tangle of papers on her desk was now totally impenetrable and she was talking of starting again from scratch. Nobody believed him, however, and he was suspected of concealing the truth for dark reasons of his own.

In order to find out the truth, Elizabeth suggested that a watch be kept on Lucia's movements, and pickets and observers were duly posted about the town to see where she went. The Padre at once began an investigation of the lead on the top of the church tower, although why he needed binoculars to examine what was under his feet was a mystery. Evie spent a lot of time in the stationer's, debating what shade of writing-paper she wanted and frequently darting out into the street to examine the colours by daylight. Diva spent a whole morning in the queue at the post-office, for she always seemed to lose her place whenever she got to the front, so busy was she, craning her neck to see what was going on in the street. A comparison of notes and sharing of information gleaned from other sources enabled the Watch Committee (as someone frivolously called the group) to work out a probable itinerary; but, since there was no way of knowing in which order the various places of interest would be visited, all this patient reconnaissance seemed to have been in vain.

As usual, when a great deal of effort is expended with no tangible results, resentment began to manifest itself and a scapegoat was sought. Lucia, being in charge of all the arrangements, was the likeliest candidate for this unappealing part, and the fact that she never stopped in her frantic movements to wish them good-morning or release any snippet of useful information fuelled the flames of ill-feeling that flickered around the tea-cups and Bridge-tables of Tilling.

'She's deliberately keeping out of our way,' said Elizabeth, speaking not for herself alone. 'She wants the Queen all to herself, and no one else is to be allowed even a sight of her. Why, I wouldn't be surprised if the visit took place at dead of night and Queen Mary was shown round by the light of a lantern.'

'She can't very well invite us all to take tea with Her Majesty,' said Georgie, forgetting that his place at the Royal tea-table was assured.

'Well, you will certainly meet her,' said Evie, 'because you are Lucia's prince consort, or whatever she calls you. It's us who will be kept out.'

Mr. Wyse, as a member of an old and distinguished family, and Susan, who was an M.B.E., felt very strongly about this subject, and, although Mr. Wyse at least did not allow his displeasure to manifest itself in any way, his silence was sufficient to encourage Elizabeth to develop her theme.

'The least she could do,' she said, pouring milk into her cup, 'would be to tell us the route by which the Royal party is to travel. How else can we ensure that Her Majesty gets a friendly and patriotic welcome? It won't look very well if the streets are all deserted. Very apathetic we will seem and Her Majesty will say "Very well, I shan't visit Tilling again, if that's how they feel." '

'Lucia has been very busy, you know,' Georgie started to say, but the atmosphere of cold hostility that greeted his words caused him to fall silent. In addition he felt slightly guilty that he, who was in no respect remarkable or outstanding, should be assured of an audience

202

when everyone else was excluded. As a result, his privileged position seemed to lose its charm for him, and he even toyed with the idea of being indisposed on the day of the visit. But that would seem rude, so he gave it up. Nevertheless, it was with a heavy heart that he returned to Mallards and to the fusillade of complaints about the head gardener that constituted his welcome.

'My request for snowdrops and violets — for simple charm is, as you know, to be the keynote of the proceedings — was met with plain rudeness,' she said. 'Instead, I was offered daffodils and narcissi — just think of it, Georgie — and bright yellow tulips. Yellow, mind you, not red, which I believe the Queen admires. We might as well offer Her Majesty a bunch of carrots and brassica.'

'It is a little late for snowdrops,' said Georgie diffidently, but Lucia swept his words away as a liner might sweep away a fishing-boat.

'And then I find that the child I had selected to present the bouquet — the only one who would possibly do — has been allowed to catch mumps and is confined to bed. Why the authorities thought fit to ignore my suggestion that the child be kept out of school, and thus away from the risk of infection, until after the visit, I cannot hope to understand. It is almost as though someone were trying to sabotage my plans.'

Georgie did not not even try to reply to this. Instead he sat back in his chair and attempted to think of pleasant things, such as picnics by a river or walks in a formal garden. Sadly the river-banks and flower-beds of his imagining were lined with daffodils and narcissi and staringly yellow tulips, so he gave it up. All through dinner the tirade continued, so that he got indigestion; and, when in a lull in the narrative, he meekly suggested a piano duet to soothe away the tribulations of the day (Lucia's own favourite specific for troubled minds) he was briskly informed that there was no time for such indulgence, and went early to bed.

'I hope it rains,' he said bitterly, and switched off the light.

Alone of the ladies of Tilling, Elizabeth took no thought for the morrow, what she might wear. She knew that, even as she sat and sipped tea at Grebe, a measured quantity of the finest silk was being rushed from Macclesfield to clothe her. Secure in this knowledge she evaded with skilful and infuriating guile all attempts to wheedle from her details of her costume. Let them guess as much as they liked, she would outshine them all. Her only concern was lest she should outshine Her Majesty, but that was improbable. True, the material she had requested seemed to have been a long time in coming; but she had been promised it for Thursday. Thursday had come, and there would be plenty of time to have the dress made up. The pattern she had chosen was one that would display the silk to its best advantage and the dressmaker had promised to hold herself in readiness for its delivery. So Elizabeth walked into town and collected her parcel.

'Good morning,' she carolled as she entered the shop, then noticed to her irritation that Evie was lurking in a corner, feigning interest in some purple ribbon. So she lowered her voice and asked if her order were ready, taking care not to mention the type of material, for Evie's ears were sharp.

'Yes, Mrs. Mapp-Flint, your order arrived this morning. That'll be nine shillings and elevenpence altogether.'

This struck Elizabeth as decidedly cheap for the very finest Macclesfield silk, but her upbringing and her natural frugality had instilled in her the importance of never acknowledging a bargain.

'Dear me,' she therefore said, 'what a price things are these days.'

To her surprise the draper agreed with her and for a moment she felt unaccountably suspicious. But Evie had moved up towards the counter and was nonchalantly inspecting a card of buttons, so instead of opening the parcel and having a look at the contents, she thanked the draper and took the parcel straight to the dressmaker. There she found Diva, fussing endlessly about her tea-rose georgette, so she thrust the package into the dress-maker's arms, giving her a terrible look to ensure secrecy, wished Diva good-morning and hurried on her way. She spent the rest of the morning engaged in casual shopping, welcoming now the desperate attempts of her friends to wheedle her secret from her and leaving them with a fine selection of erroneous impressions.

This pleasant occupation filled up the time until lunch, and she returned home with a light and happy step, to find Major Benjy engaged in a fearsome argument with Withers. The accusation was that Withers had burnt a hole in the trouser-leg of his second-best suit, to which Withers replied austerely that it was not a flat-iron but the terror that flies by night which had done the damage, damage that would not have occurred had her request to be allowed to put the Major's garments into mothballs been granted. Elizabeth resolved this bitter dispute with Solomon-like diplomacy, accepting that the damage had been done by moth, and scolding Withers for not putting the clothes into mothballs on her own initiative. This seemed to satisfy both parties, to some extent at least, and tranquillity was restored. Having obtained silence, Elizabeth sat down to think about the forthcoming event and plan what her rôle in it might be. Ought she to ignore the whole affair, as being devalued by Lucia's com-mandeering of the Royal party and the entire occasion; or ought she to follow each step with diligent attention, the better to be able to offer constructive advice and criticism after the visit was over? As Mayoress she had a duty to perform the latter function, yet Lucia had not yet seen fit even to request her presence, which was an insult not only to her but to the office she held and to the people of Tilling, whom, in some nebulous way, she represented. This fierce internal debate was interrupted by the distant clamour of the telephone, and after a short while Withers, still sullen after her rebuke, came to inform her that Mrs. Pillson was on the line and would like to speak to her.

'Elizabeth, dear!' Lucia's voice, unmistakable even across the vast expanse of cable. 'So glad I managed to catch you at last. I've been ringing all day. You dear thing, how elusive you are!'

Elizabeth drew in her breath to rebut this charge of flightiness, but the delay proved fatal. Lucia continued. Lucia, it seemed, never needed to stop for breath.

'Could you possibly spare me a minute this afternoon — just to discuss your official rôle as Mayoress in the Royal Visit. I'm sorry it's such short notice, but you can have no idea how terribly busy I have been, and every time I manage to find five minutes to telephone you, Withers says you are out! Oh dear!' and a wistful sigh floated through the receiver. 'Everything seems to be happening at once. Anyway, could you be especially kind to poor tired me and spare half-an-hour at — let me see' — pages, beyond doubt those of an engagement-book, rustled at the other end — 'ah yes — twenty-past three? Cadman will call for you in the motor.'

The voice fell silent just long enough to allow Elizabeth to say 'Yes', and then bade her farewell and was replaced by the dialling tone. As Elizabeth put the instrument down, she was reminded of an unfortunate lady in mythology who was for ever being pursued by a persistent, buzzing gadfly. Lucia's telephone manner made Elizabeth sympathize with that poor sufferer. She ate her lunch with a troubled heart, pondering the new difficulties that had arisen. She could not refuse to co-operate, for her office demanded that she render all possible assistance to the Mayor in her official capacity. But she foresaw only too clearly that her part in the pro-ceedings would be that of a subordinate, a mere instru-ment of ceremony, like the mace or the chain of office. Furthermore, by taking part in Lucia's self-glorifying production, she would risk being identified with it, and the disdain which she had carefully fostered in the town would fall on her as much as on the true author of the proceedings, Lucia. She could not hope to have any say in the organisation of the event, or to alter its structure in any degree. She would probably not even be told what the intinerary was. On the other hand, she would almost certainly be allowed to join the Royal tea party, and that was a great consolation.

As a result of these speculations she arrived at Mallards determined to play a purely honorary part in the proceedings; modesty, she would insist, forbade her seeking any of the limelight.

'But Elizabeth, *carissima*,' cried Lucia in apparent consternation, 'think of your official *rôle*, your position as Mayoress! You represent the women of Tilling. I shall need you at my side throughout the day. This is no time for self-effacement. The ceremonial traditions of the town demand your presence — more, your active involvement.'

'Too kind of you, Lucia,' replied Elizabeth, rather startled, 'but I am so unused to mixing in such society. Why, I should be tongue-tied and unable to speak. It would be far better if you, who have had so much practice . . . all those duchesses and princesses we have heard about so often.'

But Lucia was set on her purpose. If anything were to go wrong with the Visit, she wanted Elizabeth to be involved as deeply as herself, so that the blame might be shared equally. On the other hand, she could not bear the thought of Elizabeth taking the credit for a single particle of the hard work that she, and she alone, had put into this affair.

'Just by being there,' she said, 'you will be performing the essential function that I have described to you. Look at it from my point of view, dear. Think how I would feel,' and as she spoke a brilliant thought came to her, 'if everyone were to say that just because I have had to do so much of the work myself, I had taken no account of popular feelings about the Visit. People might say that I had deliberately kept them out and told them nothing, just to keep the glory for myself!'

'Perish the thought!' said Elizabeth.

'Not everyone is as sensible as you, Elizabeth dear, which is why I want you to be my eyes and ears in the town, right up to the day of the Visit. Tell me what people are saying and thinking, what they would like to see, and so on. Then I can consider all reasonable suggestions, reject the obviously impracticable and incorporate such as are feasible into our programme. And you could do something else for me, if you would; you can tell everyone how things are going — what progress we are making with the itinerary and so on. So that when people come up to me and ask questions, I won't have to stay and answer, I can just say "Ask the Mayoress, she will tell you." Now you *will* do that for me, won't you?'

This was clearly a move of diabolical cunning on Lucia's part. Not only would the blame for Lucia's secrecy be shifted entirely on to the shoulders of her spokeswoman, but Elizabeth, as liaison between Town Hall and High Street, would be personally responsible for every discarded suggestion and rejected innovation, blamed by everyone for the dismissal of their contributions. She would be directly implicated in any failure, but unable to claim any credit for a success. She had, in short, been caught in a trap. Once her reluctant agreement had been elicited, she was dismissed from the Presence and sent back to Grebe, with instructions to report at eleven-o'clock sharp the next morning to be thoroughly briefed. The only thing she still had to look forward to was the Macclesfield silk. Apart from that, the future was bleak indeed.

Just as she had feared there was no shortage of idiotic suggestions from the general public for Elizabeth to convey to Lucia, none of which Lucia found herself able to accept. The Padre, for instance, had the idea of a pipe-and-drum band to accompany the Queen throughout the town. Elizabeth had reported this and Lucia had explained patiently to her the difficulties that made the suggestion impossible (which Elizabeth already knew): that there was not one single bagpiper in the town and precious few drummers; that it seemed strange (to say the least) that Tilling, as far from Scotland as it is possible to be on the British mainland, should affect a Caledonian air for the Visit. Yet, when Elizabeth reported to the Padre that his suggestion had been rejected, he grew quite angry, not with Lucia, who had originally called for suggestions and thus was obviously open-minded, but with Elizabeth, whom he suspected of presenting his case ineffectually.

With this terrible burden on her back, Elizabeth went for her first fitting. The pattern had been a complicated one and there was little time — today was Friday, the Visit was on Monday, the dressmaker would have to work all weekend to complete it. Furthermore, the poor woman was so busy with work for the other ladies of Tilling that she was having trouble fitting them all in.

'Let me see,' said Elizabeth greedily as the dressmaker brought out the creation. She was glad to see that the worthy woman had gone to the trouble of protecting the dress with a rayon cover. But when she tried to remove the cover, she found to her horror that there was nothing beneath.

'Is that what you will be wearing on Monday, if you don't mind my asking?' said the dressmaker in a rather strange tone of voice. 'I must say, I can't keep up with these modern fashions.'

'Where's my dress?' demanded Elizabeth hoarsely.

'That is your dress, madam.'

'It can't be,' gasped Elizabeth. 'What on earth is it made of?'

'Sateen, madam. Exactly as you gave it me.'

Had she recalled them, Elizabeth would have echoed Macbeth's words to his guests, 'Which of you hath done this?' As it was, she bolted through the door and dashed along the High Street to the draper's shop. There she extracted the entire history of the sateen and Irene's devilish deception. The draper, who was a sympathetic man, listened patiently to her eloquent denunciation of Irene, Fate and the World, which, for anyone who savoured the effusions of the Tragic Muse, were well worth hearing, and then informed her that it would be quite impossible to obtain Macclesfield silk before Monday. He also reminded Elizabeth that she had not yet paid for the sateen and asked whether it should be put on her account.

This final, unspeakable blow caused Elizabeth to hurl the dress (which was still in her hand) across the counter, cry in a fearful voice, 'Charge it to Miss Coles's account!', and surge forth into the High Street.

Since Irene had no account at the draper's the bill remained unpaid for some time until that worthy man put it on Elizabeth's account as 'Sundries' and was finally paid.

14

All human beings have at least one talent, and Irene
Coles had several. She was a gifted painter (although
she tended to treat this gift as a child treats an expensive present that it does not really care for); she had a
quite remarkable gift of mimicry which she used to persecute those of her fellow creatures who roused her
displeasure; these blessings Nature had bestowed upon
her. Such gifts should have been enough for anyone, and
there were those who would have said that she did not
deserve any of them. But the Creator had bestowed upon
her one other facility, greater than any of these, which
she exploited to the best of her ability. Just as the
offspring of the rich and powerful are said to be born
with a silver spoon in their mouths, so Irene had come
into the world with the apple of Discord gripped in her
hand. In other words, she had the rare ability to irritate
people at will. This talent she had recognised at an early
age, and she had devoted her life to it.

In the pursuit of her vocation, she managed to make
herself extremely unpopular by her quite outrageous
behaviour. It was an open secret that she was a Socialist
and an admirer of Russian Communism (although before
that she had been fiercely pro-German). Her atheism,
for which she called upon God to forgive her, was a
constant thorn in the Padre's ample flesh. In her life in
Art, her object seemed always to offend; in her relation-
ships with her fellow-creatures, therefore, she could not
in all conscience spare any of them, whatever her personal feelings, without betraying her Calling. To this

rule she made only one exception, namely Lucia. Within hours of Lucia's first arrival in Tilling, Irene had adopted her as her personal goddess, so that, whatever Lucia might do or say, Irene would usually find some way of admiring it, at whatever expense to her own integrity. Her warlike nature longed for conflict, and in order to gratify this desire she was prepared to strike the most extraordinary attitudes, to deny what was obviously true and to assert what was patently false.

Under any other circumstances, therefore, she would have awoken on the morning of the Royal Visit with the express purpose of doing something to demonstrate an unreasoning Republicanism. But since Lucia had, so to speak, taken the whole affair under her wing, Irene was powerless to act. With a wistful sigh, she left unmade the banner that she had dreamt of, left her dinner bell, the faithful companion of her worst excesses, on the mantelpiece, and sat down, with the blinds drawn, to start work on a secret anti-Monarchist cartoon.

Thus it was that she missed the last frantic preparations for the Queen's arrival, and did not see the Royal Train pulling into the station or any of what followed. But curiosity is the bane of all resolutions, and she found it hard to sleep that night for wondering how Lucia had fared. So, when Tuesday dawned and the weary hours before marketing time had slipped away, she put on her reefer-jacket and a woollen hat and hurried from Taormina to find out what had happened.

The people of Tilling, had they been asked at any other time, would have said that, by and large, they had little use for Irene Coles. But on that particular day, she had a vital rôle to perform as a listener, for she was the only person in the town who had not witnessed the events of the preceding day, and to her alone could the whole story be told. Since the only point of things happening was that those who observed these things could tell other people about them, there was a great demand for an audience, and by the time Irene got back to her house, she had heard the tale from every conceivable source

212

(sometimes from two or three sources at once; surely the stuff of an historian's dream) and her thirst for knowledge had been satisfied.

She had heard how the train had been held up for five minutes by a fallen branch on the line, and how the Town Band had stood playing Elgar until they were out of breath; how the child that Lucia had chosen to replace the victim of mumps had thrust her bouquet into the Royal hand and immediately burst into tears, which Her Majesty found rather touching; how Lucia had, the night before, sent everyone handwritten notes with a suggestion as to where they might stand in order to get a good view of the Queen, and how, as soon as the Queen arrived, she had given Lucia a list of the things she wanted to see, none of which appeared on Lucia's own carefully compiled itinerary; how the Queen had apologised most graciously for this sudden change of plan and how (this was said most grudgingly) Lucia had coped splendidly.

Irene heard that, instead of the Norman Tower and the Landgate, Her Majesty had wanted to visit one house whose conservatory contained an unusual variety of orchid, and another whose owner (that wretched stockbroker in Church Square again) possessed a small but quite unique collection of Chinese jade, which the Padre, the only member of the community to have seen it, had said looked like a collection of bars of soap, but which the Queen had admired enormously. Into Irene's ears was poured the whole tale of the Queen's tea at Mallards; how Elizabeth had appeared wearing, not the Macclesfield silk that Diva and Evie had promised, but last year's brown marocain, as antiquated and obsolete as a wheel-lock musket on a modern battlefield; how, at the last moment, Lucia's best silver tea-pot had mysteriously vanished and all that could be found was a brown earthenware vessel, belonging to Foljambe; and how the Queen had smiled when she saw it and declared that it was the image of the one she used herself to pour her husband's breakfast tea. All this Irene heard, and thereat she rejoiced. But the part of the day's events that everyone was most keen to tell her about, that part which inspired the greatest eloquence, was not quite so pleasant to listen to, and the way in which it was described, not by only one or two, but by all her sources, left Irene in no doubt what the outcome was likely to be.

'Oh golly,' she said, as she let herself into Taormina, 'she's done it this time.'

What she had heard was this. When tea was finished and Lucia's motor stood outside the open door of Mallards to take the Queen to the station, the eager spectators gathered outside had seen Her Majesty emerge into the hall (she had been in the garden-room before, so rumour had it) and one step behind her, chattering away as endlessly as, according to Elizabeth, she had chattered throughout tea, was Lucia. Although the crowd outside could not make out what was said inside the hall, it seemed likely they were talking about the Tapestry curtains, for, as they spoke, Foljambe and Grosvenor appeared in the garden-room window, unhooking the curtains, with Georgie and Elizabeth directing the operations and getting under their feet. Once the Queen and her hostess were through the door and on the step, however, the spectators could hear every word that was said. To their horror they heard Lucia imply that the curtains, which she was proposing to give to the Queen as President of the Needlewomen's Guild, had been designed and executed by herself. One phrase in particular which condemned her, the one phrase which was heard and confirmed by all those present, was 'a poor, poor thing, ma'am, but mine own', which Susan Wyse had thought was a quotation, but which everyone else had said was typical Lucia, in her most pompous vein.

The next minute, Georgie, with Elizabeth at his heels, had appeared with the curtains neatly folded in his arms, and an attendant had taken them from him. Lucia had then dropped a deep curtsey (she must have been practising) and the Royal party had departed for the station, leaving behind a buzz of furious and resentful chatter. In short, Lucia had claimed for herself all the credit for the wretched curtains, which the women (and men) of Tilling had laboured so long and so hard to create. It was monstrous, unforgivable, impossible.

Of the rest of the Visit there was little to say; but about Lucia's crime, her unspeakable, unpardonable offence, there was a great deal to say, and the people of Tilling went on saying it. This was no matter to be dealt with by merely ignoring Lucia's existence, for they knew, from recent experience, that excommunication simply gave Lucia a chance to catch up on her reading. Harsh words needed to be said, and their only fear was that Lucia might hide in Mallards and not come out to hear them. Yet such was her extraordinary effrontery that she appeared that very evening at the dinner party at Starling Cottage that should have been a celebration of the Visit. She had arrived in the middle of a Declaration of War against herself, and had seemed quite surprised and upset at the accusations flung at her. Things had been said, voices raised, and Lucia had gone home without any dinner. She had also gone without Georgie, for he, who had with his own hands embroidered the largest part of those fatal curtains, when he heard what Lucia had said while he was still in the garden-room supervising their removal, was as furious as anyone. Indeed, it was behind Georgie's banner that the Great Revolt started; for a man who had taken tea with and offered sponge-fingers to the Queen of England cannot be lightly crushed beneath the heel of a thoughtless, arrogant woman.

It was as if the world of Tilling had suddenly been blown apart, and the quarrel over *County Life* seemed like a friendly dispute over Bridge by comparison.

When Georgie returned to Mallards after dinner at Starling Cottage Lucia had already gone to bed, leaving behind her on the hall-table a savagely worded note in which occurred phrases like 'extraordinary behaviour', 'entirely unwarranted conclusions' and 'extreme ingratitude', some of which referred to Georgie and some to other people, and from which Georgie, as he read it, gathered that she intended to leave for Riseholme in the morning to stay at the Ambermere Arms for an indefinite period, as she needed a complete rest from her exertions (there followed a vituperative passage about the pointlessness of ever doing anything for anybody) and a change of surroundings.

Having read this horrible epistle, Georgie crumpled it into a ball, then spread it out again and re-read it. There was no mistaking what Lucia meant: she was washing her hands of Tilling and considering a return to her former realm.

Strangely enough, Georgie slept soundly that night. Next day, while the High Street was humming with excited talk, he sat in the *giardino segreto* (or Queen Mary's Garden) and tried to think things out. Lucia had left before he had woken, taking with her Grosvenor and all her piano music. Another note, cold to the point of formality, had awaited him, requesting him to forward any letters and not to contact her unnecessarily, for fear that her rest-cure might be interrupted and thus deprived of its value. Her primary reason for choosing Riseholme was obvious, and he felt a strong wave of sympathy for Daisy Quantock, on whom Lucia would, indirectly, vent her wrath. But there was a sinister undertone to both letters; almost as if Lucia were considering quitting Tilling for good and going back permanently to Riseholme, where she had never been seriously challenged and where she could be confident of resuming unopposed supremacy. God help Riseholme if she did return; years of fighting with Elizabeth had so sharpened her teeth and claws that they would never be able to withstand her.

The possibility of Lucia's never coming back filled Georgie with horror; what would become of him? Suppose she sold Mallards and bought back The Hurst from Adele Brixton? He would either have to follow her, leaving the pleasant life to which he had become attached, or live in a state of separation from his wife in Tilling. Now that his anger had cooled a little he realised that the latter course would be unthinkable; yet so deep was the wound in his soul that he would rather be rid of Lucia altogether than allow that deed of hers to be forgiven and forgotten as if it were no more than a revoke at Bridge. Her lie about the curtains was bad enough, but that could be pardoned. What he could not let pass was her storming off to Worcestershire and the two hideous notes she had written him. Of course, it might not be entirely his own choice. He had never seen Lucia as angry as she had been the previous evening; all her self-control had melted, like chocolate on a biscuit, and she had become shrill and unpleasant. Whether this new Lucia would replace the old one, or whether the metamorphosis was purely temporary he did not know; neither could he judge how deeply Lucia was offended with him. For all he knew she might not want to see him ever again.

He tried to think of all the things that would continue to make his life worthwhile without Lucia: his *bibelots*, his furniture, his embroidery, tea parties, his cape with the fur collar. All of these would be as hollow as an egg from which the yolk has been sucked without Lucia to discuss them with or show them to. There was only one thing, or rather one person, who could brighten life without Lucia, and she was far away, he could not say where. He tried to think of her, but the thought would not form in his mind; like a suspicious animal that one tries to attract by the offer of some small delicacy, it came close, took fright and disappeared, and he could not apprehend it.

As he sat among his abandoned croquet-hoops, Foljambe drew near and announced that there was a telephone call for him. Wearily he rose to his feet and trailed into the telephone-room, where Lucia's schedules and diagrams were still scattered over the table, chairs and floor, and took the instrument.

'Georgie!' cried a beautiful, carefree voice. 'How are you?'

He started violently and closed his eyes lest the tears escape them.

'Olga!' he nearly sobbed. 'Is that you?'

'That's right, Georgie,' said the voice. 'How lovely to hear you again. Now listen, because I haven't much time. I'm in Hastings at a ghastly luncheon, and when I've escaped from them all, I'm going to leap into my car and drive like the wind to Tilling and beg a cup of tea and some divine gossip from you. So you must tell Mrs. Mapp-Flint and all the other fine ladies that you've got a cold and can't come to tea today — you and your tea parties, Georgie. What would Ceylon do without you! Give my love to Lucia. Expect me at half-past four.'

Before he could say anything she was gone. Georgie stood for a moment like a statue, the receiver in his hand, then he replaced it gently, as if he were afraid of waking it. Suddenly it seemed as if there was a faint possibility that everything might turn out right after all. As he turned to leave the room, he stooped to pick up off the floor a notebook on which was written in Lucia's small, businesslike handwriting: 'Duties and Privileges of the Mayors of Tilling'. He turned the pages, his eyes falling on that section describing the procedure to be followed if the Mayor, having been elected, should be unwilling to take office. He read it and shook his head sadly, then, replacing the notebook on the table, he went to prepare for Olga's visit.

At last, at long last, Olga arrived. The hours until half-past four had seemed like centuries, but longer, more painful still were the five minutes after that, when Georgie sat in the garden-room window and thought that she might have decided not to come after all. But at twenty-five minutes to five a magnificent Lagonda car had drawn up outside, from which had stepped Olga Bracely, looking as beautiful and natural as ever. She saw him sitting in the window and called out 'Coo-ee!' (for had she not recently taken Australia by storm?)

whereupon Georgie leapt from his place on the hot-water pipes and dashed inside the house to open the door to her.

'Now then,' she said, as Foljambe brought the tea-pot that only yesterday had poured tea for the Queen of England. 'Tell me all about it.'

'All about what?' said Georgie. Supernatural as he knew Olga to be, how could she possibly know about Lucia's desertion?

'Queen Mary, of course. Haven't you seen the papers? The moment I saw them I had to fly to your side and congratulate you. Your photograph, Georgie, in the *Daily Express*. You look just like Sir Walter Raleigh, with your beard and your cape — but why didn't you throw it over a puddle for her to walk on, and make everything perfect? Don't say there was no puddle — Foljambe could have brought some water in a jug.'

Georgie did not answer. The Visit and the tea party, a mere twenty-four hours ago, seemed so impossibly remote that he could not associate himself with them. Olga looked at him strangely for a moment and asked him what the matter was. Out came Georgie's story in a torrent, starting with the history of the Tapestry and its conversion into curtains, continuing through the events of the last few months and ending in an emotional peroration in which Georgie was able to say some of the things about Lucia that he had only been able to think since yesterday evening.

'She's impossible,' he declared, 'absolutely impossible. I never get a moment's peace. She quarrels with everyone and spends her life trying to put Elizabeth down, and then she pretends that quarrels pain her and that she couldn't care one little bit what Elizabeth does. One minute she is going on about this Tilling Festival of hers — you'd have thought she would have learnt her lesson last year when she sent invitations to all those people and they said they were too busy — and the next moment she is up to her eyebrows in musty old books, for days on end, trying to prove Elizabeth isn't a Norman.

She's thoughtless and self-centred and I've had enough of her. And now she's going to sell Mallards and go back to Riseholme, where she'll spend the rest of her life being beastly to you, because everybody there likes you and she thinks you do it on purpose.'

'Being liked, you mean?' asked Olga.

'Yes. That's how her mind works. And what am I meant to do? I suppose I'll have to go with her and leave all my friends here. But suppose she doesn't want me — there were those beastly letters. Where am I going to live? I shan't forgive her and that's final. I couldn't face moving house again — all my things might get broken or lost and there wouldn't be room at The Hurst for a lot of my best furniture.' Georgie suddenly realised that his complaints were becoming trivial, so gathering steam he went on, 'Why, the Queen of England was here yesterday and everyone should be thrilled and excited, and they're not. It's all Lucia's fault, she spoilt it. No. I shan't forgive her and that's final!'

He thumped the table, crushing a currant bun, and turned away, folding his arms, as if challenging Olga to dissuade him. But Olga simply sat for a while and thought.

'Poor Georgie,' she said at last. 'You should have married me when you had the chance and then none of this would ever have happened. No, I'm sorry, I shouldn't have said that.' For Georgie had given her such a piteous look that she could hardly bear to meet it. 'But all the same,' she said seriously, 'I'm surprised at you, Georgie Pillson. How long have you known Lucia now? Well, I don't know and I won't embarrass you by making you answer. Everyone knows that you are thirty-nine, and the mathematics won't work out. But it is a good few years and still you don't understand her. Lucia is — well, she's like some tremendously stirring period in history, that can be quite dreadful to live through, but you wouldn't have missed it for the world. No, Georgie, listen, I'm being serious. There are some people, and I, who am so much older and wiser than you, can recognise

220

one when I see her, who have a right to put upon other people, even make them miserable at times, because they're unique. Lucia's just like that. She's like an elephant, Georgie. She goes crashing through the jungle, trampling on everything and everybody, but she can get away with it because she's *bigger* than everyone else. Not better, but bigger. Now you're better than she is, much better, but never mind that; you and everybody else just have to put up with her, and, when you're really furious with her, just stop for a minute and think how funny she is.'

'Funny?' said Georgie, bewildered, 'What do you mean?'

'I mean — well, never mind. I'll tell you what, Georgie. If *I* tell you that Lucia is worth giving one more chance, will you do it, just for me? As a special favour?'

Georgie was silent for a while, as if two factions were fighting for control of his voice.

'Just for you,' he said at last. 'I'll give her another chance.'

'Splendid!' cried Olga. 'I knew you would. Now, don't you worry about Lucia not wanting to speak to you again or leaving Tilling for ever. I've had an idea that will fix everything. It'll be a surprise.'

'I hate surprises,' said Georgie. 'Tell me now.'

'Absolutely not. But I mean to give Lucia an extra-special triumph that will make her bigger and even more unbearable than ever before. Meanwhile you will have to think of something that will make Elizabeth, Diva and everyone forgive Lucia, or the triumph won't work at all.'

'I can't think of anything!' cried Georgie. 'What on earth could make them forgive her? Why *I've* only forgiven her for your sake!'

'You'll think of something,' said Olga, 'and then I shall be very proud of you. Or something will turn up. But I've thought of one reason why you and Lucia can't be parted. If she goes to Riseholme for good she'll keep Cadman with her and then Foljambe will leave too. Think of that!'

'Don't!' cried Georgie, who had been worrying about

just such a dreadful possibility. 'It would be bad enough to lose Lucia, without losing Foljambe too!'

'I thought you'd say that. So you see, your fortunes are inextricably entwined, and my gipsy blood — did I ever tell you about that, Georgie? — makes me prophesy that everything will come out marvellously and everyone will live happily ever after — except Elizabeth, of course, and she'll just disappear in a little green cloud of jealousy, which will be even better. Give me some more tea, Georgie, and I'll read the tea-leaves for you.'

So Georgie poured her another cup of tea, which was cold (but Olga did not mind) and they chatted for a while about more pleasant things — Olga's tour of Australia (where they had named an ice-cream sundae after her) and the new part that Signor Cortese was writing for her, which was to be either Viola or Cordelia, depending on whether it turned out funny or sad.

Finally, Olga looked at her watch and said that she had to go, because she was giving a party at Brompton Square and it was rude for the hostess to be more than an hour late. As Georgie was seeing her into her car she stopped and took a little stone carving from her pocket; a tiny bird with a bunch of grapes in its mouth. She pressed it into his hand and said:

'There you are, Georgie. It's a little carving I was given in Australia and I want you to have it, because it reminds me so much of Lucia when she puts her head on one side and asks you a question. Put it in your waistcoat pocket — never mind if it spoils the shape — and then, whenever you feel angry with Lucia, you'll remember your promise to me and forgive her. Goodbye, Georgie.'

And she started up the motor and was gone. Georgie watched until she was out of sight, then went upstairs to his dressing-room and unlocked the cabinet where he kept his *bibelots*. In the most honoured place of all, next to the silver thimble that might just conceivably have belonged to Marie Antoinette, he placed the little statuette; then he closed the cabinet, locked it and went downstairs.

Georgie slept late the next morning and by the time he had risen and made his usual careful *toilette* it was almost the marketing hour. He had no taste for the excitement of the High Street, especially today, for the news of Lucia's departure would have broken and that was a topic he did not want to discuss. He sat for a while and tried to think of some way of conciliating the people of Tilling towards Lucia, but could not, so he went downstairs to look at the post.

There was only one letter and it bore the crest of Buckingham Palace. Georgie was quite startled at first, and then be remembered that the Queen had been at Mallards the day before yesterday; perhaps she had left something behind. He started to open it, and then recollected that it was addressed to Lucia. He stopped, the paper-knife already half-way through the flap of the envelope, searching in his mind for a pretext for finishing what he had started. It occurred to him that Lucia had specifically requested that nothing should disturb her rest-cure; it was his duty to open this letter on her behalf.

It was from Lady Jane Hall, thanking Mrs. Pillson for a nice tea and so on; but there was also something about the curtains. He read it and rubbed his eyes. The words seemed incomprehensible and his mind could not encompass them. Slowly and in a clear voice he read the paragraph aloud and then it made sense. Just to make sure he read it out again.

'The Queen also commands me,' he declaimed:

to thank you on her behalf, and on behalf of the Needle-women's Guild, for the exquisite curtains that you presented to the Guild through Her Majesty. The Queen is full of admiration for the skill and artistry with which the work is executed and wishes me to congratulate on her behalf your husband and the other men and women of Tilling who, as you informed Her Majesty, designed and executed this magnificent piece of embroidery.

Georgie bit his lower lip, which hurt; he did not know what to do for the best. Should he drown himself at once, or would it be better to tell everybody about the letter first? He considered this problem for a moment, and a third possibility occurred to him. Ought he to telephone Lucia in Riseholme and tell her that her name had been cleared by no less a person than the Queen herself, then tell everyone, and *then* drown himself? No, for one's words tended to get muddled up as they travelled down those many miles of cable, and he particularly wanted Lucia to understand his message. He then reflected that the shortest way to the River Rother from Mallards was along the High Street, so he might as well spread the news as he went.

He called to Foljambe that he was going out, grabbed his military cape and the first hat that came to hand, and dashed down West Street, causing a motor-bicycle to swerve and himself nearly colliding with an errand-boy delivering fruit to Taormina.

He did not have much further to go, for the people of Tilling had gathered outside the poulterer's to discuss Lucia's departure. The Royce was drawn up outside the shop and there was Mr. Wyse craning over Susan's fur-clad shoulder. There was Diva and the Padre, and beside him Major Benjy, and facing them Elizabeth and Evie (the cat and the mouse, thought Georgie irrelevantly). They were already excited about something. How much more excited they would be presently!

'Good morning, Mr. Georgie,' Elizabeth had started to say, but she had got no further than 'Good' for Georgie had leapt upon the group like a small lion attacking a herd of rather statuesque buffalo, and with no more preliminaries than a rather breathless 'Listen to this!', he read out the important paragraph. When he had finished, he handed the letter round and everyone (except Diva, who had been buying fish and did not want to mark the immaculate parchment) took it and read it.

'So you see,' cried Georgie, 'she didn't take all the credit for herself, as we thought; she gave it to us, when

224

it was really all her idea and she did the designing. It must have been when she was talking to the Queen in the hall, when you couldn't hear, and that bit about a poor thing but mine own must have been about the idea, not the whole thing. And now we've accused her of something horrid she didn't do and she's gone off to Riseholme and she'll never come back!'

His voice tailed off, and there was absolute silence. Then everyone started talking as quickly as they could. They had known that she had gone, but not that she had gone to Riseholme, and certainly not that she had gone for ever. Diva stood wringing her hands and moaning 'What shall I do?' to herself, while the Padre shook his head sadly and Evie squeaked 'It wasn't *me!*' over and over again. Major Benjy shot a nervous look at his wife and edged away, muttering something about being late for the tram. Only Elizabeth seemed unaffected by remorse and fear, for something that Georgie had said — perhaps it was that phrase about never coming back — had filled her soul with music, and she whispered 'God save the Queen' under her breath.

When a semblance of calm had descended on the hysterical throng and they had all dispersed, looking miserable, Georgie went back to Mallards. On the way, he stopped at Taormina to tell Irene, who cried 'Yippee!' and kissed him on the forehead, at which he recoiled, but put it down to the excitement of the moment. As he rang the bell of Mallards (for he had come out without his key), he remembered Olga's prophecy of the day before about something turning up that would solve everything.

'I wonder how she knew?' he said to himself, as Foljambe opened the door. 'But, after all, she knows everything.'

15

The news was not good. When Georgie tried to telephone Lucia at the Ambermere Arms, he had been told,
as he had been told every day for the past week, that she
was unavailable. His letter had not been answered,
except for a very polite note asking him, in future, to
forward her mail unopened. This he had done — and
there had been quite a flood of letters for her, with
curious postmarks and unfamiliar handwriting — and
there seemed to be little more that he could do. Twice he
had walked to the station with his suitcase packed,
resolved to go to Riseholme and confront her; but on the
first occasion he found that he had come out without any
money and, when he returned to the station, his courage
failed him.

Apart from Elizabeth, everyone was very worried; but
Elizabeth had (so she thought) risen to the occasion quite
splendidly. It had occurred to her, almost before
Georgie had finished speaking outside Mr. Rice's shop,
that since Lucia had, so to speak, deserted her post as
Mayor, someone had better deputise for her, and she
had proceeded to open two jumble sales and a Sunday
School Bazaar before the Corporation realised that
Lucia had gone away. When Elizabeth explained to them
that Lucia was unlikely to return, the Councillors were
all deeply affected; one of them, a usually very cheerful
man who worked for the Sanitation Department, was
quite cast down and declared that Lucia was the best
Mayor that the town had ever had and that no one else
could have organised the Royal Visit so splendidly. To

this Elizabeth felt compelled to reply that no Mayor worth her salt would have abandoned her responsibilities so wantonly, and demanded a vote of no confidence. At this Irene, who, it may be remembered, had displaced Elizabeth on the Council, demanded that Elizabeth be ejected from the Town Hall, and Elizabeth felt it wise to depart. She had, however, continued to deputise for Lucia at various functions, despite the fact that an official deputy Mayor had been appointed, with the result that a Produce Show was opened twice and the new Pumping Station had two foundation stones.

So dispirited had the town become that Elizabeth's activities went almost without comment. When Diva reported to the morning shoppers that Elizabeth had claimed the use of the Mayoral car and, on being refused, had gone on sitting in it for quite five minutes, declining to leave, the news was greeted with apathetic murmurs and the comment from the Padre that they could expect a great deal of such behaviour frae Mistress Mapp-Flint now that Lucia had gone awa'.

It was this fear of Elizabethan domination that most worried the citizens of the town. All of them could remember the days before Lucia's coming, when Elizabeth had held unchallenged sway, and that had been bad enough; but Elizabeth's character had been hardened and embittered in her constant war against Lucia, and the events of the past year alone had given her a fine store of grudges to be worked off. Mr. Wyse, in particular, thought of Elizabeth's portrait and trembled at the prospect of the retribution that must follow, while Evie was under no illusions about what was likely to happen to her if Elizabeth remembered (as she undoubtedly did) certain words she had spoken on that occasion. Already Elizabeth had picked a quarrel with Diva over a petunia in the garden at Grebe which Paddy had dug up in a fruitless search for some long-forgotten bone; as if there was not enough unhappiness in the town without creating new miseries! Yet there was no earthly chance of their displacing Elizabeth on their own; Tilling Society needed a leader, or else it would simply collapse.

'Lucia was horrible to us at times, I agree,' said Evie as she poured tea for her guests at the Vicarage. 'Just think of that *County Life* business. But,' she lowered her voice, 'she was never as bad as Elizabeth.'

'Where is Elizabeth, by the way?' asked Georgie nervously. 'Didn't you invite her?'

'She invited herself,' said Evie, 'but you know she's always the last to arrive. I expect she will turn up in a minute and tell us all about what she's been doing. That's why I didn't dare invite Diva, or she would have been unpleasant to her again. Oh, I can't stand any more of this!'

'Susan and I are contemplating a visit to Capri,' said Mr. Wyse. 'We wrote to Amelia yesterday. Heartbroken as we will be to leave Tilling, especially,' he said miserably, 'in the summer, when the town is quite at its best — the strawberry season, you know — I do think that after the events of the past few weeks, a holiday — an extended holiday — might be advisable. Then we have a standing invitation to visit my cousins in Whitchurch; and in October there is a suggestion that we might go to Scotland, for the shooting, you understand.'

'I ought to go and visit my sisters,' broke in Georgie. 'I haven't seen them for ages.'

'Your mention o' the Highlands fills me with a sudden longing to see the bonny heather again,' said the Padre hurriedly. 'What do you say, wee wifie?'

Evie said that it was a splendid idea; indeed had her husband declared that he had heard the call of missionary work in Mashonaland, she would probably have consented to go with him, for the thought of being left behind as Elizabeth's only remaining subject would have been far more terrifying than going to dwell in the Dark Continent. At that moment, however, Elizabeth arrived with Major Benjy, looking very hot and uncomfortable in his second-best suit and a stiff collar, for as the husband of the Mayor's (unofficial) deputy, he had been called upon to dress respectably.

'How cosy this is,' said Elizabeth brightly as she sat down at the tea-table. 'So sorry I'm late, Evie dear, but I had to pop into the Town Hall on my way. Any news?'

There was an awkward silence, and Georgie became aware of Elizabeth's eye upon him, fixing him like a butterfly to a collector's tray.

'I might be going to stay with my sisters,' he said. 'It's so long since I went to see them last and they did send me a card at Christmas.'

'Mr. Georgie!' exclaimed Elizabeth. 'How could you think of such a thing! Is it not bad enough that we should be without poor Lucia?' (Elizabeth always called her 'poor Lucia' these days, rather as in Homer the sea is always described as 'wine-dark'.) 'No, we cannot allow you to go away and leave us all.'

Georgie did his mental arithmetic and worked out that without him, even if she pardoned Diva, Elizabeth could not compose two tables for Bridge. He realised suddenly that she would not permit him to leave; he was a prisoner in Tilling, chained, like a slave to a treadmill, to Elizabeth's Bridge-table. He uttered a faint groan, which Elizabeth seemed to take for a symptom of indigestion, for she told him not to eat his cake so quickly. The would-be fugitives looked at each other in despair.

'Such a pity that Diva could not be here,' Elizabeth continued. 'Poor thing, she does take on. Just because I had occasion to utter a mild rebuke — that dog of hers, so unruly — she has become as sullen as a spoilt child and won't come out of her house.'

'Surely not?' quavered Georgie. He had not realised that Diva was under house arrest.

'I haven't seen her since,' said Elizabeth. 'How that wretched animal causes trouble for her, knocking things over and damaging people's property. I wouldn't blame her if she got rid of it.'

'But she's very attached to it, isn't she?' murmured Evie.

'Perhaps. But she will have to choose which she values most, her dog or her friends. I won't have it in the house, and I advise you to do the same. Such a dreadful creature, forever tracking mud all over the carpets. My Benjy is quite firm that if he ever sees it in our garden again he will add it to his other trophies.'

A look of horror crossed the Major's face, for he was appalled at the thought of such a brutal and illegal act.

'Steady on, girlie,' he said, and nearly upset the cake-stand.

'Well, I hope such a course of action will not prove necessary,' said Elizabeth firmly. 'I expect that when Diva realises how unpopular she is becoming as a result of that animal's activities, she will give the wretched thing away or send it to a dog's home. Now, let us talk of more pleasant things.'

Georgie escaped from the tea party as soon as he could and stopped off at Wasters to tell Diva of the threat to Paddy. Diva had been taking solace in violent gardening and had, after a long struggle, succeeded in defeating a forsythia.

'There,' she said, surveying the battlefield, 'it'll look twice as good next year.'

Georgie looked at the devastated shrub and averted his eyes. 'I'm sure it will,' he said with a shudder. 'Listen, I've got some very bad news for you.'

Then he told Diva what Elizabeth had said, whereupon Diva wailed loudly and rushed into the house. Georgie followed her, fearing that she might do something desperate.

'She can't,' cried Diva, 'not Paddy. All he did was dig up a petunia — and it was dead already, Elizabeth had been mulching it. I shall have to go away! I'll go and stay with my sister-in-law in Harrogate. She wouldn't follow me there.'

'She wouldn't let you go,' said Georgie. 'She needs you to make up two tables for Bridge.'

At that moment Paddy himself appeared, with a long-dead thrush held lovingly in his jaws. Diva, in an access of tenderness, tried to clasp him to her, making him sprint for the safety of the cupboard under the stairs.

'Why doesn't Lucia come back?' sobbed Diva, and

Georgie, who was much moved, in spite of his fear of dogs, took his leave without another word.

Still more letters awaited Georgie at Mallards and he sat down to redirect them all to Riseholme. He had finished the last one when he realised that it was addressed to himself and not to Lucia. It was in Olga's handwriting. He opened it with his finger, cutting himself with the thick paper as he did so, and devoured the contents:

Dear Georgie,
Don't be surprised at all those letters arriving for Lucia, and be sure to send them on to Riseholme as quickly as you can.

Love, as ever,
Olga.

After several attempts, Georgie gave up trying to understand this cryptic message and had gathered up Lucia's mail, readdressed to the Ambermere Arms and ready to be posted, when Foljambe, her normally impassive features betraying a certain excitement, told him that Mrs. Pillson was on the telephone. Georgie hurled himself into the telephone-room and lifted the receiver.

'Yes?' he panted.

'*Georgino caro*,' warbled Lucia, '*come sta? Va bene?*'

'*Molto bene*, thank you,' gasped Georgie, 'and all the more *bene* for hearing your voice!'

'How *dolce* of you to say so, *caro*. Such a delightful *vaccazione* I've been having. All well with you, I hope. Any news?'

It was as if nothing had happened. Of course, she would have read his letters and from them found out that the awful mistake had been discovered and that everyone was truly sorry. Nevertheless, to chirrup away in Italian as though the horrors of the past week had not occurred — Olga was right. Lucia was bigger than anyone in the entire world, and with her giant stride she could cross chasms and abysses as though they were mere cracks in the pavement.

'Now listen carefully, *mio caro sposo*, Lucia has some-fink to tell *Georgino*. Can *Georgino* guess?'

'No,' said Georgie — then feeling that he might have seemed rather abrupt, he added, '*Georgino* so vewwy *stupido*.'

A silvery laugh, untarnished by distance, tinkled in his ears. 'Nonsense, and me *cattiva* Lucia to tease 'oo. But tell me first, have you missed me? And has Elizabeth been simply dreadful?'

'Yes to both questions. She's been opening things and laying foundation stones as if she were the real Mayor, and she's making Diva get rid of Paddy.'

'No!' For a moment the serenity of Lucia's voice might have been disturbed and steel seemed to replace silver. 'We must see about that when I get home.'

'You're really coming back?' cried Georgie.

'Of course, *caro*. I shall be arriving at eleven-o'clock tomorrow. But don't you want to know the answer to my riddle?'

'Yes, please. Is it something exciting?'

'Very exciting. All those lovely letters you've been sending on to me — guess who they're from? No? Very well. They're from all those people we invited to take part in the Tilling Festival last year — you remember, when they were too busy and couldn't accept. Well, now they've all written to ask if we are having a festival this year and can they take part — and some others, too, whom I do not recall having invited, very important people, some of them. Remarkable, *non è vero?*'

'Astonishing,' replied Georgie. 'So what are you going to do?'

'Do? Why, organise a festival for them all to come to, of course. Georgie, there's not a moment to be lost. I am writing to them all, just to tell them that there *will* be a festival and that I will send them the details soon. Then, tomorrow I'll get to work properly. *Arrivederci, Georgino.*'

Georgie hung up the receiver and, hazy with bewilderment, sat down and tried to get on with his embroidery.

But he could not concentrate and his mind kept dwelling on Olga's peculiar note and Lucia's extraordinary revelation. When the truth finally dawned on him he became so excited that he accidentally speared himself with his needle and did not notice for several minutes. He badly needed to tell somebody, but there was nobody that he could tell.

He could not continue with anything as mundane as embroidery so he went upstairs to his *bibelot* cabinet and reverently drew out the stone bird with the grapes in its mouth. Although it was not his day for dusting and polishing his collection, he rubbed the bird delicately with his softest duster. As he did so, he pondered whether he should tell Lucia when she arrived; but she would probably rather not know that it was Olga who had begged, cajoled or bullied all those terribly famous people into offering their talents to the Tilling Festival. How Olga had managed it he couldn't imagine, but, of course, to Olga all things were possible.

Even now he was restless and went into the telephone-room to tidy it up before Lucia's return. The pile of re-addressed letters need not be posted now, but traces must be removed of things that might have an unpleasant association for her when she came to start work on this great new project. Once again, his eye fell upon the little book with the notes on Mayoral duties that Lucia had been translating and the thought of one passage came into his mind. He found the place and read it through again.

Soon it would be time to dress for dinner at Starling Cottage. The start of Elizabeth's reign had been one long succession of social events, all of them so far perfectly horrible. With Diva still under embargo, three of them would have to sit and watch while the other four played Bridge. Then he remembered that this tyranny would soon be over, that Lucia was coming back. There was some news to cheer up the miserable gathering. It occurred to him then that although *he* did not like surprises, he had no reason to believe that Elizabeth felt the same way; or, for that matter, Lucia. . . .

When Elizabeth and Benjy rang the bell of Starling Cottage they could hear the sound of merry, cheerful conversation, with frequent cries of 'No!' and 'How fascinating!', such as had not been heard in Tilling for a little while. Everyone seemed particularly pleased to see them and there was no shortage of volunteers to yield places to them at the one Bridge-table that could be furnished. Elizabeth had Mr. Wyse for her partner, and Benjy had Susan, and, as the rubber progressed, Elizabeth strained to hear what Georgie and the Bartletts, sitting at the other end of the drawing-room, were saying. But their voices, although excited, were low and indistinct, and so she gave up the attempt and tried to concentrate on the game, which she and Mr. Wyse were winning by a large margin. Benjy, too, seemed to be acting strangely, although he showed no obvious signs of intoxication. Was he up to something too? Elizabeth thought hard and deduced that his strangeness of manner — a rather pronounced obsequiousness, an unwonted note of chivalry in his Bridge-playing — had begun shortly after he had come in from drinking his port in the dining-room. . . .

'Do you think it was wise to let Benjy in on the secret?' whispered Evie nervously.

'Of course,' replied Georgie. 'He suffers more than any of us.'

'Oh look,' said Evie, 'they've finished their rubber. Now?'

'Now,' said Georgie firmly, 'and be careful.'

'Let me see,' Elizabeth was saving, 'I make that three shillings and sixpence you owe us, Benjy-boy.'

'Are you sure?' said Benjy. 'I made it four shillings myself.'

'Nonsense,' said Elizabeth. 'Three and six.'

Benjy insisted on paying Susan's losses as well as his

234

own, saying that his errors had brought about the disaster, and he counted out the money into Elizabeth's hand.

'Thank you, dear. Now shall we have another rubber for the poor outcasts?'

'Not for us, thank you,' said Georgie, 'we've had such fun just watching. You played that last hand splendidly, Elizabeth.'

The praise was, in fact, merited, for Elizabeth had revoked quite palpably and the skill with which she had covered up this error was of a high order. She thanked Georgie for his compliment and Georgie thanked her back. Then there was silence and the Padre nudged Georgie with his elbow. But Georgie seemed speechless, and so the Padre said:

'I believe Mr. Georgie has somewhat to ask ye, Mistress Mapp-Flint. Go on, man. Speak.'

Georgie coughed nervously and asked Elizabeth if she would like to come to tea tomorrow. Elizabeth pondered awhile under cover of flicking through her pocket-diary, for there was something strange about all this; but she could not see any reason why she should not accept. So she thanked Georgie and Georgie thanked her again. Then, quite suddenly, everybody seemed to notice how late it was, and soon only Elizabeth and Benjy were left. So, although it was still quite early, Elizabeth said goodbye to the Wyses and she and the Major started on the long journey back to Grebe.

'Something very odd is going on,' said Elizabeth, as they turned left in front of Mallards and went down West Street. 'And I have no idea what it can be.'

'Same here, old girl,' said the Major innocently.

As soon as they were out of sight, shadowy forms began to creep stealthily towards the door of Starling Cottage. At first, an observer would have taken them for the smugglers and pirates whose spirits haunted Porpoise Street. But, as the door opened and light poured through it, they could be plainly recognised as Georgie and the Bartletts, followed by Diva and

Irene. They went into the house and the door closed behind them.

'*Buongiorno, Georgino!*' cried Lucia, as she stepped into the house that she had possibly renounced for ever. 'Ah, how pleasant to be back in dear Tilling again after my holiday.'

Now it was in Georgie's mind to suggest that it had not been a holiday at all and to have a serious talk with her; but he remembered the elephant and decided against it. One cannot talk seriously with an elephant.

'And how was dear Riseholme?' he therefore cried as lightly as possible. 'How I wish I could have come with you.'

'As beautiful as ever, except that dear Adele has planted parsley — think of it, Georgie, parsley — in Perdita's garden and decorated Midsummer Night's Dream in salmon-pink silk and Art Deco. How does *The Rubaiyat* put it, *caro*?

"They say the lion and the leopard keep
The courts where Jamshyd gloried and drank deep."

Or some such words. And poor Daisy has become quite eccentric with no one to keep her in order — I believe that dear Adele and Colonel Cresswell quite encourage her. She could speak of nothing but vegetarianism, and when I went to dinner with her what do you think we had? Barley-bread and rye-bread and millet cakes and Malvern water to drink — for she will not drink the water from the tap, which she says is full of bacteria. She declared over and over again that she would not allow a living thing to be killed for her benefit — she was wearing tennis-shoes, for leather is quite forsworn — and when I told her, as gently as possible, that cereal plants and flax are living things too, and all the vegetable kingdom, come to that, she grew quite distraught. I had hoped that my time in Riseholme might have had some lasting effect, but there. *Alles vergängliche ist nur ein Gleichnis*, as Goethe so succinctly puts it.'

236

After a week without her, Georgie found that this burst of concentrated Lucia (*The Rubaiyat*, vegetarianism *and* Goethe) quite disoriented him, like a waft of powerful gas, and he did not know what to say. But there was no need for him to say anything, and scarcely any opportunity.

'And now to business, Georgie. So many letters. Who is this? — the paper-knife, dear, if you please. Thank you. Ah, Signor Cortese, no less — you remember him, Georgie, his glorious *Lucretia*, first sung in your little cottage at Riseholme.'

Lucia's brow clouded over and Georgie guessed that Signor Cortese, who was Italian, and who knew little English, had written his letter to Lucia in *la bella lingua*, for Lucia, after staring at the letter for a while, put it back in its envelope, said 'Dear Signor Cortese!' and moved on to the next one.

'From Miss Olga Bracely, Georgie,' she said, and fixed him with her bright, piercing eye. Perhaps she had guessed everything — how Olga had rounded up all these distinguished people like a sheepdog, and had driven them into Lucia's fold — or perhaps not. 'I am sure we shall be able to find something for dear Olga to do. In fact, if she can spare the time, I think we ought to ask her to join our Festival Committee. What do you say, dear? Such a capable, influential woman.'

What Georgie said can be guessed and Lucia turned to the rest of her letters and called for strong black coffee. Georgie, feeling drained, tottered into the drawing-room. Then he took something from his waistcoat pocket and hugged it to his bosom.

Lucia stayed in the telephone-room until luncheon, and throughout the meal remained blithe and light-hearted, chattering away gaily in a virtually incomprehensible mixture of Italian and baby-talk. For a moment, Georgie believed that she had forgotten all about the Tapestry curtains and her tempestuous departure from Tilling; but an elephant never forgets. Suddenly, in the middle of a sentence, she put down her fork and looked Georgie in the eye.

'That reminds me,' she said (they had been talking about Shakespeare). 'We shall need some new curtains for the garden-room. Something bright and cheerful, now that summer is upon us.'

After lunch, Georgie was thoroughly briefed on the Festival, and the list of names that Lucia read out to him was quite staggering. Omnipotent as Olga was, she could not have mobilised so many legions of the illustrious. The project had started to gather its own momentum; Great One had mentioned it to Great One, suggesting that it might be rather fun, and no one had wanted to be left out. So thrilling was the prospect that Georgie lost all track of time, and it was only when he glanced out of the garden-room window and saw a large number of people standing outside that he remembered that his own particular triumph was about to take place. Fortunately, Lucia had her back to the window and had not seen. But where was Elizabeth? Had Benjy's nerve failed him, and had he betrayed the secret? But there she was, striding up the hill, and Major Benjy behind her, looking extremely nervous. It was time.

'Excuse me for a moment, Lucia,' said Georgie, and he slipped from the room. From the drawer of the desk in the telephone-room he took Lucia's notebook; then he opened the front-door and descended the steps. Everyone was there; the Padre and wee wifie, Diva, in tearose georgette, with Paddy on a chain, Susan and Algernon Wyse, on foot, and Susan hedged about with sables, quaint Irene, carrying something in a brown paper-bag; and the Mapp-Flints, he trying vainly to hide behind Diva, she on the point of flight. But Irene saw her and drew from its paper-bag the dinner-bell.

'Stay right there, de Map,' she cried, 'or I'll follow you all the way back to Grebe.'

'Is everyone here?' cried Georgie. 'Very well, then. Ring the bell, please, Miss Coles.'

Irene rang her bell and cried out 'Oyez, oyez!'

Elizabeth, seeing her chance, tried to edge away, but Lucy, Irene's gigantic maid, blocked her path and she

238

knew that escape was impossible. Georgie cleared his throat and began to read from the notebook.

'If the Mayor should refuse,' he tried to say, but a lump the size of a tennis-ball had found its way into his throat and he stopped.

'You're useless,' said Irene. 'Give it to me!'

She snatched the book from his hand and rang the bell again. 'Listen, people of Tilling,' she sang out in a loud, carrying voice. 'Extract from the Ancient Duties and Privileges of the Mayors of Tilling, used thereof from time out of mind, which Men's mind cannot think the — what's that word? Oh, yes — contrary. If the Mayor should refuse, and if the Mayor, so chosen and elected. . . .'

Lucia, hearing the bell, looked round and saw what looked like a mob assembled in the street. At first, thoughts of Bolshevism and Revolution filled her mind, then she recognised their faces. Georgie and Irene, and Elizabeth looking very bad-tempered, and all her friends — and what was Irene reading?

'. . . All the whole commons together shall go sit beneath her house and entreat until such time as she come forth. . . .'

For a moment she did not understand; then she understood. Everyone was calling out 'Lucia!' or 'Come forth!' Even Elizabeth, with a face like a thunder-cloud, managed to shriek, 'Do come forth, you sweet Mayor!' while Major Benjy was roaring like a lion and waving his hat. She rose and left the room.

'Now where's she gone?' gasped Georgie, hoarse with shouting. 'It's at least three minutes since she left the garden-room.'

'Shout louder!' yelled Irene. 'Come on, Mapp. Shout!'

So they shouted.

Lucia called Grosvenor and ordered tea and cakes for ten.

'Very good, madam,' said Grosvenor impassively. 'Oh and, madam, your chain is not quite straight.'

'Thank you, Grosvenor,' said Lucia, and adjusted it slightly.

She put her hand on the door handle and observed that the fingers trembled slightly. She frowned, and the trembling stopped. She opened the door and stepped out, her Mayoral robes sweeping the ground beneath her, the feather in her hat touching the lintel. A deafening cheer greeted her and, as the sun, emerging from behind a cloud, cast a sparkling light upon the Mayoral chain, she raised her hand for silence.

'You dear people,' she said. 'How you all work me!'

THE END

Mapp and Lucia
E.F. Benson

'I have not laughed so much at any novel as *Mapp and Lucia*
since I read the early Waughs'
TERENCE DE VERE WHITE

At last they meet – the two most formidable ladies in English
literature collide in genteel and deadly enmity. Lucia, now
widowed, shakes the dust of Riseholme from her elegant feet
and, with Georgie Pillson as devoted courtier, prepares to
conquer the high society of Tilling. She brings her musical
evenings, her Italian, her poetry, and her ambitious snobbery.
And Miss Mapp, her features corrugated by chronic rage and
curiosity, can only prepare to defend her position as doyenne
of Tilling. The town is split in an exciting and scintillating war
of garden parties, bridge evenings, and staggeringly simple little
dinners.

Mapp and Lucia is the fourth of the Lucia novels, a chronicle
of life in two English country towns described with malicious
delicacy and wit.

'I might have gone to my grave without ever knowing about
Lucia or Miss Mapp. It is not a risk anyone should take lightly'
AUBERON WAUGH

0 552 99084 1

BLACK SWAN

Lucia in London
E.F. Benson

Lucia, Queen of provincial society, now launches herself onto
the London scene. The crème de la crème of social climbers,
Lucia never falters as she dons her real (seed) pearls and
prepares to attach the beau monde, wheedling her way into
parties where she has not been invited and coaxing the rich
and titled to come to tea.

Lucia In London is the second of the famous Lucia
books by E.F. Benson. Comic masterpieces, these novels of
manners are brought to life by sharp, satirical social
observations and are as deliciously funny today as they were
when first published in the 1920s.

"He was a master of a certain kind of light fiction, and he
can delight even though one knows that his satire is ultimately
friendly . . . He is clever and funny, but he writes for his
victims"
THE SPECTATOR

"The flow of his comic inspiration never dwindles"
ELIZABETH HARVEY

"Here she is again, the splendid creature, the great, the
wonderful Lucia . . . I must say I reopened these magic
books after some thirty years with misgivings: I feared that
they would have worn badly and seem dated. Not at all; they
are as fresh as paint. The characters are real and therefore
timeless"
NANCY MITFORD

0 552 99076 0

BLACK SWAN

Miss Mapp
E. F. Benson

'The flow of his comic inspiration never dwindles'
ELIZABETH HARVEY

Here is the redoubtable 'triumphantly arch of all arch
villainesses', Miss Elizabeth Mapp of Tilling — a schemer,
a woman of fine habits and low cunning who spends her
days in the delightful bow window of her delightful period
house, light opera glasses in hand, noting and annotating
the business of her neighbours. Not a thing escapes her
gimlet eyes, from the purchase of a basket of over-ripe
red-currants, to the unfortunate drinking habits of
Captain Puffin.

Miss Mapp is the third in the sequence of the famous Lucia
novels. Deliciously funny, outrageously U, quintessentially
English, Benson's comic characters have come alive again
for another generation.

'He was a master of a certain kind of light fiction, and he
can delight even though one knows that his satire is ultimately
friendly . . . He is clever and funny, but he writes for his
victims'
THE SPECTATOR

'My greatest reading pleasure in 1967 was the discovery of
E. F. Benson's "Lucia" novels . . . I enjoyed them so much
that I borrowed (and was tempted to steal) two more of the
series. I confess myself a Lucia addict'
TERENCE DE VERE WHITE

0 552 99083 3

BLACK SWAN

Queen Lucia
E.F. Benson

"We will pay anything for Lucia books"
NOEL COWARD: GERTRUDE LAWRENCE: NANCY MITFORD:
W.H. AUDEN

Queen Lucia is set in the middle-class, garden-party
world of the 1920s, a society dominated utterly and ruthlessly
by the greatest arch-snob who has ever existed. Lucia and
her cohorts – Georgie with his dyed hair, embroidery, and
piano duets, Daisy Quantock with her passion for the new
and exotic – capture the mood and flavour of a whole period,
and the nuances and rivalries of English life are described
engrossingly and with a rapier wit.

If the pens of Evelyn Waugh and Jane Austen had mated,
Lucia would have been the offspring.

"At long last, here she is again, the splendid creature, the
great, the wonderful Lucia"
NANCY MITFORD

"To describe her as a snob would be to describe Leonardo as
a talented man"
MICHAEL MACLIAMMOR

0 552 99075 2

BLACK SWAN